rae of sunshine

USA TODAY BESTSELLING AUTHOR
MICALEA SMELTZER

rae of sunshine

© Copyright 2014, 2016 Micalea Smeltzer

All rights reserved. This book or any portion thereof may not be reproduced or used in any manner whatsoever without the express written permission of the publisher.

This is a work of fiction. Names, characters, businesses, places, events and incidents are either the products of the author's imagination or used in a fictitious manner. Any resemblance to actual persons, living or dead, or actual events is purely coincidental.

Cover Design: Emily Wittig

Photography by Regina Wamba at Mae I Design

Edited by Wendi Temporado of Ready, Set, Edit

one

...

THE THING about starting over is it isn't as easy as people say.

It's impossible to become a completely different person.

You can change your hair.

Your makeup.

Even your name.

But at the end of each and every day, you're still the same person you were yesterday and the day before that.

I've spent the last year trying, and failing, to become a different person. The shitty events of my life have certainly changed me, and I'm not the same carefree girl I used to be, but I'm still Rachael—or Rae as I prefer to be called now—because no matter how far, we run we can never escape ourselves.

It might be stupid, but I feel like hiding behind the new nickname gives me a bit of anonymity. Not that anyone at Huntley University is going to know who I am or what I did.

My eyes flutter closed as I feel the breeze tickle the skin of my cheeks, and I inhale the scent of lilac.

For the first time in a year, I feel peaceful and centered. Like maybe I'm where I belong—which is funny, since I didn't even want to go to college after everything that happened.

I open my eyes and grab one of my duffel bags from the car and my camera case.

My camera has always been like a limb to me—an extension of who I am. Even after everything that happened last year, I couldn't give up photography. It brings me peace when everything else in my life is chaos. I slam the door closed and lock my car, since I have other stuff to get later, and I don't want anyone trying to steal something. For now, I just want to get to my dorm and check things out.

I pull the piece of paper out of my pocket with the housing information on it. I already have it memorized, but for some reason, I find it necessary to read it again. It brings me some strange sense of peace. Like it is a lifeline or something.

I bow my head and step onto the sidewalk.

I haven't taken more than two steps when I fall.

Only, I don't fall—I'm knocked to the ground by the force of a very heavy male body.

I can smell his sweat—even more potent than the lilacs dotting the campus—and it isn't the stinky kind of sweat. Oh, no, he smells delicious. Like he's been rolling around in the sheets naked for hours having the hottest sex imaginable.

"Fuck, I'm so sorry!" the guy exclaims, rolling off of me. He reaches down to pull me up, and when he does, I end up plastered against his chest. It's hard and smooth, not a blemish in sight. He keeps a tight hold on me so I can't scramble away. "Are you okay?" His eyes roam over my body as he surveys any damage he might've caused, lingering longer than necessary on my body.

"I'm fine," I assure him, finally looking at his face and holy hotness; it should be illegal to be that good looking. Brown hair hangs in his eyes—eyes that are so blue they could only be categorized as cerulean. Stubble dots his defined jaw, and his lips are kissable. They don't make guys like this where I'm from. *Not. At. All.*

Clearing my throat, I take a step back, bowing my head so that my hair hides my suddenly flushed face. I can't believe I was ogling the guy who knocked me down. Or any guy, for that matter. I haven't allowed myself to look twice at any guy in over a year. Not since …

I shake my head free of my thoughts and reach down for my camera case. Luckily, it's heavy duty, and I don't need to worry about my camera being damaged when it's contained inside.

Without a second look at the guy that knocked me over, I dust the dirt off my camera case and walk away. He might be hot, but I'm not going down that road.

He jogs after me, undeterred by my rapid departure. Of course. "Whoa, whoa, whoa." He grabs my arm. "You're not getting away that fast."

I look at him, and then at the spot where we fell. There is

a football lying there, and I assume it's the reason he ran into me.

"Uh—" I point to the fallen ball "—it looks to me like you have a game to get back to." My pulse thuds in my throat at the feel of his hand on my arm. I feel a light sweat break out across my skin. I can't understand my body's reaction to the stranger. For the first time in a year I feel ... *alive*. It makes no sense.

I pull my arm from his hold, since he hasn't let go. Unfortunately, it does nothing to alleviate the feelings he produces inside me.

He sees the ball and looks behind him. That's when I notice the other sweaty guys watching us. They are all good looking, but they have nothing on the Adonis in front of me.

"They can wait." He grins, looking boyish. "What's your name?"

I can't understand why Hottie-McHot-Pants is talking to me. I'm nothing special. From the looks of him, he has to be a junior or a senior, and I am a freshman. Besides, if he's interested in an easy lay, he needs to look elsewhere; I'm not looking for a relationship or a hookup.

"Why do you want to know?" I counter. I can't help but be flippant. All I want to do is go to my dorm, and he's keeping me from doing that.

He chuckles. "I mean, I did lay on top of you, so I figured I should at least know your name."

My cheeks heat further, and I bite down on my tongue. Something tells me he isn't going to leave me alone until I tell him my name. "Rachael," I answer automatically. "But I prefer to be called Rae," I hasten to add.

"Rae," he repeats, a small smile causing his lips to crook at the corners. "I like it." He holds out his hand. "I'm Cade."

I look at his hand like it's going to bite me and then at his face before taking a step back. "I didn't ask for your name."

He lets his hand fall and smiles like he isn't at all upset by my actions. Chuckling, he says, "Well, now you know it."

Giving him an awkward smile, I turn to leave.

I only make it three steps before he calls, "Rae?"

I swivel around to face him and tilt my head to the side. "Yeah?"

"I'll see you around."

It isn't a question. It's a statement. I can tell Cade is the very determined type. Unfortunately for him, I'm very determined not to know him or anyone. I'm here to get my education and disappear again. I'm not looking for any connections. Connections mean feelings, and feelings mean attachments, and attachments make you do stupid things.

As I walk, I notice I'm missing the piece of paper with my dorm information, and I almost go back to get it. But since I have it memorized, and going back means taking the chance of running into Cade again, I decide not to.

The amount of people bustling around campus makes me feel a bit uncomfortable, but it's easier to blend in and appear normal so I have to learn to deal with it.

I jog up the steps of my dorm building and breeze inside. I'm nervous, but you wouldn't know it if you saw me. I'm a master at concealing my emotions. Muttering my room number under my breath, I stop outside the door when I find it.

I take a deep, steadying breath, and wrap my hand around the knob.

This is it.

This is the moment that will forever change my life.

I know it.

And then I walk into an explosion of Pepto-Bismol.

"What. The. Fuck?" I gasp, looking around at all the pink.

Pink bedspread. Pink rug. Pink pillows. Pink blanket. Pink chair.

Pink *every*thing.

"My eyes!" I cry as I slap a hand over my face.

"You must be my roommate!" an overly chipper voice sing-songs.

I lower my hand and— "Gah!" I gasp in shock. The pretty light-haired brunette in front of me even wears a pink shirt. Thank God her shorts aren't pink or I might've had a heart attack. *Death by Over Exposure to the Color Pink*—now, that's a headline.

I can't believe I'm going to have to live with *this* for the next ten or so months of my life. *Kill. Me. Now.*

I look down at my dark hair and black clothes. I don't see how I'm going to get along with the Barbie Doll in front of me. We are clearly polar opposites.

"I'm Thea." She holds out a hand. What is up with everyone wanting to shake my hand today?

Skirting around her, I head toward the plain side of the small room.

She follows me, either oblivious to the brush off or ignoring it. "You must be Rachael."

"Rae," I correct her, dropping my bag on the bed and refusing to turn around. "I prefer to be called Rae."

"Oh, okay. Rae is a pretty name. I mean, so is Rachael, but Rae is cooler. I—"

"Do you ever stop talking? Or breathe?" I wheel around to find her all up in my personal space.

"Sorry." She frowns, wringing her hands together. "I'm nervous."

"Obviously," I mutter. "Look, Thea?" She nods. "I'm not here to make friends. So, don't expect any late-night talks with me, or nail painting, or whatever else it is you've conjured up in your head."

"Oh." Her face falls.

I turn back to my duffel bag and dump my clothes on the bare bed. I need to go back out to my car and get everything else. My mom made sure I had everything I needed, since she knew I'd never do any shopping on my own. I've changed a lot in the last year, and I no longer cared about much of anything.

I haven't always been such a depressed person, but then life dealt me a pretty shitty card, and I handled it my own way. Nothing I did could make me forget that day.

Once all my clothes are put away, I head toward the door.

"Where are you going?" Thea speaks up from where she

lounges on her bed. I still have to repress my gag reflex from all the pink.

"To my car," I answer, glaring at her.

"Cool, you want some help?" she asks, bouncing up. Before I can answer, she invites herself by saying, "Okay, good."

She's like an overeager Golden Retriever. I don't quite know what to do with her peppy personality compared to my doom and gloom. Something tells me this is going to be a long year.

As we walk through the building, she says, "My brother goes to school here. He's kind of a big deal."

"Is that so?" I ask, not interested at all in hearing about her brother.

"Yeah, he's the quarterback of the football team." She bounces along.

"Is that important? I don't really like football."

She stops walking and grabs my arm. Her mouth hangs open in shock. "How do you not like football?"

I shrug. "I just don't."

In another lifetime, I liked lots of things that I don't anymore.

"Are you from here?"

Here happens to be Colorado.

I huff, irritated with all her questions. "Yes."

"And you don't like football?" He mouth gapes open. "But it's like ... necessary to the way of life."

I snort and tilt my head. "*Oxygen* is necessary for life, not football."

She shakes her head and starts walking. I don't know where she's going since she has no idea which car belongs to me.

I point to my car when we have almost reached it. "It's that one."

"It's cute," she smiles.

I laugh at that. Cute is certainly not the word anyone would ever use to describe my clunker of a car. Looking at Barbie, I'm pretty sure she probably drives a cute little Volkswagen. I had a cute car once, but that was ... before.

Before what?

Before I destroyed everything.

With Thea's help, it won't be necessary to make another trip out to my car. We walk back to our dorm, and I notice the guys playing football are gone. Maybe if I was a normal girl, I'd tell Thea about Cade. Then we'd laugh and talk about how hot he was. But I'm not normal, not anymore.

Luckily, Thea doesn't talk much on the way back.

She ends up spending several hours on her computer while I fix up my side of the room. There's nothing personal on my side. It doesn't scream *This is Rachael Wilder's Room!* It could be any girl's room on any campus at any school. The day that ruined my life effectively stripped me of my identity. I ghosted along, a fragment of the girl I used to be. I think my parent's had hoped college would snap me out of this 'phase', but day one was a resounding failure.

"I like your comforter," Thea says, looking over at my side of the room.

I eye her bubblegum confection of a bedspread and look

down at my gray and yellow one. "Yeah, it's the life of the party."

She lets out a laugh and looks around at all the pink. "I guess we can't all be as bright and colorful."

"And thank God for that," I crack a smile, smoothing my hand over the bedspread before sitting down. "One of us has to be tame."

"So," she bites her lip, closing the lid on her laptop, "I was wondering if you'd want to go to a pool party with me?"

I narrow my eyes. "How on Earth is there already a party at this place? Isn't today the first move-in day?"

"It's not tonight," she corrects me. "It's Sunday, and it's kind of a big deal around here. Only certain people get to go, because it's invite only. Since my brother is, well, my brother, I was invited, but I won't know anyone but him and his friends, and I don't want to be alone. Please come?"

A pool party is *not* my thing, and I haven't worn a bikini in a year. However, looking at her pitiful face and pleading eyes makes it impossible to say no.

"Fine, I'll go on one condition," I warn, staring her down so she doesn't get too excited.

"Thank you! Whatever it is, I don't care!" She claps her hands together.

"I'm not swimming," I tell her. "I *can't* swim," I add, to avoid any possible questions about why I don't want to swim.

"What do you mean you can't swim?" Her perky nose scrunches together. "Everyone knows how to swim."

"Not me," I sigh. I *can* swim, but I'm not the strongest

swimmer. The real reason for not swimming has more to do with not wanting anyone to see the scar on my abdomen than with my weak swimming abilities.

She frowns. "Well, that's fine. Most girls lounge around anyway, or at least, that's what my brother said, but he probably just doesn't want me to wear a bikini. He gets all pissy when guys look at me," she rolls her eyes. "Typical brother."

I don't have a brother, so I don't know. I shrug, because she seems to want some kind of response.

Thea stands from her bed and stretches her stiff muscles. "I'm starving. Do you want to grab something to eat?"

Food. I'd completely forgotten about dinner ... and lunch. All I had at breakfast was an apple. My mom would've clucked her tongue and given me a lecture for already failing to take care of myself on the first day of school.

I'm a bit afraid to agree to go with Thea, though. Despite my warning, she seems all too eager to band together and become besties.

But I'll hate myself if, God forbid, I let her go by herself and something awful happens to her. I don't need a fourth death on my hands. Yes, fourth.

"Fine," I agree grumpily. "Let's go."

She smiles and tucks a piece of her strawberry-blonde hair behind her ear. She grabs her purse, and guess what? It's pink. Of course. Its bright color is a stark contrast to my skull and crossbones messenger bag.

Thea and I head to the dining hall. I'm surprised when she doesn't fill every second with chatter. Instead, it's almost peaceful walking across campus with her at my side. She doesn't know who I am or what I've done. We are strangers, and she can't judge me for my sins. There is something comforting in that. For the last year, I've hated myself, and the looks from others haven't helped in that—seeing the judgment in their eyes. My parents and therapist always assure me that what happened isn't my fault, but that's a lie. I might not be in prison, but I'm stuck behind bars of my own creation.

I miss the old Rae—or Rachael, as I was called then. I miss the girl that laughs and smiles with her friends. I miss the girl that loved her parents and didn't resent them. I miss the girl that always looked for the positive in life. I miss *everything* about the old me, but I killed her when I killed *them*.

"Rae!" Thea calls, and I halt in my steps. I turn around to look at her and find her standing outside two glass double doors of a brick building. "The dining hall is this way," she nods at the building.

Oh.

I backtrack hastily.

"It's okay." Thea smiles, despite the fact that I haven't apologized for my mistake. "I wouldn't know where anything is if it wasn't for my brother." She opens the door, and I follow behind her.

"You talk about your brother a lot, don't you?" I comment, heading to the counter. I wrinkle my nose in distaste at the cheeseburger they are serving for dinner. If that's a cheeseburger than I'm a duck. I pick up a bowl of salad; that seems like the safer of the two options. Thea picks that as well.

I follow her to a table and take the seat across from her.

"I love my brother; so why wouldn't I talk about him?"

I lift my head, confused at first, until I realize she's answering my question. I shrug indifferently and take a bite of salad.

She stares at me. "You don't talk much."

I shrug again. "I don't have much to say."

"Everyone has something to say," she counters with a raised brow.

"Not everyone."

She sighs heavily and tosses her salad around with the fork. She's growing frustrated with me, and I don't blame her. If roles were reversed and I had to deal with me, I'd get huffy too.

After a few minutes of tense silence, she speaks. Her pale green eyes sear me as she stares at me, her lips turned down in a frown. "You know, we don't have to be best friends, but we do have to live together. We should at least try to make it as civil as possible and try to get along."

"I thought I was trying," I grumble. I look away from her eyes and begin to pick at the silvery polish on my nails.

She blows out a breath, causing her bangs to flutter against her forehead. Finally, she cracks a smile. "If that's what you call trying then you're doing a pretty lousy job."

"So I don't get an A for effort?"

"Definitely not." She rests her head in her hand. "No stickers for you."

"Stickers?" I ask with a raised brow.

"Yeah." She laughs, and it's light and musical sounding.

"You know, like teachers give school kids stickers when they do something good."

I screw my face up in displeasure. "What kind of school did you go to? No—" I hold up finger "—let me guess, some preppy private school."

Her cheeks turn pink—her favorite color, how appropriate.

"How'd you know?" she asks.

I narrow my eyes at her fancy clothes. "You have rich kid written all over you."

I leave out the part that I *am* one of those rich kids. I just don't dress or act like it anymore.

"Is it really that obvious?" She pales, her hands fluttering over her body.

It's almost funny. *Almost.*

"No," I say to put her out of her misery. It really isn't as obvious as I made it sound, but since I come from an upper-class family, I can always pick out people who run in the same circles.

"Oh good." She visibly relaxes, and we finish our meal in silence.

It had been twilight when we left our dorm, but on the way back it's completely dark. Luckily, there are lights every few feet so you don't have to worry about monsters lurking in the shadows. I don't know why I'm worried. After all, all the monsters live inside me now.

"I'm going to bed," Thea announces when we step into our room. "It's been a long day."

I nod in agreement. She grabs some pajamas and goes to

change in the bathroom. We're lucky that our bathroom is only shared between the two of us. I wouldn't have been pleased if we had to share with another dorm. I don't like people in my space, and it's bad enough that I'm stuck with a double.

I begged my parents to pull some strings to get me a single, but they refused. They told me I needed to stop locking myself away in suffering and make new friends. "Live your life, Rachael," my mom told me before I left, her hands on my shoulders. "Just because they're dead doesn't mean you are."

But she's wrong. I am dead.

two

...

WHEN I WAKE up on Saturday morning, it's still dark outside.

I can't remember the last time I slept in. My body runs on very little sleep. Sometimes I think it's a miracle I haven't fallen over dead yet. I know that living, and suffering for what I've done, is my punishment. It's why I'm still here. Living while my friends are dead.

I've tried so hard not to remember anything from *before*, but it's impossible.

That day is always going to haunt me. There is no flushing it from my memory. I have to learn to live with it to survive.

I scrub my hands over my face and let out a soft groan so I don't disturb Thea. The last thing I want to do is deal with her at this time of the morning. I need some time to myself before she wakes up.

I slip out of bed and into my running clothes as quietly as possible.

Rachael didn't run, but Rae does.

I find that when I run, I can't think about anything else. My thoughts cease to exist. When I run, I'm free from my sins.

I open the door and ease it closed so that she can't hear the lock click. Hopefully, she'll still be sleeping when I get back. Classes don't start until Monday, so it isn't like she has to get up early.

I move through the building like a ghost and out the double doors.

I stop on the steps and inhale the crisp morning air. It's chilly, but I don't mind. Unfortunately, I know that means there won't be many mornings left where I can run outside. I'll have to use the school's gym—I won't like it, but I refuse to give up running.

After a few stretches, I take off.

Immediately, I feel that rush I always get—like I'm in control. I haven't been in control of my life in a long time.

My feet thump against the concrete sidewalk as I jog around campus. I keep my pace steady, but a little on the fast side. When I first started running, I used to run so hard and fast that I'd throw up. But now my body is used to it, and I can run for hours without getting tired.

I begin to sweat, despite the cool air, and my hair sticks to my damp forehead.

My breath is heavy and the steady beat of my heart in my chest soothes me.

I'm so absorbed in the humming of my body that I don't notice when someone falls into step beside me, but soon, their presence becomes overwhelming.

I flick my gaze over to the stranger and find that it's no stranger at all.

It's the tackler. *Cade*, he said his name was.

My steps falter, and I trip.

Down I go, scraping my knee against the cement. I hiss between my lips at the sharp sting.

Jesus Christ. All I do around this guy was fall. Granted, the first time he knocked me to the ground so that doesn't really count.

"Are you okay?" he asks, dropping down beside me. His voice is a husky gasp as he inhales sharply, his chest heaving with each breath. His t-shirt is damp with sweat. As is his hair. Clearly, he'd been running for a while before he joined me.

I glare at him with heat in my eyes. "Why the fuck were you running beside me?"

"You looked lonely," is his response.

I narrow my eyes. "I wasn't."

I clumsily come to my feet and start to walk, trying to shake off the stiffness in my limbs from the fall.

"Are you mad?" he asks, catching up to me easily with his long-legged stride.

I stop in my tracks and look up at him. "Yeah, I'm mad. That's twice you've made me fall. If this is how you pick up girls, you need to try a new method. This one is seriously lacking."

He throws his head back and laughs—the kind of laugh that shakes your whole body. I like the sound of his laugh, too. It's warm and happy sounding. I never laugh anymore, and I wonder if I do, will it sound like Rachael's? Or will it be different?

"You're funny."

"I was serious." I tilt my head, putting a hand on my hip.

He grins down at me, and I see that he has a dimple in each cheek. The heavy scruff on his cheeks helps to camouflage them, but they are still there. They give him an almost boyish appearance.

A lock of brown hair sweeps down to hide his blue eyes. He grins at me, completely unfazed.

"You're different."

I look up at him and nod. "You're right."

He narrows his eyes with his hands on his hips. He looks at me like I'm some intricate puzzle he's trying to piece together. When he doesn't say anything, I start to walk away again. My legs feel okay, so I start jogging.

Cade joins me once more, and I'm not even surprised.

When we circle the fountain that sits in the middle of campus, I'm tempted to push him in just so he'll leave me alone. But I don't.

Cade continues to run with me—even though I know from his appearance he has to have already run *a lot*.

Neither of us speak, but when you're running hard, there isn't much breath for small talk.

My dorm appears in front of me, and I run harder. I

don't say goodbye to Cade as I jog up the steps and into the building. I feel his eyes on me, though.

I swore I wasn't going to look, but when the doors closed behind me I allow myself to turn.

He stands on the sidewalk outside the dorm, staring at where I stand—although, I doubt he can actually see me.

I wonder what Cade finds so fascinating about me.

Most people are afraid of me, and I don't blame them. They should be afraid; I'm a killer.

I step away from the door and head up the steps to my room.

Thea is still sleeping, a light snore echoing through the room. I shake my head and grab my stuff so I can shower.

By the time I'm done in the bathroom, Thea is stretching her arms above her head and blinking sleep from her eyes.

"Did you get up early?" She yawns.

I nod, heading to my side of the room to make my bed.

"I hate mornings." She runs her fingers through her wild and tangled hair. "Would you mind waiting for me to shower, so we can get breakfast together?"

"I can wait," I assure her.

"Great." She slowly peels her body out of bed and grumbles unintelligibly all the way to the bathroom.

While Thea is getting ready, I spend the time unpacking the last of my things—which is mostly my clothes. I haven't brought much with me decoration wise. Looking at Thea's side of the room, I think I might have to remedy that fact, because I'm not sure I can handle all the pink.

Thea takes her sweet time doing her hair and makeup.

I'm about ready to throttle her by the time she says she's ready. I'm starving, and she's holding up progress.

I follow her out of the building, and instead of turning to head toward the dining hall, she goes the other way.

"Where are you going?" I ask.

She shrugs. "My brother told me about this neat little diner on campus. I thought we'd check it out. My treat." She smiles.

When she looks at me like that, I find it impossible to say no.

I don't want to like her. Hell, I want to *hate* her. But something tells me it's impossible not to like Thea. She's one of those people that are so vibrant and full of life that they're impossible to ignore.

Five minutes later, we stand in front of the diner. Thea pushes open the door, and a bell chimes pleasantly.

"Take a seat anywhere!" one of the waitresses calls as she bustles behind the counter.

I follow Thea to a booth in the corner. The place is busy, but not too crowded. Menus are already on the table, and we each pick one up.

"Hmm," Thea hums. "Everything sounds so good. I don't know what to get."

"I think I'm going to get the waffles," I shrug, setting the menu aside.

"Those do look good." She licks her lips as if she can taste them already. "I think I'll get them too."

By the time a waitress finally makes it to us, we place our drink and food order. When the waitress leaves, I long for her to return, because her departure mean I'm going to be forced to talk to Thea.

"So ..." Thea drums her fingers against the table. "I guess we should get to know each other, since we're going to be living together and everything."

I cross my hands on the table and sit back. "Is that really necessary?"

Her lips quirk. "Yeah, it kind of is." Leaning forward, her voice lowers, "I know you said you don't want to be friends, but frankly I think that's stupid, Rae. We're going to be living together for quite a while, and we should try to get along. I can tell you're the type of person that pushes people away, and while I can respect that to an extent, I refuse to tiptoe around my roommate."

Whoa. This girl is nothing like what I thought when I first met her. I thought then that she was a clueless bimbo, but she sees more than I give her credit for.

"Okay, then." I shrug, hoping I'm not making the wrong decision. "What do you want to know?"

"What are you studying?"

Easy enough. I didn't expect that. I figured she'd go right for the jugular and ask me why I'm so fucked up. Thea's full of surprises.

"Photography. You?" I don't see the point in going into deeper details with her. The less I say, the better.

She bites her plump bottom lip and looks down at the table. "Undecided." Her eyes flick up to meet mine. "Yeah, I'm one of *those* people."

I give her what I hope is a reassuring smile. "There's

nothing wrong with not having it figured out yet. You'll get there."

She cracks a small smile in return. She reaches over for the saltshaker and slides it back and forth across the table between her hands. "I hope so. Sometimes it really sucks living in my brother's shadow. He's got it all figured out, and he's good at everything. I'm just me ... and sometimes I don't even know who I am."

I try my best to hide my surprise at her honesty, but I fail.

She lets out a soft laugh that holds no humor. "Sorry to get so deep on you." Her eyes flood with sadness. "I don't have many friends. Actually, I don't have any real friends. Most girls just want to get close to me because of my brother. But you ... You don't know him. I feel like I can trust you."

"I'm not a good person," I tell her, swallowing thickly. "You don't want me as a friend. I've done things. *Horrible* things. I—"

Thea shakes her head. "No. I think you're wrong. I think you're beating yourself up over something that's stupid."

I doubt killing three people counts as stupid, but I'm not telling her that. I don't want to see the fear in her eyes, or the hatred. I get enough of that back home. The whispers and glances have often become overwhelming. It's why I spent the majority of the last year locked inside my bedroom.

"I'm not a good person, Thea," I repeat. I need her to understand that.

Her eyes soften, and she reaches for my hand where it rests on the table. I flinch at the touch, but refuse to pull my hand back.

"You say that, Rae, but I think you're wrong. Often times it's all too easy to delude ourselves into believing one thing than it is to see the truth in our own eyes. I may not know you that well, but I do see you. I see the pain in your eyes, and I know something haunts you. We all have demons, but the thing is, we usually think they're worse than they really are."

I open my mouth to reply, but am cut off by the waitress appearing with our food.

While we eat, Thea chats about random things—the campus, her brother, how nervous she is for classes. I think she hopes she can distract me from our previous conversation, but it isn't working.

I want to dismiss her words, but I can't, because a part of me wonders if she's right.

I know what I've done is wrong, horrible, despicable, and a bunch of other things, but am I torturing myself because it's easier than moving on?

three

. . .

SUNDAY STARTS MUCH the same as Saturday. I get up early, before the sun rises, and go outside to run.

Cade joins me halfway through.

We don't speak today, and I try my best to ignore him. I'm learning that Cade isn't easily ignored, though.

Just like yesterday, I turn to look at him once I am safe in the dorm.

He stands watching me, arms crossed over his chest and his head tilted to the side.

I back away and up the steps, and still, I feel his eyes on me. It isn't an unpleasant feeling, and while it should be creepy, it doesn't seem that way. I wish I could figure out what he wants from me, but I don't dare to ask.

I'm considering changing my running schedule, but after some deep thought about it, I decide against it. I want to run in the mornings, and I'm not going to let Cade ruin my schedule. I can ignore him or avoid him. Problem solved.

Back in my room, I grab my towel, clean clothes, and my shower caddy.

If yesterday served as the norm, Thea won't be up for another hour or two.

I'm dreading this afternoon—aka The Pool Party.

I hate myself for agreeing to attend. Parties are not my thing. Especially ones involving water and half-naked people.

I push all thoughts of the hell I'll have to endure later out of my mind and let the hot water relax my sore muscles.

Soapsuds cling to my skin and hair before swirling down the drain.

Around and around.

Away.

Gone.

I stare at those white suds like they hold the key to the universe.

I wish I could leave so easily.

Just disappear and cease to exist.

My fingers absentmindedly rub against the scar on my abdomen. I should've died, but I didn't.

Miracle, the doctors said.

Curse, I chanted.

Most days, the pain of my past is crippling. I've learned to deal, but it doesn't make the memories any easier to bear. I lost my whole life in one instant—seconds was all it took to shatter my life, and I'm the one to blame for it. *I* did this to myself. I'm responsible for everything. At least, I can own up to it unlike some people. I've accepted what I've done. I don't try to put blame on anyone else. Nope. This is all me.

My body begins to shake as I cry.

In the safety of the shower is one of the only times I ever allow my emotions to get the better of me.

The water washes the tears away and the spray helps dull the sounds of my sobs.

I don't cry much about it. Tears don't solve anything. They don't have magical healing powers that make everything better. They don't erase the past, but sometimes, I have to let them out.

Eventually, I turn the shower off and step out onto the cold tile. It's brown and dingy. The whole dorm needs a good cleaning. Maybe after the pool party I can stop at the store and get some cleaning supplies.

Cleaning, like running, is good for me. It's mindless and numbing. It allows me to focus on what's in front of me and not the horrors that haunt me every minute of every day.

I reach out and swipe my hand over the mirror, wiping away the condensation. My hazy reflection appears before me. My eyes are red-rimmed and purple shadows bruise the skin beneath them. I rarely sleep these days, and when I do nightmares haunt me. Well, not *nightmares*. Memories.

Memories are crippling.

In the last year, I've often wished for a magic wand that would erase my memory and take away all the painful things. The problem is, *everything* is painful—the good, the bad, *all of it*.

I turn away, not able to take another second of looking at the girl in the mirror. I hate her, and I don't want to be her.

I want to be someone new.

With a sigh, I get dressed. Despite the last of the summer heat lingering in the air, I dress in ratty black jeans, a black t-shirt with a band name on it—a band I don't even know if I like or not—and tie a checkered black and red shirt around my waist.

I line my eyes in heavy black eyeliner—a shield from the world around me.

My dark brown hair curls around my shoulders.

I'm ready to face the world, even if I don't want to.

I push open the bathroom door and find Thea sitting up in bed. She stretches her arms above her head and yawns.

"Morning," she smiles brightly.

I nod in acknowledgement.

"Are you still coming to the party?"

"Yeah." I sigh. It would be rude to ditch her now, and I'm working hard at trying to be nice.

"I'm going to shower and go get something to eat. You wanna come with me?"

"Sounds good." I force a smile, sitting on the end of my bed. I know if I was smart I would've left without her. I don't need Thea complicating my life. But selfishly, I don't want to have to face the crowded campus alone, so that's why I agreed.

She gets up and gathers her stuff before going into the bathroom. A moment later, I hear the shower come on.

I sit back on my bed and grab my computer. I flick through some old photos, marking ones I want to edit later.

An hour later, Thea is ready to go.

The dining hall is as loud as a concert when we arrive. Although, a concert I would've enjoyed. This ... not so much.

I grab an orange and a bowl of cereal—Trix, because those delicious things aren't just for kids.

Thea and I sit at a table with a few other people. They don't acknowledge us, and we pretend like they don't exist. That's college for you.

I don't mind being ignored, though. In fact, I prefer it. I don't like having to fake being interested in conversation when I'm not. I'm *trying* to make an effort with Thea, to at least keep things civil since we have to live with each other, but there is no way we'll ever be best friends forever.

After all, forever never lasts.

"So," Thea starts, taking a bite of blueberry muffin.

I raise a single brow, waiting for her to continue.

"Are you wearing that to the pool party?" She eyes my clothes.

"Yeah." What's wrong with what I'm wearing? I'm not going to swim.

She wrinkles her nose with distaste, but doesn't say anything for which I am thankful.

"I'm glad you're coming with me." She smiles genuinely, seeming to forget my clothing choice. "Parties like this aren't my thing." She sighs heavily. "They're not really my brother's thing, either, but he has a part to play. At least, that's what he tells me."

I push my bowl of cereal to the side of the table and start peeling my orange. "Do I get to meet this mysterious brother of yours?"

She laughs, flipping her curly, strawberry-blonde hair over her shoulder. "Of course."

"You seem fond of him," I comment.

"I am."

Something tells me those are the only words I'm going to get out of her. She doesn't know, but those two words give me a wealth of knowledge. They tell me that her parents probably weren't great. Either they were abusive or strict. Thea had obviously come to rely on her older brother. She looked up to him.

Sometimes, I wished I had a sibling I felt like that with, but then after everything that happened to me, I'm sure I would've pushed them away like I did everyone else.

I can't bear to be close to anyone anymore.

Emotions are complicated and messy.

"Do you have any brothers or sisters?" Thea asks suddenly.

I shake my head and grin. "Nope. I'm perfect. My parents had no need to reproduce a second time."

Thea's lips quirk into a smile, and finally, she laughs. "Wow. I didn't know you had it in you," she sobers. "You actually made a joke. I'm impressed. I'll have to tell that one to my brother. He'll argue that he's the perfect one and I'm the pesky little sister."

"I doubt that." I might not have met her brother yet, but from everything she said, it was obvious that they were close and he loved her.

We finished eating and headed back to our dorm so Thea could get ready.

The fact that she needs to primp again baffles me. She already spent an hour getting ready before we could get breakfast. I can't fault her too much; Rachael had been the same way—concerned about having her hair perfect, her makeup done, and her clothes pristine. Rae didn't give a shit.

She comes out of the bathroom with a tank top and jean skirt overtop of a bikini. Thank God it didn't take her another hour to get ready or I might've lost my mind.

"What time do we have to go?" I ask.

She looks at the clock beside her bed. "Now."

"Great." There is no enthusiasm in my tone.

Since Thea doesn't have a car, I drive. That's fine by me; it puts me in control. If this thing sucks, I can leave whenever I want.

We end up at a community pool that has been closed off for the party. The place is already packed, and I feel my anxiety grow. My hand tightens around the steering wheel—like I could sear myself to it and not have to go. This is the last place I want to be. Why did I agree to this? Oh, right, I'm trying to be a good person.

Taking a deep breath, I slip out of my car and follow Thea over to the fence. She bats her eyes and tells the guy standing there her name.

He waves us inside.

What the hell is this? A club? The guy is literally holding a clipboard and crossing off names.

Thea says hi to someone and then hisses under her breath to me, "God, I hate her. She's such a bitch."

"Oh, look!" She claps her hands together excitedly and points at two lounge chairs that are free. "Perfect spot!"

"Yippee," I groan.

She looks at me over her shoulder and laughs. "Most people would die to be at this party."

"I'm not most people."

"No, you're not," she agrees.

She drops her tote bag on one of the lounges, and I take the other. I look extremely out of place in my grunge clothes compared to all the preppy hipsters surrounding me. Several people give me dirty looks. I resist the urge to show them my middle finger.

"Ignore them," Thea says, catching on to what's happening.

"I am," I tell her.

I don't mind people staring at me when they don't know me. It's when they hear my story and look at me with pity or horror that I can't stand it.

"Oh! Look! There's my brother!" Thea cries. "Cade!" she calls. "Cade! Come over here and meet my friend!"

Ice slithers through my veins, wrapping around my heart and nearly stopping it.

First off: Cade? It can't be ... but I don't imagine there are very many Cades.

Secondly: friend? Since when are Thea and I friends? I don't know much about her besides the fact that she has a brother, doesn't have a major, and has horrible taste in colors.

"Hi," a warm voice chuckles softly. "I'm Cade Montgomery."

I know that voice. *Fuck*.

I look up slowly, and there he is. "Cade." He stands there smiling cockily, those dimples winking at me. His blue eyes sparkle with laughter—and I'm not sure if he is laughing *at* me, or with me, at the irony that he's Thea's brother. Seriously, what are the freaking odds?

His smile widens as I stare at him. Despite introducing himself, he knew it was me sitting here. "Rae," he replies. His eyes skim over my dark heavy clothes, but he makes no comment on my lack of swimwear.

Thea's mouth drops as she looks between us. "You two know each other?"

Cade starts to reply, but I cut him off. "If being tackled to the ground by this ogre counts as knowing each other, then the answer is yes."

Thea's brows furrow. "You tackled her? I'm confused. Ohhh, is 'tackled' a code word for sex? I'm not good at reading between the lines."

I shake my head. "He tackled me. As in the normal sense of the word tackled."

"Why'd you do that?" She turns to glare at her brother.

"It was an accident." He chuckles, scrubbing his hand through his longish hair. "I can see that you've recovered just fine." He looks me up and down.

I roll my eyes.

"So ..." He smiles slowly. "How've you been, Rae?"

I resist the urge to snort since he saw me this morning. True, it isn't like we had chat while we run, but his question is still ridiculous.

I stretch my legs out on the lounger and close my eyes. "I've been just dandy, and right now I'm in need of a nap." I'm not one for small talk. Small talk leads to long talk—is that even a thing?—and I'm not here to make friends.

I crack on eye open and find Cade grinning down at me.

"Stop staring at me," I groan, opening both eyes. "I can't sleep with you watching me."

He chuckles and lifts his arms, encompassing the chaos around him. "How can anyone sleep with all this noise?" He crouches down beside me, in the space between the lounger I occupy and the one Thea is stretched out on. Lowering his voice so that there is no chance of Thea hearing, he says, "You can't avoid me, Rae."

"I'm not trying to."

He stands up slowly and smiles crookedly. "See you in the morning," he whispers.

And then he's gone.

Air whooshes out of my lungs. I didn't even realize I was holding my breath.

"What the hell is going on between you and my brother?" Thea asks, slipping her sunglasses down her nose so I can't avoid her gaze.

"I have no idea."

And that is the honest to God truth.

"I'm going to get a drink." Thea sighs, standing up and adjusting her bikini top so that her ample chest is covered. "You want anything?"

"Something strong."

She laughs. "I'm sure that won't be problem."

I receive more stares once Thea leaves my side, but no one bothers me. I lean back on the lounger and take several steady breaths to calm myself.

Once upon a time, this was my scene. My friends had been just like these people. And I was the girl over there in the pool clinging to her boyfriend's shoulders.

But not anymore.

Apparently, I'd been too happy and life had seen fit to toss a bucket full of misery my way.

The sunlight bathed Brett in a halo, making his red hair glow. He smiled at me and walked forward.

"I was beginning to think you weren't coming."

"I'd never miss your birthday." I smiled as he wrapped his arms around me and kissed me squarely on the mouth in front of everyone.

"Stop sucking face," Sarah groaned, "the rest of us want to party."

With a laugh, Brett pulled away, keeping ahold of my waist. "It's good to see you too, Sarah."

"It's hot, and I'm going swimming. Are you losers coming?" She looked at Brett and me, then at Hannah who hovered somewhere behind us shyly. "Come on," she coaxed, stripping off her clothes down to her bikini.

Without waiting for any of us to respond, she ran forward and jumped into the in-ground pool at Brett's house. The pool was large, but with all the people at the party currently swimming, it seemed smaller.

Brett grinned down at me. "You ready, Rachael?"

I smiled nervously. Brett knew I wasn't a very good swimmer, and it always made me nervous getting in the water.

"You won't let go?" I asked, a slight begging tone to my voice.

"I'll never let go," he promised.

I nodded and he took my hand. Together—because the two of us had been inseparable since we were in diapers—we ran forward and jumped into the water.

Beneath its cool depths, Brett's arms wrapped around me, and his lips smashed against mine.

For the first time in my life, I wasn't afraid to drown.

Thea sits down, a peculiar look on her face. "What's wrong?" she asks.

"Nothing," I sigh, taking the drink she offered me and shaking off the remnants of the memory.

I take a sip. I'm not sure what it is, but it's definitely strong.

"Cade said not to accept a drink from anyone but him unless you get one yourself."

I raise an eyebrow at her and lift my drink. "Am I safe accepting this one from you?"

She laughs. "Yes. You're hot and all, but I prefer guys."

Laughter bubbles out of me. It feels strange and foreign, but good at the same time.

Thea's smile is pleased, almost as if she sensed I didn't laugh often.

I didn't wanted to make friends here.

I wanted to lay low, get my degree, and get the hell out of here.

But watching Thea and the other rowdy college students around us, I can't help but wish for more. The real college experience. Not what I had planned to do, which was basically shut myself up in my room when I wasn't in class.

I know it's stupid, but I feel like if I go on and live my life that I am betraying the people I lost. Their lives were cut short, so shouldn't mine be?

My therapist disagrees. Like my parents, he's spent the last year or so trying to convince me to move on. I can't.

I know I've disappointed my parents with my inability to let it go. I hate seeing the pain etched on their faces, knowing that I'm responsible for putting it there.

I knew they hope that college will be good for me—that getting away from home and the glares from everyone that knows what I've done will give me a chance to "spread my wings and fly". My mom's words, not mine.

Being away does help, but I still can't escape the crushing memories. Not just what happened on that fateful day a year ago, but what happened before. I can't escape the good times or the bad times, and it's crippling.

"Do you ever think about the future?" Brett asked as we lay in the tall grass, gazing up at the stars.

I curled my body around his, resting my head against his chest where I could hear the steady thumping of his heart.

"What do you mean? Like, college?" I asked.

"No, about us ..." he whispered, his fingers tangling in my hair.

Brett and I had been best friends since we were infants. We grew up in the houses next to each other, and since neither of us had siblings and were the same age, we'd always played together. As we grew older, that friendship turned into more. I couldn't imagine my life without Brett in it.

"Well—" I wiggled, trying to get comfortable "—I see myself marrying you one day, preferably after college, and having cute little redhead babies." I laughed, reaching up to tangle my fingers in his hair.

"I want that too, Rachael. I want to grow old with you by my side." Maybe it was a strong declaration to make at sixteen years old, but I knew Brett meant it. I never doubted his feelings for me. I knew he was it for me. I would never love another guy the way I loved Brett. It just wasn't possible. This was once in a lifetime.

"Hey." Thea snaps her fingers in front of my face. Once she has my attention, she asks, "Where'd you go?"

"Nowhere." I sigh, looking away so she can't see the moisture in my eyes. I don't know what's making the memories so much worse today, but I have a pretty good idea that it has something to do with Cade and the feelings he stirs inside me.

She sits back on the lounger and eyes me. "You zone out a lot," she states.

It's true.

"Yeah," I agree. There's no point in lying.

She stares at me as if she's waiting for me to elaborate. She shouldn't hold her breath.

Luckily, I'm saved from saying anything more thanks to the guy who shows up beside Thea. He grabs a chair and smiles at me before turning his attention to her. Immediately, her fair cheeks flare with a blush. She sits up and leans toward him. I don't think she even notices that she's trying to get closer to him.

I can't blame her, though. The guy is gorgeous, but he doesn't compare to Cade in my opinion.

He has light-brown hair and heavy scruff covering his cheeks and chin but it isn't enough to be considered a beard. He has searing brown eyes and an easy smile. He seems friendly enough and not a creeper. Thea seems to know him.

"Hi, Xander." She looks up at him and—I kid you not—bats her lashes.

"Thea." He nods, fighting a grin. "You are?" He lifts his gaze to me.

"Rae," I answer, looking between the two. "Thea's roommate."

"Ah." He nods. "I'm Xander."

"Oh." She shakes her head, as if just now realizing I'm still here. "This is Xander." She looks at me and points at the guy.

I laugh. "Yeah, he just told me."

"Oh," she says again, and her cheeks redden. "Right." Biting her lip, she looks at Xander and back to me. "Xander is a friend of Cade's; we grew up together."

Now I understand. Someone is crushing on her brother's best friend. That sounds messy and complicated, but from the looks he's giving her, the feelings are reciprocated.

"Interesting," I comment when it becomes obvious I need to say something.

Satisfied, Thea turns back to Xander and begins chatting away.

It isn't long before another guy shows up. His name is Jacen but he goes by Jace. He's good looking—I'm beginning to think that it's a requirement to go to this school—with straight blond hair. He has piercing green eyes and an overall broody vibe to him. A colorful tattoo covers the whole sleeve of one of his arms. He sits in a chair beside Xander, a beer bottle dangling from his fingertips. Apparently, he is a friend of Cade and Xander's. Like me, he doesn't seem to belong here. Not in his black jeans and white shirt. He keeps glaring at anyone that stares at him for too long.

It isn't long until Cade joins us. I didn't even see him approach. I *felt* him. His presence is that potent.

It bothers me that without even trying he's managed to needle his way under my skin.

Instead of grabbing a chair, he sits down on the end of the lounger I occupy.

I promptly pull my legs up to my chest.

He chuckles, his gaze flicking my way as a strand of hair falls into his eyes. A knowing smile tugs up his lips.

He doesn't acknowledge my reaction for which I'm thankful.

He falls into easy conversation with the others, and I ignore them for the most part. While they chat, I look around at all the people gathered. There has to be at least a hundred people. I've been to large parties before, but now I just feel out of place. I'm not sure where I belong anymore. I'm lost, floating away at sea.

Eventually, I bring my attention back to the group gathered around me. The last thing I want to do is look like I'd zoned out again. Thea is going to start thinking I'm weird if she didn't already.

I'm uncomfortable in my current position. I turn so I'm sitting sideways on the lounger, and Cade uses my movement as an opportunity to scoot closer to me.

My body tenses up at his proximity.

His arm brushes against mine, and I shiver.

I'm not sure if I love or hate my body's reaction to him. I'm going with hated, because it's completely unfair that one guy can affect me in such a way.

Not even Brett—I cringe as I think his name—made my body react like this. I am drawn to him like a fly to honey—which only ends in disaster.

I'm not dumb or naïve enough to believe that Cade sees something in me. Guys like him—hot jocks—want one thing and one thing only, and that's an easy lay. He won't get that with me.

"So, Rae." Cade turns to look at me, his blue eyes sparkling. "What brings you to Huntley University?"

What a stupid question.

"Uh ... I wanted a degree, and college seemed like the most logical place to achieve that."

Jace's lips quirk in a smile and Xander chuckles.

"You're a sassy little thing, aren't you?" Cade grins.

Thea watches her brother and me with a careful gaze.

Little thing? Considering I'm five-foot ten, I can't remember the last time I was described as *little*.

I eyed Cade, but he's unfazed by my glare. He's something else.

"It was a compliment," he finally says.

"If that's what you call a compliment, then you're really shitty at them."

Xander snorts and Jace actually cracks a full smile.

"Excuse me." I stand up. I don't know where I'm going, I just know I have to get away. Cade is making my brain fuzzy.

I haven't made it far when some idiot bumps into me. A small scream escapes my throat as I stumble.

There's no ground to break my fall.

I go straight into the swimming pool.

I hear Thea's scream just before my head submerges.

Water stings my nose, and since I wasn't been prepared to go face first into the pool, water enters my lungs.

My vision grows spotty, and I float down.

Sinking.

Drowning.

Gone.

———

The light was bright, and the pain was intense.

For a moment, I thought I was dead, but then I realized if that was the case, everything wouldn't hurt so bad.

I slowly blinked my eyes open, and the room came into focus.

A hospital.

Why was I in a hospital?

What happened?
Why couldn't I remember?

"Oh, thank God!" my mom cried and crashed into my arms.

I winced, and she immediately let go, apologizing profusely. "Oh, Rachael, I thought we'd lost you."

"Wh-What happened?" I tried to get my voice to work, but it came out all crackly sounding. By some miracle, she understood. She appeared reluctant to say anything, but at my insistence, she finally told me. With each word that left her mouth, I retreated farther and farther into myself.

I gasp, coughing up water. Even when the water leaves my lungs, I keep coughing. I know people surround me, but I'm too embarrassed to look at them for the moment.

I slow my breathing and try to take steady breaths.

"Are you okay?" A warm hand lands on my shoulder.

I turn to look at Cade. He's soaked, and water drips from his shaggy hair onto my shoulder.

"Are you okay?" he asks again.

I nod. "D-Did y-you?" I stutter, still trying to catch my breath. "Did you jump in after me?"

"Thea said you couldn't swim." He shrugs "So, of course, I jumped in after you. A bit too late though. You'd already sucked down a lot of water. I had to give you mouth to mouth."

Mouth to *what?* Oh, hell no. You have to be freaking

kidding me. I was unconscious for my first kiss with Cade? Not that I wanted to kiss him, but it is still completely unfair and embarrassing. And all these people have been a witness to this. Great. I'll be the laughing stock of the whole college before I even have my first class.

Cade seems to sense my embarrassment.

"Back up, everyone," he warns with a voice that brooks no argument, "you're crowding her."

After a pause, everyone backs away, except for Thea. I find myself thankful that she is still crouched by my side. I don't know what to make of this new feeling of fondness toward my roommate. Thea has this calming quality to her and an overall sweetness that makes it impossible not to like her. I'm not looking for a friend, but something tells me Thea isn't going to stand for that.

Cade grabs the back of my neck, his hand warm against my chilled skin, and slowly lifts my head. "Are you okay?" he asks for a third time since I never answered him.

I nod slowly. "Yeah, I'm okay." I'm still struggling to catch my breath, but I am otherwise unharmed. Thanks to Cade. Great, now I am indebted to him.

He wraps his muscular arms around my shoulders and helps me up. My legs are shaky. I think I'm still stunned from the events that transpired.

"I have some spare clothes in my Jeep," he explains, guiding me toward the gate with Thea on my heels. "I don't expect you to stay, but I don't want you going back to your dorm soaking."

It really surprises me that Cade seems to have such a

caring heart. I always assumed jocks were selfish cocky assholes. Not this guy.

He leads me over to a black Jeep Wrangler. It's jacked-up on large wheels with no top on. "Hold her," he commands Thea.

She grabs ahold of my arm and steadies me. I keep shivering.

Cade reaches into the backseat of his Jeep and pulls out a red duffel bag. He shuffles through it and pulls out a heather-gray shirt. "I have some shorts in there if you want those too."

"This is fine," I say, reaching for the shirt.

He won't relinquish it, and I am too weak from nearly drowning to put up much of a fight. He lays the shirt on the driver's seat of his Jeep and reaches for the one I was wearing.

"What the hell are you doing?" I swat his hand away.

"Helping you." He looks at me like I've lost my mind. Turning to Thea, he asks, "How'd you guys get here?"

"Rae drove," she answers.

"Get your stuff and go get her car and bring it over here. I want you guys to go back to the dorm."

My eyes widen. I don't want Thea to leave me alone with her brother. The guy is dangerous in a too-sexy-for-his-own-good kind of way, and I don't need any kind of temptation.

"I don't want to drive Thea away from the party," I say.

Cade grins slowly, and I know I'm in trouble. That smile spells dangerous. "I can take you back to your dorm. Thea, grab Rae's bag." I completely forgot I'd left the bag where we'd been sitting.

Thea nods, eyeing her brother and me with a shrewd look. She can't seem to figure us out. I see Xander waiting for her by the gate. She seems reluctant to leave me alone, but eventually, she leaves to do as her brother asked.

Cade tugs at my shirt, and this time, I am unprepared since I was watching Thea abandon me.

He manages to get it off of me before I can stop him, and I know the moment he sees.

Air hisses between his teeth, and his fingers hesitantly brushes against the raised pink skin on my stomach.

"What happened?" he asks. I'm surprised that there is no disgust in his tone.

"Something I don't want to talk about," I growl angrily. I don't like for people to see the scar. It raises too many questions I don't want to answer.

Cade sighs and his damp hair falls over his forehead. "Okay."

I balk in surprise. I can't believe he's letting it go so easily. He helps me into the dry shirt that is much too large. It smells like him—fresh cut grass and rain. He pulls his own shirt off and tosses it into the duffel bag. He doesn't put a dry one on which means that his perfect chest is on display for me. A man's chest shouldn't be a work of art, but Cade's is.

"I don't have another clean shirt," he explains when he sees me staring. Somehow, I doubt that.

Thea returns with my bag and hands it to me.

"I can take you back to the dorms if you want me to," she says timidly.

"I'm fine," I assure her. "I can drive myself." I'm already pulling my car keys out of my bag.

"Nice try." Cade snatches the keys from my hand and tosses them to his sister. "*You—*" he points at her "—can drive her car home when you're ready to leave. I'm taking Rae back to the dorms."

I resist the urge to stomp my foot like a child. I do *not* want to be alone with Cade Montgomery.

But nobody argues with Cade, that much is obvious. What he says is law around here.

Fuck that.

He can take my keys, but he can't take my legs. I'm walking back to school. It might be an eight-mile walk, but I don't care.

While he's distracted with talking to Thea, I walk away.

I haven't even made it off the property when he catches up to me. He grabs me around my waist and tosses me over his shoulder.

"Put me down!" I beat his back, trying to wiggle out of his grasp.

He chuckles. That's right, he *laughs*. That is his only response.

He opens the passenger door of his Jeep, sits me down, and buckles me in.

He climbs in the driver's side and speeds out of the parking lot before I can finagle my way out of the car.

"Who are you?" I snap.

"I'm Cade," he answers with a smile. "Did your tumble into the swimming pool 'cause you to lose your memory?"

"There's nothing wrong with my memory. I was just assuming you were the President or some member of the royal family with how fucking bossy you are."

He chuckles, speeding toward the dorms. "I have never met a girl like you before."

"I can't figure you out," I mutters, not even bothering to comment on his previous statement. Of course, he's never met a girl like me. Most girls aren't murderers.

"Elaborate." He glances my way with a crooked smile.

I huffs a sigh and glares at his profile. Handsome or not, he's currently pissing me off big time. "It's obvious you're a big deal on campus. Guys want to be you, and girls want to fuck you, just to say they did. And yet, you're following me around like some lost little puppy dog. If you're trying to make up for knocking me down that day, consider yourself forgiven. It was an accident. And I don't like you running with me. You need to stop that. I like to run by myself."

"No can do." He shakes his head.

I bite down on my tongue to contain a scream. "Why?"

"Because I like running with you. I like *you*. Like I said, you're different. Even now that you know who I am it doesn't matter to you. It's refreshing. I'm used to people only wanting to be close to me because of my name or because of where I might be going with football. You. Don't. Care."

"You're right. I don't. You mean nothing to me."

He smiles, his blue eyes twinkling. "You don't mean that. You like me. Admit it."

"I don't know you, how could I like you?" I counters, my arms crossed over my chest. Thank God we are almost back at campus and I can get out of his car and out of this shirt that smells a little too good.

"Then let me take you out."

"No."

"No?" His brows lift with surprise. "I don't think anyone's ever told me no before," he whispers, rubbing his hand over his heavily-stubbled jaw.

"There's a first time for everything. I'm not interested."

"You will be," he says with surety.

"You're really cocky, you know that, right?" I glare at him. True, he's gorgeous with that shaggy brown hair and blue eyes and that smile and ... I need to stop, because I'm pretty sure I could go on for days about him.

He chuckles huskily and smiles. "And you really know how to cut a guy down, you know that, right?" He mimes my words.

I roll my eyes and let out a sigh of relief when he turns into the parking lot. Freedom is in sight. I can get away from Cade and pretend this whole mouth-to-mouth thing never happened.

But when I get out of his Jeep, he follows.

Instead of stopping at the steps of my dorm, he saunters inside like he owns the whole damn place.

"Hi, Cade," a smooth and sexy sounding female voice calls after him.

"Hey," he replies, flashing her the same smile he gave me. I roll my eyes. Right there is proof that I am nothing special to him. I am a challenge, and that's all.

I shake my head, and my wet hair swishes around my shoulders.

Cade continues to follow me. At the top of the stairs, I turn around sharply and come face to face with his bare chest. No wonder the girl downstairs had been so keen to say hi.

I push all thoughts of his bare chest out of my mind, though. "You can go now. I'm at my dorm. I'm alive. I don't need your help."

"Don't be silly, Rae. I'm your friend, and I'm not leaving until I know you're okay."

"You are *not* my friend," I seethe, slashing my hand through the air.

"Yes, I am." He grabs my hand and drags me down the hall.

He stops in front of the right door, and I almost ask him how he knows which is mine when I realize that Thea is his sister, so of course he'd know.

I open the dorm door and don't bother protesting when he follows me inside. I don't know Cade, but I know enough to see that he isn't going to leave until he's ready.

"Sit." He points at the bed that's obviously mine.

"Um, I live here. Stop bossing me around." I purposely refuse to sit even though I'm exhausted.

He narrows his eyes. "God, you're frustrating."

"So I've been told." I lift a shoulder in a small shrug.

He shakes his head and heads into the bathroom. A moment later, I hear the shower turn on.

He pokes his head out of the doorway. "Come on."

I blanch, "No way. I'm not showering with you. Are you crazy?" Cade is clearly off his rocker. I have never in my eighteen years of life met a guy like him.

He throws his head back and laughs. "Did you seriously think I meant for us to shower *together*? I'm not that presumptuous, but if you'd like for me to join, I'm happy to accommodate your fantasies."

My mouth falls open in shock. I step into the bathroom and push him out. "Get out!" I yell before slamming the door in his face.

His answer is to laugh. I can hear him through the closed door.

I strip off my damp jeans and pull his shirt over my head.

The hot water does wonders to revive me, and I take extra time washing my body and hair—just killing time in the hopes that Cade will be gone when I'm done.

When I finally step out of the shower, the small room is steaming. Since I was been flustered earlier, I hadn't grabbed clothes. I slip Cade's shirt on once more and open the door.

I let out a scream when I see him lying on my bed, arms crossed behind his head, and smirking like he owns the place. "Why are you still here?"

"You have my shirt."

My face turns red. "You're ridiculous," I shriek. Before he can say anything else, I grab my clothes, go back into the bathroom, and change.

This time when I open the door, ready to throw the shirt at him, he's gone.

He's infuriating.

I walk over to my bed and find a note lying on top of the pillow. I reach out and picked it up.

I was only kidding. The shirt looks better on you anyway. Keep it.

-Cade

I stare at the note, dumbfounded.

Cade Montgomery is the most annoying and infuriating person I've ever met.

So why can't I shake him?

four

· · ·

SOMEONE WAS SCREAMING. *I thought it was Hannah.*

"Rachael, stop!"

I looked up and the world disappeared, replaced by a blinding white light.

The screeching of metal was worse than the screaming.

Pain lacerated my side, and I sucked in a sharp breath. I tasted blood on my tongue.

The world that had been filled with noise just moments before was now eerily silent.

"Brett? Sarah? Hannah?"

Nothing.

And then, just when the darkness threatened to take me, I heard their voices.

"You did this. You killed us. You'll pay for this, Rachael."

I wake up with a gasp, the nightmare clinging to my skin in the form of sticky sweat. My heart thunders in my ears.

I've had the same nightmare since ... since it happened, but it always has the same effect on me.

An alarm blares through the room—the reason for waking me—and Thea covers her head with her pillow.

"Turn it off," she groans.

"It's your alarm," I tell her.

"Shiiiiiit," she groans. "I hate mornings."

She sits up and her hair sticks up wildly around her head. She slaps her hand against the annoying clock, ceasing its cry. It's then that I realize the time.

"Oh, crap." I scramble out of bed, looking for clothes. My first class starts at eight, and it's already seven-thirty. I won't have time to run. I can't believe I didn't wake up at six or even earlier like I normally do. But after the catastrophe of a pool party last night I guess that explains my current state of exhaustion.

I shimmy into a pair of jeans and grab a t-shirt out of the drawer. I try to make my curly hair look halfway decent, but it's pointless.

Grabbing my bag, I run out the door without even saying goodbye to Thea.

I make a pit stop for coffee and a sandwich, because food is a must at this point and we don't have anything in our dorm yet. Luckily, I have a few minutes to spare.

After ordering and grabbing my stuff, I scurry out of there; I don't even take time to look around the place. I have a one-track mind and right now I am focused on getting to class.

That's my downfall.

When I turn to head out the door, I collide with a solid chest and stumble back. I know that scent. I became intimately acquainted with it yesterday while wearing his shirt.

He reaches out and grabs my elbow to steady me. I look up into his too-blue eyes that cause me to pause. Why does he have to be so gorgeous with that dark hair and smile? Why does he have to make me feel so good?

"Rae." Cade grins, his lips quirking up at the corners. "We really need to stop meeting like this." He winks and releases my arm.

"Yeah," I mumble in reply, because I am too busy gawking at the outline of his chest concealed behind a gray t-shirt. He's wearing a leather jacket on top and his jeans are a dark blue. He smells like dessert, and I want to take a bite. I haven't let myself think such thoughts in a year, and I hate that this one guy can frazzle me in such a way. He doesn't know me, and I don't know him. Therefore, this ... this *connection* between us shouldn't exist, but it does. I've never believed in destiny or soul mates, but I do believe in Cade Montgomery, and there is more to him, to *us*, than I want to accept.

I shake my head and side-step him as I head to the door.

He follows, and I'm not the least bit surprised. I can feel him hovering behind me, his body a heavy and warm presence.

I look over my shoulder at him as we step onto the sidewalk and the door closes behind us. "Weren't you getting coffee?" I ask, walking away.

He jogs after me. "Can't we share?"

"Uh ..." I look at him like he's lost his mind.

He continues to speak, completely unfazed by my dumbfounded expression. "I mean, I did give you mouth to mouth, so my saliva has already been in your mouth. It's not like sharing a cup of coffee would be gross or anything."

Fucking Montgomery. I can't find a sound argument for that, and he knows it.

"Fine," I agree, stopping in my tracks. As we stand there, I take several sips of the heated liquid and hand it to him. "Your turn."

He chuckles and takes the paper cup. As he sips, he starts to walk. "You coming?" he calls over his shoulder.

I roll my eyes and follow. After all, he has my coffee.

"You know," I tell him as I fall into step beside him, "you're like that annoying homeless dog that shows up at your house and won't go away once you give it a little attention."

He snorts and grins down at me. "Are you saying I look like a homeless dog?"

"No, I'm saying you act like one," I explain.

"So, you think I'm good looking?" His eyes sparkle with mischief.

I want to smack my forehead. *Walked right into that one, didn't you, Rachael?*

I decide to not even bother trying to talk my way out of this one. Instead, I say, "Oh, please, you're very aware of what you look like. Don't act like you're clueless to the effect you have on the female population. Unfortunately—" I look him up and down "—your charm and looks don't work on me.

I'm saving you the trouble here, Cade. Leave me alone. You're not going to get any more from me than this right here." I wave a hand between the two of us.

He tilts his head slightly to the side and studies me. "I never said I wanted to fuck you, Rachael." His voice lowers and he steps forward. I shiver as he reaches up to play with a piece of my hair. "Although, if that's what you wanted, I doubt you'd resist. I see the way you react to me." His lips brush my cheek, and I gasp. "Just. Like. That." He steps away, his point having been proven. "And while I'd like to fuck you until neither of us can walk, that's not the reason I talk to you. I want to be your friend, Rae."

"I don't need friends," I spit, like the mere idea is repulsive.

An elegant brow rises on his forehead. "Everyone needs friends."

"Not me."

"Even you." His eyes narrow.

I snatch the coffee cup from his hand and give him the most withering glare I can muster—which frightens most people, but, of course, Cade just continues to smile like I've handed him a damn lollipop.

"You're determined to make me not like you, which makes me even more determined to like you."

"Wow, that was quite the mind bender, Cade," I tell him as I start walking away. "I'm late for class, so please stop wasting my time."

"Hey," he calls after me, and I turn, "you're the one that talked back. You don't have to talk to me, Rae. But you do."

With that, he turns on his heel and saunters away, his point having been made. *Again.*

I walk into my first class with not a moment to spare. I slide into a seat beside a guy with spiky black and blue hair just before the professor walks in.

If Cade Montgomery had caused me to be late I might've lost my ever-loving mind. Like a full-on *Toddlers and Tiaras* kind of hissy fit.

After what happened last year, I gave up on my dreams of photography and going to college. I killed three people. I didn't deserve my life, whether or not I was technically guilty of their deaths or not. I still felt I needed to be punished, and I'd done it by closing myself off from everything and everyone. However, my parents and therapist had been persistent in the fact that I needed to go to college. I have to admit, now that I am here, I'm glad they'd been so pushy.

This might be exactly what I needed all along.

A fresh start.

five

. . .

MY FIRST TWO weeks of classes flew by, and I began to settle into my new life. Despite my thoughts on first walking into my dorm and meeting Thea, she was actually pretty cool. In fact, I kind of even liked her. I hadn't wanted to make friends here, but Thea was pretty impossible to ignore, and she was determined to be my friend. We met up for lunch and dinner every day and often hung out in our dorm and around campus together.

I haven't seen Cade at all in the last two weeks—not since our run-in at the coffee shop.

That should've been a good thing, but instead, I find myself looking for him every chance I get. From whispers on campus and what I've gathered from Thea, he is like a superstar here. I thought guys like him—you know, the super-hot jock types—*craved* attention, but Cade stays hidden. He's a pretty unusual guy.

Since he seems to have disappeared, that means my

morning runs have been relatively quiet and pretty boring. I never thought I'd like having someone run with me, but leave it to Cade to ruin it for me. Now running doesn't seem as much fun without him. On the few mornings we ran together, we didn't even speak much, but Cade seemed to calm and center me. He has a weird effect on my body. I want to hate it, but I don't. Cade makes me feel alive when I've been dead inside for far too long.

I know it would be better if I stayed away from him—far, far away—but I'm not sure I am strong enough for that. Something about him draws me in, and I am too weak to resist—just like I can't seem to resist becoming friends with Thea. The Montgomery siblings are pretty impossible to dislike. They both have a magnetism to them and it's nice to have people in my life that don't know what I've done. Back home, I'd been judged and looked down upon—not that I could blame anyone for their hatred. What I'd done had been wrong, so very wrong. But I was human, and I craved normalcy, and for the first time in a year, that's what I am finally feeling. Normal. I almost forgot what it felt like.

I know I'm being silly to even be thinking about Cade. After all, I haven't seen him in a while, but the jock has invaded all my thoughts.

Realistically, he's probably avoiding me and has found someone else that actually returns his feelings—because while he might've made me *like* him, it doesn't mean I want him in that way. You know, a sexual way, because I so am not going there. Sex complicates things, and when feelings are involved ... Yeah, that is a bomb I want to avoid at all costs.

"Hey." Thea smiles, appearing in the doorway of the bathroom where I stand brushing my hair. "We should go out tomorrow. We've been cooped up on campus for too long. I'm bored."

I resist the urge to wince. "Going out isn't exactly my thing."

"Is anything your thing?" she counters. *She has a valid point there.*

"Not really," I reply honestly. Once upon a time, it had been, but not anymore.

She juts out her bottom lip and brings her hands together in a pleading manner. "Please," she begs. "Please, please, please? We don't have to go to a club or anything like that. Ooh! Ooh!" She suddenly raises one arm excitedly, like a little kid in school desperate to be called on because they know the correct answer to the teacher's question. "I know! This weekend is the end of the carnival! Let's do that! It'll be fun!"

I want to say no, but I find myself saying, "Okay." Apparently, it's impossible to say no to Thea. Actually, it's more than that. Despite my vow to not make my friends here, I am actually desperate for it, and I want her to like me. Yeah, I'm weird, but at least I'm aware of it.

She lets out a shriek and wraps her thin arms around my neck. "Thank you, thank you, thank you!" she chanted. "This is going to be so much fun!"

You would've thought I told her that her favorite actor was going to be sleeping in our room with how excited she is.

"Yay." I shake my hands around, feigning excitement.

Thea backs away into the dorm room and grabs up her bag. "I better go; I'm going to be late for class."

I look down at my phone and pale when I see the time. Crap. I'm going to be late too. I'm losing track of time more often thanks to my wandering thoughts.

I grab my bag from the room and run out the door. Thea hurries behind me, and once we exit the dorm, we head our separate ways. She tosses a cheery, "See you later" my way, but I don't reply.

I breeze into class with a few minutes to spare. I take a seat next to a girl with purple hair, a sprinkling of freckles across her nose, and a pierced eyebrow named Novalee. I've seen some of her photos, and she is amazing—the kind of photographer I'm envious of.

She glances up when I sit down, and I force a smile. She does the same.

Our professor comes in and begins the lesson. Before it's over, he starts discussing a project that will run all semester long and we are to work with a partner. He's hoping since each of us have such a distinct style we will be able to learn something from each other, and at the end of the semester, we are to turn in a collage showcasing our collaborated work.

"Find someone to work with—" he waves his hands dismissively "—and then you can get out of here."

I turn to Novalee, and she's already looking at me. A single brow arches on her forehead, but she doesn't say anything.

"Want to work together?" I ask.

"Sounds good." She shrugs, picks up her bag, and leaves.

I think I've finally found someone that hates talking as much as I do.

"I don't know what to wear." Thea pouts with her hands on her hips as she stares into her overflowing closet.

I quirk an eyebrow and peer over her shoulder. "It looks to me like you have plenty of options."

She wrinkles her nose. "Not really."

I sigh. She's already been standing here shuffling through clothes for a good thirty minutes. It's safe to say that she is tap-dancing across my last nerve.

"Come on, Thea," I groan, not even bothering to try to hide how irritated I am. "Just pick something and put it on so we can go."

"Okay, okay," she intones, picking a random dress off a rack.

Despite the fact that I am standing here, she strips down to her underwear and slips the dress on. It's a pretty pale-blue with flowers on it. She fluffs her hair and touches up her makeup.

"Reeeadddy," she sing-songs.

I stare at her for a moment and then glance at myself in the floor-length mirror she has on her side of the room.

It's safe to say I look like a piece of crap next to Thea. I'm dressed in a worn pair of jeans and a black t-shirt, my curly hair is all over the place, and I smeared on the bare minimum of makeup.

True, Thea took a lot longer to get ready than me, but she looks stunning.

"Why are you staring at me?" she asks. "Do I have lipstick on my teeth?" She swipes a finger over her teeth.

"No, you're good," I assure her. "I was just thinking that it's completely unfair that you look like that, and I'm well ... me." I wave to my drab attire.

She smiles slowly. "Why don't you let me dress you? I'm sure I have something that'll work for you."

Considering I'm five-foot ten and Thea can't be more than five-foot four, I doubt she has anything that will fit me. I'm slender all over and she has the kind of curves girls envy and guys drool over.

"I doubt your clothes would fit me," I tell her.

She waves a hand dismissively. "We'll make it work."

She shuffles through her clothes once more. "A-ha." She grins, producing a short and flowy mint green dress.

"I don't think that will cover my ass," I state. The thing is really short, and it would be even shorter on me.

She rolls her eyes and thrusts the dress into my hands. "Just put it on. If it's indecently short, then that's what tights are for."

Clearly, there is no arguing with Thea; she has an answer for everything.

I slip into the dress, and surprisingly, it isn't *that* short on me. It still exposes a lot of leg, but I'm not worried about flashing anyone my lady bits.

"See?" Thea claps her hands together. "I knew it would work. Now sit." She points to the bed.

I do as she asks and she begins to braid my unruly hair to the side. A few shorter pieces escape and frame my face.

"You're so pretty, Rae. It's not fair."

I resist the urge to snort at those words coming from Thea, of all people.

After she finishes with my hair, she raids my closet for shoes. I don't have many options that will match the dress, so she settles on my lone pair of black flats.

She hands them over and gives me a look—the kind of look that says I'm in trouble.

"We need to go shopping. Like at a mall. You need real clothes."

I let out a small laugh as I slip the shoes on. "Last time I checked, those were real clothes."

"You know what I mean. You need some more ... sparkle, and less doom and gloom." She wiggles her fingers like she's doing jazz hands.

I pause and quirk a brow. "Did you seriously just use the word *sparkle?*" My eyes widen. "Oh, let me guess, you were one of those girls that paraded around on stage in a tutu for a pageant?"

Her cheeks heat. "They're not tutus, they're dresses, and I only did that till I was like ..." She pauses, thinking. "Twelve. Then I put a stop to it."

"Do you have any crowns with *sparkles?*" I giggle. *Whoa, I actually giggled.* That's new.

She puts her hands on her hips. "Stop making fun of me."

"All right, all right," I relinquish, standing up. I smooth my hands down the front of the dress. "Are you ready to go?"

She nods. "Yep ... Oh, and I probably should've told you ..." She bites down on her bottom lip and gives me a sheepish look.

"Told me what?" My eyes narrow and my heart pumps faster with fear at her next words.

"My brother will be there."

Oh, shit.

I school my features and stand up straight, feigning that I am unaffected by what she just told me.

"Oh. That'll be ... fun?" It comes out sounding like a question. Since I haven't seen Cade in two weeks, not since the coffee shop incident, I'm not sure where we stand. It looks like I am about to find out.

"Yeah, when I told him we were going he wanted to tag along. Jace and Xander are coming too." She shrugs. "So it won't be just the three of us."

I let out a breath I didn't know I was holding. "No worries. It's fine."

"He keeps asking about you," she whispers, her lashes lowering. "I'm sorry for being nosy, but did something happen between you guys?"

My mouth falls open in surprise. "Absolutely not. I'm not the kind of girl that jumps into bed with every guy that walks by me."

"Okay," she says the word slowly, staring at me, "then what is going on? And don't tell me nothing, because I know there's something."

"Honestly?" I shrug and she nods. "I don't know. He knocked me over within my first ten seconds on campus and then there was the pool thing and the coffee thing and ..." I trail off, purposely not telling her about the times he ran with me, because my runs are *my* thing, and for some reason, I don't want her to know. It's one of the only times I am ever free of my thoughts, and I don't want to share that with her. "Yeah, that's about it. He asked me on a date one time, and I said no. I don't want a relationship and he's your brother. That would be majorly awkward. He's not my friend. I don't really know where we stand."

She eyes me for a moment and lets out a soft sigh. "He likes you."

I shrug again. "So?"

"My brother doesn't like many people or trust them. I mean, he's nice to *everyone*, but it doesn't mean he likes them ... Not in the way he likes you."

"Cade doesn't like me in any different way," I reply easily.

Her expression says *yeah right*. "I've known my brother a lot longer than you have, and trust me when I say he *likes* you." Her face softens. "He's a nice guy, and he deserves to have someone in his life. Someone like you."

"Whoa, whoa, whoa." I hold my hands up in defense. "Get that look out of your eyes right now. I can see you planning our wedding already. I've only been around your brother a few times and yes, he's nice. But he's also ridiculously cocky and annoying. I don't want or need a boyfriend. I'm just fine on my own."

She sighs. "Whatever. But I seriously wouldn't be mad if you liked him back."

I bury my face in my hands. "What is this? Elementary school?"

Thea's eyes lighten and she grins. "College. Elementary school. Same thing."

I crack a smile at that and we finally leave.

The carnival is only about fifteen minutes away from campus, but it takes us another ten minutes to find a place to park. It looks like everyone else had the same idea.

Thea's phone chimes with a text message, and she looks down at the screen.

"Cade said they're at the entrance."

I nod because I don't know what else to say.

I follow her to the entrance, tugging at the bottom of the dress. I suddenly feel very naked, and I kinda want to run back to my car and hide.

"Stop fidgeting," she scolds.

"Sorry," I mumble and let my hands drop. My arms feel awkward at my sides so I cross them over my chest, which only serves to make me look grumpy.

"Honestly, Rae." Thea groans. "At least try to smile."

I try to force my lips up.

She wrinkles her nose. "On second thought, don't smile. That looks even creepier."

Thea, Queen of the Blunt Comments.

I finally lower my arms and take a deep breath.

I can do this.

It's just a carnival, and I am going to have fun. It doesn't matter that Cade is here.

The entrance comes into view—a silly arch made of balloons—and there stand the three guys waiting for us.

Xander and Cade have their heads bowed together in conversation while Jace stands a few feet away smoking a cigarette and tugging at the beanie he wears.

Cade looks up then, almost like he sensed us, and a huge smile spreads over his face making his eyes crinkle at the corners. That smile ... It's like a kick to my gut. It reminds me of everything I can never have again.

"Hey—" he chuckles, stepping forward "—look who it is. My Rae of Sunshine."

I roll my eyes at his jest-filled comment. "Ha, ha, ha," I fake laugh.

"Come on—" he grabs my wrist "—admit that it was a good one. In fact, I think it might be your new nickname."

I try to pull away from his grasp, but he is too strong for me. He wraps a paper band around my wrist and secures it. Seeing the question in my eyes, he explains, "You have to wear a band to get in." He holds up his own wrist and wiggles it around.

"Oh." I nod. *Of course.* "You didn't need to get one for me. I could've bought my own."

"That's what friends are for." He shrugs, smiling lazily.

"You're not my friend," I say the words firmly.

He chuckles and scrubs a hand over his jaw. "I beg to differ, but if you say we're not, then I'll have to work that much harder to convince you that we are."

I feel flustered by his words and very confused. I haven't seen him in a while, and he is acting like we are close, which most definitely isn't the case. He baffles me.

"I don't understand you." The words tumble out of my mouth before I can stop them. I want to smack myself in the forehead for saying anything, because I *know* he'll make me explain.

"Why is that?"

As we walk forward beneath the balloon arch, I shrug. "It's just ... I haven't seen you in a while, and you're acting like ..."

"Like what?" he prompts, shoving his hands in the pockets of his jeans and gazing down at me.

"I don't know." I shrug.

He chuckles. "Oh, you know."

Ugh. I stop in my tracks and tilt my head back to look at him—which is saying something since a lot of guys are shorter than me. "You act like you know me, and you don't. I haven't even seen you in two weeks."

His eyes lighten, and he smiles. Over his shoulder, I see Thea watching us closely. "Someone's been keeping track."

I roll my eyes. "Definitely not."

He shrugs off my words. "I've been busy. Coach has us practicing morning and evening. Plus, I have classes. As for the not knowing you part ..." His voice lowers, and he takes a step forward and cups my cheek. I shiver at his touch and back a step away so that his hand falls away. "I really want to get to know you."

"Why?" I ask, incredulous. There is nothing special

about me. I'm just ... Rae. Rachael Wilder. The girl who killed three people. The girl who is angry at herself and the world. The girl who should've died that day. The girl who should not be standing here having any sort of conversation with the likes of Cade Montgomery.

"Why wouldn't I?" He gives me a significant look and saunters away, catching up with Jace and Xander.

I stand there in shock. Cade confuses me like no one else. I truly can't figure him out. I shouldn't even want to know anything about him, but I do. I so do. *Damn him.*

Thea scurries to my side. "Still want to tell me there's nothing going on with you and my brother?"

I gape at her for a moment. "I have no idea what just happened."

"Mhmm," she hums in disbelief.

"I swear," I assure her as we start walking once more. The whole place smells like popcorn and funnel cake. I feel my stomach do a flip at the thought of all the buttery and sweet goodness I could devour. "You know, your brother is kind of strange."

She laughs. "So are you. Maybe that's why he likes you."

I give her shoulder a light bump with mine. "That wasn't funny."

"I thought it was." She smiles.

The carnival isn't that big, and it isn't long until we've ridden everything. Despite my best efforts, I'm actually having fun. In fact, I'm downright giddy with excitement.

"I'm going to get a bottle of water," Thea tells me after we get off one of the spinning rides. I feel dizzy and press a hand to my forehead to steady myself. "You want anything?"

"Water is good," I reply, leaning against one of the game booths for support.

"I'll be right back," she calls over her shoulder before bleeding into the crowd.

My skin is warm despite the cool temperature, and I feel almost drunk—drunk on life, maybe, because for the first time in a long time, I am happy to be *alive*. I guess having fun can do that to you. I will have to remember to thank Thea for this. I'd been reluctant to come, but this has been the best thing for me. In fact, I'm starting to think that Huntley University is going to change my life. Maybe it already has.

For some reason, I find myself spinning around with my arms spread wide. I can't stop grinning, and since the sun has gone down, all the colorful lights blend together in a swirl.

It's beautiful. Magical.

"What are you doing?" Someone is laughing at me.

"Living."

I forgot what it was like to be so happy and carefree. To be just a girl. It's amazing, and I don't want to lose this feeling. I don't want to go back to feeling so morose, but I know that just like Cinderella at the ball, my time is almost up. I'm determined to enjoy this and hang onto this feeling for as long as I can.

I finally stop spinning, and when I do, it's Cade that stands in front of me. I'm surprised I didn't recognize his voice since it usually fills my body with such warmth.

"Hi," I say stupidly with a goofy grin on my face. I seriously feel drunk, but I haven't had anything to drink. I sway unsteadily again, and he reaches out to steady me. "Thanks," I mumble, clinging onto him. I'm glad I haven't eaten anything yet. Between the ride and my own spinning adventure, I'm starting to feel sick to my stomach.

"No problem." He doesn't let go. In fact, he draws my body even closer to his. Where I am soft, Cade is hard. I fit perfectly against the side of his body, and I resist the urge to rub myself against him like a cat.

I really need to get away from him, because in my current state, there is no telling what I might do or say to him.

"I think we should go on the Ferris Wheel," he suggests, his hand lowering from my elbow to my wrist. He chuckles when he feels my pulse jump.

I've been in love once. I thought Brett was my forever, my everything. I thought we'd get married and have kids. Grow old together. But that can't happen anymore.

Right now, with Cade touching me, and the way my body reacts, I can't help but wonder if everything with Brett had been a lie. Well, maybe not a lie, but just not ... *right*. Because this? This feels right. Perfect, even. Cade makes my pulse race and goosebumps dot my body. I don't even know him, but he pushes all my buttons and makes me want him when I shouldn't. After what happened to me, I'd vowed never to love anyone ever again. Loving someone and losing them is too painful. But staring up into the depths of his blue eyes makes me want to take the plunge. I'd never known that someone you just met could have such a hold on you, but

Cade does. I don't want him to, but that doesn't stop the feelings.

"Did you hear me, Rae?" He reaches out and plucks the end of my braid.

"What?" I ask, blinking rapidly to clear my thoughts.

His lips quirk into a smile. "I said we should go on the Ferris Wheel."

That's probably a really bad idea, but right now, it sounds like the best thing ever. "Sounds good." My voice seems to catch in my throat as I stare up at him. I'm trying to make sense of my feelings, to find some explanation, but there is none.

Cade nods toward where the Ferris Wheel sits in the distance. "Let's go." I nod and follow along.

I completely forget about Thea and the fact that she is supposed to be coming back and will worry when she finds me gone.

Cade and I stand in line side by side. I lean my head back and look up at the clear night sky. I take a deep breath and feel my heart begin to slow, the high from earlier beginning to disappear.

Slowly, I come back into myself, and I turn to look at Cade. He's watching me closely with narrowed eyes. Back home, when someone looked at me like that, I used to duck my head and run away, but Cade doesn't know what I've done, so I stare right back at him. Now that my mind is clearing, I'm angry at myself for agreeing to go on the Ferris Wheel with him. This only spells trouble. The kind of trouble that used to be fun, but I want no parts in anymore—no matter how nice or good-looking Cade is.

"Go out with me," he states.

I snort. "Didn't we already have this conversation?"

"We did." He grins. "But that time you said no, and today is a new day so maybe you'll say yes."

"No."

He puts a hand over his heart and winces. "You wound me."

"I don't date, Cade." I look away and stare at the back of the head of the girl in front of me. She has pretty chestnut hair, and she's smiling at the guy beside her who I assume is her boyfriend. My stomach dips. That used to be me. I look at Cade again. That could still be me if I allow myself such things.

"Okay ... So, how about we go out as friends then? No date." He raises his hands in mock surrender.

I let out a laugh that holds no humor. "We're not friends," I say for what feels like the hundredth time.

He sighs heavily, and for the first time since the day he knocked me over, I can sense his frustration with me. Good. Maybe he'll leave me alone. He should. I am no good for him, and the sooner he learns that, the better.

"Why don't we go grab a burger next weekend as *acquaintances* getting to know one another?"

Jesus Christ, he won't let it go.

"Fine," I relent. I can use this as an opportunity to show him how fucked up I am and why he should run the other way.

His eyes widen in surprise. "Great. I'll text you a time when I know something."

"I never gave you my phone number."

He grins. "I'll get it from Thea."

Of course he would.

I'm about to make an excuse to leave and forget the whole Ferris Wheel thing, but then it's our turn to take a seat. Cade puts his hand on my waist, and I lose all rational thought. He guides me forward, and I sit down.

He takes the spot beside me, and since he's so large and the seat isn't that big, we end up plastered together. Maybe that has been his plan all along.

My heart picks up speed, and I grab ahold of the railing to hide the shaking in my fingers.

Up we go, and I feel his eyes on me, but I refuse to look at him. I keep my eyes focused on the stars above and pray he can't see my heart pounding in my throat.

The wind is cool on my face, and I find myself shivering.

Cade lifts his arm and wraps it around me, drawing me even closer. His warmth envelopes me and my breath leaves me in a shaky gasp.

"I'm not trying to make a move," he whispers, like he senses my unease, "but I could tell you were cold, and it's not like I can take my jacket off and give it to you." He lifts his shoulders in a small shrug and uses his free hand to point to where we are strapped in.

"Where are your friends?" I ask, desperate to steer the topic away from the fact that his arm is wrapped around me.

"They were getting something to eat."

"Thea was getting us water," I blurt. "She's probably worried about me."

Cade chuckles, and his breath stirs the hair on top of my head. "We'll have to find her once we get off this thing then."

I nod in agreement.

It grows quiet between us, and neither of us seems to know what to say. It surprises me that for once, Cocky Cade seems to be at a loss for words.

I look around us, and I thought the kaleidoscope of colors had been brilliant on the ground, but from above like this, it's even better.

My mouth is gaped in awe like a small child. I've been to carnivals before, but I've never let myself appreciate one. I've been too focused on other things.

Too soon, we are getting off the Ferris Wheel and going in search of Thea and the guys. A part of me wants to get back on and escape the world for a little bit longer.

Cade doesn't try to hold my hand—which I am thankful for, but also find surprising.

After five minutes of looking, we find all of them sitting at a picnic table eating hotdogs. My stomach rumbles at the sight.

I sit down beside Thea and try not to drool on her food like a hungry dog.

"Here." She hands me a water bottle. "Got this for you."

"Thanks," I reply, twisting off the lid.

"I couldn't find you, but it seems someone else did." Her eyes flick across the table to her brother who grins in response.

I shrug. "Yeah. He wanted to go on the Ferris Wheel."

"Of course he did," she mutters, dipping a fry in ... Is that mayonnaise? *Ew*.

Cade drums his fingers against the table. "I'm going to get some food; you want anything?" he asks me.

I turn away from Thea to face him. "I can get my own food."

"I'll get you a hotdog." He grins and pushes away from the table.

Jace and Xander look up from their food at me. "Can you believe it?" Xander asks Jace.

"Nope," Jace replies, shoving a fistful of fries in his mouth.

"What?" I ask, since it's clear whatever they are referring to has something to do with me.

Xander shrugs. "Nothing."

"Bullshit," I mutter.

Jace snorts. "I like you." He takes off his beanie and lays it on the table. His blond hair sticks up in every direction, but he doesn't seem to care.

"Don't let Cade hear you say that," Xander chides. "I think he just might punch you."

Jace grunts in response. "She's a cool chick. Just voicing my opinion." He raises his hands.

I turn my attention to Xander. "What did you mean by your first comment? The whole, 'can you believe it?' thing."

Xander sighs and sets his hotdog on the paper plate. "It's just that Cade would never normally do that for anyone. I'm not saying he's rude to everyone else, he just ..."

"He distances himself from people he doesn't really know," Thea inserts. "But with you he doesn't. He's just Cade; there's no façade around you. He lets you see the real him."

"I'm still kinda lost." I frown, looking between the three of them.

Thea tries to explain. "Cade is used to people wanting something from him because of who he is. He has to keep a shield up or he'd lose his mind. Do you have any idea how many girls have thrown themselves at him in the hopes of getting pregnant because they think he's going to go pro and they want to trap him?"

I absorb her words. That has to be hard. "I'm just not interested in your brother that way." Lie. My body definitely is, but my mind is firmly against it.

"Then maybe you could at least try to be his friend," she speaks softly. "He needs more of those."

Friends? Cade's *friend*? Can I do that?

I'm not so sure.

I'm not sure I can be anyone's friend anymore, but I feel like maybe Thea and I are friends now. So maybe I can try to make the effort with Cade. After all, my plans to lay low and keep to myself have failed miserably.

"I'll try," I sigh, and Thea brightens at my words.

"Try what?" Cade asks, putting a plate down in front of me

"It's not important." I smile at him in the hopes of distracting him. "Thanks for this."

"No problem." He waves a hand dismissively.

We all eat and make idle chat. When we're finished, everyone is ready to leave. We head back to the parking lot and start to go our separate ways.

"Rae?" Cade calls when Thea and I part from the group.

"Yeah?" I turn around, my brows raised in question.

"Thank you."

I open my mouth to ask him what he's thanking me for, but before I can respond, he turns his back to me and disappears into the darkness.

six
...

THE ALARM on Thea's nightstand pierces the room.

She sits straight up, her hair puffed around her head like a fluffy cotton ball, and groans. "I swear that alarm is the spawn of Satan." She smacks her hand roughly against the top. "Die, motherfucker. Die."

I snort, pulling my damp hair back into a bun. I'm already back from my run and freshly showered.

"You know what else should die?" She turns sleepy eyes my way and then answers before I could respond. "Monday. Monday should die a fiery and painful death." She flops down on the bed and covers her eyes with the crook of her elbow. "I fucking hate mornings."

I laugh. "I think we've established that."

"And you don't help," she continues. "You're always so chipper in the mornings."

"Chipper?" I question. That isn't a word I've ever used to describe myself.

"Okay, maybe not *chipper*, but you're definitely a morning person." She lowers her arm and cracks her eyes open. "Look at you dressed and ready to conquer the world. It's not fair. I don't even feel like brushing my teeth."

"Ew, Thea. That's gross." I move across the room for my backpack and camera case. I'm hoping to get a morning shoot in; the campus is so pretty in the early hours.

"Hey, at least I'm honest." She rolls over then, but rolls too far and falls face first onto the floor. I slap a hand over my mouth in the hope that she won't hear me laughing at her. "If this is a sign of what's to come today," she mumbles, turning onto her back, "then I want a fucking do-over."

"Sorry—" I offer her a hand "—life doesn't work like that." *I wish*.

She takes my hand, and I help her up. "Thanks," she grumbles, heading for the bathroom. "I'll see you for lunch."

I nod even though she can't see me. "See you later," I call, heading for the door.

Since I have awhile before my first class, I spend my time walking around campus, snapping pictures here and there when something piques my interest. I don't know why, but the moment I raise the camera to my eye, I always see the world in a different light. The chaos diminishes, and I see only the beauty.

In the distance, I see a guy sitting against a tree with a book in his lap. He's completely absorbed in the words on the page and nothing around him seems to matter. I focus on him and snap his picture.

He looks up then, and it's like someone kicked me in the

gut. *Cade.* He grins, and I smile in response as he raises a hand to wave me over.

I stand still for a moment, reluctant to join him. But I don't see how I have much choice unless I run away.

I close the distance between us, and he smiles up at me from where he sits on the ground.

He lifts a hand to shield his eyes from the morning sun. "Well—" he chuckles warmly, his blue eyes making my stomach flip "—if it isn't my morning Rae of Sunshine."

"Still with the silly nickname?"

"Always." He shrugs, causing his gray sweater to pull taut across his shoulders. "I like it."

"It's stupid," I mutter, still standing there looking at him.

"That's your opinion." He pats the spot of grass beside him. "Join me for breakfast. I'll share."

That's when I notice he has a to-go box of breakfast food from the diner Thea and I went to a while ago.

When I don't move, his voice grows stern. "Sit, Rae."

I sit; he's rather bossy, and I can't seem to ignore his orders.

"Eat. You're too thin." He points to the smorgasbord of food he has.

"You know—" I pick up a piece of buttered toast "—most guys think there's no such thing as too thin."

"Bullshit." He chuckles. "That's something girls believe because they're often times way too self-conscious. Guys like curves. We want something to grab ahold of." He raises his hands in the air, miming that he's grabbing some invisible breasts. "No one wants to cuddle a twig."

I shake my head and nod at the book in his lap. "What are you reading?"

"Do you really want to know?" He chuckles, bowing his head so that the longer strands of his hair hide his face from sight.

"Yeah." I pick up the fork and take a bite of scrambled eggs. I'm not worried about using the same fork as Cade. After all, he already drank my coffee, and we can't forget the mouth to mouth incident.

He lifts the book in the air, and I try to hide my surprise.

"Harry Potter? Interesting choice of reading material," I comment.

"I like fantasy books," he admits. "Historical ones too, like old westerns, but mostly fantasy. I mean, who hasn't at least once wished they could be a wizard?"

I bow my head, and a small smile graces my lips. "I will admit to at one time thinking it would be really cool if I could do magic."

He grins, setting the book in the grass. "Ah, something we agree on."

I don't know why, but I lift my camera and take a picture of the book. It looks so pretty lying there with the grass sticking up around it and a few fallen leaves.

"What's with the camera?" Cade asks, picking up a bottle of water and taking a sip.

"You know how you like to play with a ball?" I smirk. Waving my camera around a bit, I explain, "This is my toy. My life, actually." I lower the camera into my lap and stare down at it.

He picks at a piece of toast. "So ... is that what you're studying?"

I nod and tuck a piece of hair behind my ear. "Yeah. I mean, I know realistically I'll probably never be able to travel the world and take pictures like I want and I'll more likely be stuck doing weddings and family portraits, but as long as I have my camera and can use it, I'll be happy." I let out a breath and look up for his reaction. He watches me with a calculated gaze, thinking deeply. Before he can say anything, I ask, "What are you studying?"

"Architecture."

"Really?" I reel back in surprise. I didn't expect that. "I thought you'd say like sports medicine or something like that."

He throws his head back and lets out a bellowing laugh. "Is that all you think of me? That I'm some dumb jock that only thinks about football?" I nod, because it's true. He chuckles low and shakes his head. "You don't know me at all, Rae. I'm quite looking forward to getting to know each other better this weekend." He winks.

I pick at a piece of grass, ignoring his comment about this weekend, because frankly, I'm trying to forget about it.

"Why architecture?" I venture to ask.

He shrugs, playing with the lid of the water bottle. "You know Xander?" He waits for my nod. "Well, his dad owns a company, and we've been friends forever. When I was little and I'd go to his house, I was always fascinated with the blueprints. Cooper, his dad, picked up on my interest, and he started taking Xander and me to sites they were working on. It always astounded me how this building would start out as lines on a piece of paper," he says passionately, "and turn into this real place that people used." He shrugs. "I knew then that's what I wanted to do for the rest of my life."

"Where does football come into it?" I ask.

He grunts unintelligibly and looks away. "I like football. I don't *love* it. But … but my dad does. He started me young, and I just continued with it because that's what was expected of me, and I wanted to make him proud." His face grows sad, and he looks away.

"He wants you to go pro," I state. I've heard enough from Thea to know that Cade is talented enough to make a career out of football.

Cade looks back at me and nods.

"But you don't want that."

"No." He sighs, running his fingers through his longish hair. "I don't want that life. I just want to be normal. The spotlight? It's not my thing."

"You're a strange guy." And he is. I thought most guys in his position would be ecstatic at the prospect of going pro. The money. The women. The lifestyle. But not Cade. He's right when he said I didn't know him at all and I'd passed too many judgments on him. Maybe … maybe I *could* be his friend.

"You're a strange girl," he counters with a small smile.

"Touché." I laugh lightly, plucking a piece of grass from the ground and twisting it around my finger.

"You know," he says as he lies on the ground, crossing his arms behind his head. The movement causes his shirt to ride up, exposing the lower muscles of his smooth stomach. A light dusting of hair starts at his navel and disappears beneath the top of his jeans. I look away hastily, my cheeks heating, and pray he didn't see me staring. "It really sucks how people judge you by what you do and not by who you are."

I wince, because that's exactly what I'd done with Cade, and look how wrong I'd been. And people judge me the same way, too.

"I'm sorry," I whisper, surprising us both. "I hate when people judge me that way, and it's exactly what I did to you."

He turns his head toward me. "I didn't expect an apology, Rae, but thanks. It's not just you though. *Everyone* judges me. Even the professors." He sighs heavily. "You have no idea how many classes I've walked into and they take one look at me and make some smart ass comment because of what I do. They think that I just want a free ride, and that's not what I want at all. I *want* to work hard and get my degree. I want to be an architect and build someone's dream home or an old-fashioned church that will stand the test of time. I don't want to be that guy they think I am. I'm *not* that guy."

"I know." And I do. I see it now. I stand up and dust loose grass off my jeans. "I'm glad we had this conversation, and I don't mean that in a sarcastic way. I'm truly happy we did." I back away slowly, and he watches me. When I am far enough away that he'll barely be able to hear me, I say, "I'm looking forward to this weekend."

And I am.

Thea drops down into the seat beside me, her backpack slamming on the table. "Monday's suck, and I need a cupcake. Or a brownie. Or ice cream. Something loaded with sugar, stat."

"That bad, huh?" I frown, picking some of the extra bread off my sandwich.

"Yes," she groans, smacking her head against the table. Raising her head, she says, "You know, maybe it wouldn't be so bad if I actually knew what I wanted to do with my life and I wasn't taking all these stupid classes that bore me half to death."

I feel bad for her, because that really has to suck. "Surely there's something you like that could be a potential career."

Her plump lips turn down into a frown, and she pouts. "Nope. Nothing." She lowers her head to the table once more in the shelter of her arms. Her body begins to shake. "I'm such a failure."

"You're not a failure," I assure her. My hand hovers above her back, not sure whether or not I should try to offer her comfort. Eventually, I give her a small pat and pull my hand away hastily.

She peeks her eyes up at me and sniffles. "I totally am. This is *college*. I'm supposed to have it all figured out and I'm clueless."

"You *will* figure it out," I assure her. "Give it time."

I've known I wanted to be a photographer from the moment I first picked up a camera at ten years old, so I've never been in Thea's position, but I can imagine it would be pretty miserable.

"You really think so?" She sits up, wiping her hands beneath her eyes.

"I know so." I nod reassuringly. "Don't get yourself too worked up about it. One day something will happen, and you'll know what you want to do. Don't stress yourself unnecessarily."

She nods at my words and then surprises me by hugging me. I slowly lift my arms to hug her back. "You're a good friend, Rae."

I open my mouth, ready to tell her that we aren't friends, but that would be a lie. Somehow, Thea has weaseled herself into my heart and become my friend. I haven't had one of those in a long time—I've come to deny myself such things. But it feels good knowing I have someone like her in my life. I hug her back with renewed force. I'm not alone anymore.

"You're a better friend," I whisper in her hair, because it's true. She can never know the real me and what I've done, but she can know the me that I am now.

She pulls away and gives me a shaky smile. "I'm sorry for crying on you."

I crack a smile. "It's okay. But seriously, you need to stop stressing yourself."

"I'll try to be better." She straightens her clothes and stands up. "I better get something to eat. Class on an empty stomach is not fun." She forces a smile and flounces away with a little more pep in her step. Now *that* is the Thea I know.

By the time she returns, she is in a much better mood.

She sets her food down and eyes me. "So, my brother asked me for your phone number."

He told me he was going to, but that news still sends a shiver down my spine.

"He did?" I act clueless.

"Mhm." She grins, peeling the top off her yogurt. "Would you like to explain *why* to me?"

I shrug and squirm in my seat, reluctant to tell her of our plans. I mean, it isn't like it was a date or anything, but if I tell her the truth, it will certainly sound that way.

"Rae?" she pleads, giving me puppy dog eyes. *Damn her.*

"We're going out for lunch or something. I really don't know the specifics." When she brightens, I hasten to add, "It's *not* a date." Nope. Definitely not a date.

She grins like the Cheshire cat. "Yeah, right."

"Seriously," I assure her. "Ask him."

"I will." She turns to her food and the subject is, thankfully, dropped.

I finish eating and look at the time on my phone. "I better go," I tell her. I still have time before my next class, but I am supposed to meet up with Nova so we can discuss our project.

I walk across campus and stand by the bench she told me to wait at. My head swivels in every direction, looking for her purple hair. At least she won't be hard to miss.

When she doesn't appear in a few minutes, I sit down on

the bench, checking my phone to see if I missed a text from her canceling our plans, but there's nothing.

The whirl of a motorcycle catches my attention, streaking across the parking lot.

It screeches into a spot a few spaces down from where I sit. The rider removes their helmet and purple hair tumbles forward.

Holy crap.

It's official: Nova is not only the weirdest person I've ever met, but the coolest as well.

She catches sight of me and waves. I slowly lift my hand and wiggle my fingers. I'm still in shock.

She walks over to me, swiping her fingers through her hair.

I stand up, shaking my head. "Let me get this straight. You're a photographer, you have purple hair, *and* you drive a motorcycle?"

She laughs, squinting from the sunlight. "Yeah."

"Can I be you when I grow up?" The words tumble out of my mouth.

She laughs, a real genuine laugh. It surprises me at first since I've barely ever seen her smile.

"Sorry, I don't think it works that way." She hops up on the bench, sitting on the part where your back is supposed to rest.

I sit down once more. "So, this project ..." I start. "My photos are typically people or nature and very straightforward. Yours are ... wow." I've seen several pieces of Nova's work in class, and to say I am envious of her talent is an understatement.

She cracks a smile. "My photos are conceptual. I see things that aren't necessarily there. When I take a photo, I don't just see a bench." She waves her hand to where we sit. "I see what I can do with the bench. Maybe I want it floating or in a tree or upside down." She shrugs. "You get the picture, no pun intended."

"What do you think we should do then?" I ask, nervously wringing my hands together. Conceptual photography is *way* out of my comfort zone, but I've always wanted to try.

"Marry the two concepts, obviously. You'll dull me down and make my photos more realistic, and I'll help you spice yours up."

"Thanks ... I think," I mumble.

"Sorry." She lets out a small laugh. "I meant no offense."

"I know," I reply. It's pretty obvious that Nova is a blunt type of person. She doesn't sugarcoat things. I kind of like that about her, but I know it could become annoying.

"Will you be free this weekend?" she asks.

"Uh ..." I start. Cade hasn't told me which day he wants to go out or given me a time. "I should have some free time, but I'm not sure when yet."

"You can let me know then." She hops off the bench. "I don't have any time after classes this week, but I should next week."

"Sounds good." I nod and stand. "We'll figure something out."

She unzips her leather jacket and nods. "See you later." She turns on her heel and disappears around the corner of a building.

I head to class, hoping this project doesn't turn into a disaster.

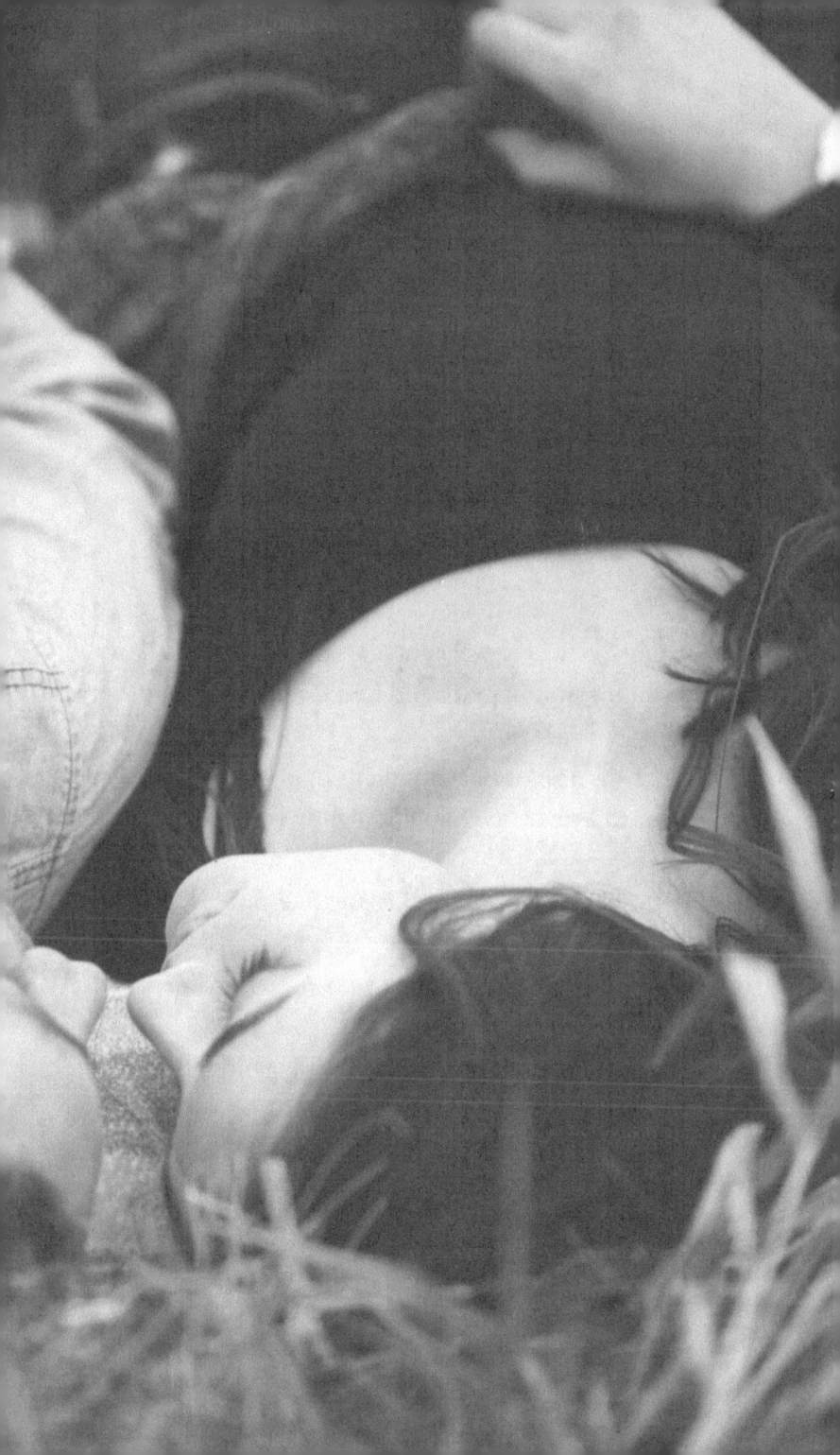

seven

. . .

I'M STARTLED on Wednesday morning when I walk outside for my morning run and find Cade sitting on the top step.

He seems lost in his thoughts and doesn't hear me approach, so I sit beside him and lightly bump his shoulder with mine.

He pushes his hair out of his eyes and smiles. "Hey, Rae of Sunshine."

I sigh but make no comment on the nickname. "What are you doing here?"

He shrugs. "Coach gave us the morning off. I thought we could run together."

"Don't you want a break?" I question. If this is a chance for him to relax and sleep in, I don't understand why he's here.

He shakes his head, his lips curving up. "Nah, I'd rather run with you."

He wants to run with me? Even though they shouldn't, his words please me. I stand up, hiding my smile, and descend the rest of the steps. "I guess we better start running then." Without giving him a moment to join me, I take off. It doesn't take him long to catch up. He shortens his strides to match mine. I don't mind having him run with me this time. In fact, I find his presence almost comforting. I haven't liked him, don't *want* to like him, but just like his sister, he's weaseled his way into my life and made it impossible to resist him.

By the time I would normally start heading back to my dorm, Cade slows to a walk. He grasps my arm and tugs slightly. Nodding his head in the other direction, he says, "Come this way."

I follow him, because apparently all rational thought was flushed down the toilet the moment I saw him sitting on the steps.

He finds a grassy spot and sits down, drawing his knees up and draping his arms overtop.

I sit down too, plucking at my damp top.

"Why are we here?" I ask, my breath coming out as a pant.

"No reason." He shrugs, flicking his hair out of his eyes. "I just wasn't ready to say goodbye to you." He grins boyishly.

"Hey, you shaved." I can't believe I just now noticed.

He chuckles and scrubs a hand over his bare jaw. "Yeah, Coach doesn't like us to look homeless when we have a game and interviews, so it had to go."

"Homeless?" I laugh.

"Coach's words, not mine." He holds his hands up defensively.

"So, you have a game coming up?" I'm not into football so I never keep track of such things.

"Yeah, on Saturday." He looks away briefly at a spot where a flock of birds are fighting over a crumb. "Will Sunday work for our ... non-date?"

I laugh at his terminology. "Sunday is fine."

He stares at me for a moment, his blue eyes like twin flames. "Will you come to my game?"

"I-I—" I stutter. I wasn't expecting him to ask that, and I don't know how to respond. "Football isn't my thing."

"Please?" he begs. "I want you there."

I don't know what to make of that.

When I don't reply immediately, he says, "If you won't come for me, will you at least come for Thea? It's a home game, obviously, and I don't want her being harassed because of who I am."

Cade knows exactly what to say to weaken my resolve. *Damn him.*

"I'll go," I finally relent. "For both of you," I add, and he grins. I like Cade's smile; it lights up his whole face and soften his chiseled features.

"Thank you." He reaches for my hand and grasps it briefly before letting go.

My hand tingles with warmth where he touched it. I school my features so he can't see how much that single touch affected me.

A part of me wants to believe that the reason Cade has such an effect on me is because I've spent so long without human contact like this. But I know deep down that isn't the case. It is just Cade.

"What are you thinking about?" he asks.

"Nothing." I lower my head.

"Liar." He chuckles warmly. "That wrinkle between your brows says otherwise." He waves a finger toward my face. "Come on, tell me. Don't make me beg."

I shrug casually. "I think about lots of things."

"Not going to tell me?" He pouts.

"No." I laugh. "I'm not."

"Does that mean you were thinking about me?" His eyes sparkle with laughter and he fights a smile.

"You're really full of yourself," I mutter, suppressing a laugh as I shake my head and look away.

"I'm right, aren't I?" Even though I'm not looking at him, I can feel his smile like a caress on my skin.

"No," I say defensively.

His answering smile says he doesn't believe me.

"I'm hungry." He rubs his stomach.

"Okay?" It comes out as a question.

"Let's go to the dining hall and get something to eat," he suggests.

When I start to protest, he presses a finger against my lips, promptly shutting me up.

"There's no harm in breakfast."

He's right, but still …

I look down at my sweaty clothes and back at him. "I'm kind of gross."

"So am I." He plucks at his white t-shirt. "Come on, Rae, we can be sweaty together."

I snort in a very undignified manner. "That sounded kind of perverted."

He taps my forehead with his long fingers. "I think you have a dirty mind, because that was a completely innocent comment."

He hops up in one lithe movement that I am instantly envious of. It's amazing that a guy his size can move like that. He certainly isn't small—not with his height and those muscles—but he moves so gracefully.

He holds his large hand out for me, and after a second of thought, I take it. He hauls me up and against his chest. My breath leaves me in a gasp. My body curves against his hard lines, and my eyes flick up to his. Time seems momentarily suspended. He stares at me for a moment, and then his eyes dart to my lips. My tongue flicks out to moisten their surface. Blood roars in my ears as it rushes through my body. I can't think about anything other than Cade and how good this feels. He reaches up, smoothing his fingers against my cheek. My eyes close, and my breath comes out in a shaky gasp. His touch feels heavenly and forbidden all at the same time.

When I open my eyes and look into his, I see that they've darkened into a stormy blue.

Neither of us move or even breathe.

Then he releases me and the spell is broken.

I look down at the ground, hoping to hide my embarrassment.

He grasps my chin and forces my head up. "You feel it too." His eyes sear into me, leaving a brand.

I gasp but don't get a chance to reply. He turns and walks away. When he realizes I'm not following, he turns around, his hands shoved in the pockets of his basketball shorts. "You coming?"

"Yeah." I shake my head and jog after him.

I make no comment about what he said. I figure that's better, because I'm not sure I can lie. I did feel it—whatever this thing between us is.

When we arrive at the dining hall, it's relatively empty.

I fix a bowl of Froot Loops and Cade gets Captain Crunch. I can't help smiling at our childish choices.

We sit across from each other at one of the many tables.

When Cade isn't looking at me, I study him. I notice dark circles beneath his eyes and wonder what had causes them. Loss of sleep, obviously, but *why*?

Before he can notice me staring and make a cocky comment, I look away.

The silence between us is oddly comfortable. I've never been this content to sit with someone and not speak, but with Cade, it's okay. He feels like someone I've known forever, which is weird since I've known him for no time at all.

When we've both finished eating, Cade grabs my bowl and throws our trash away.

I expect to head separate ways, but he falls into step beside me.

"Thanks for having breakfast with me. I'm sorry I wasn't feeling very chatty. I just …" He twists his lips. "I have a lot on my mind right now." He forces a smile.

"I can relate to that," I assure him.

"I didn't want you to think I was being rude since I'm normally so chatty."

I grasp his arm briefly and squeeze it in comfort. "You don't need to explain anything to me. I get it. Trust me, I do. Probably better than most people. And honestly, I'm kind of surprised you even like me and want to spend time with me. I haven't exactly been the nicest person to you." Taking a shaky breath, I tell him, "I'm going to work on that."

His smile turns genuine and then to a full-blown grin. "Is that so?"

I nod, smiling because his grin is so damn infectious. Everything about Cade is infectious—no, magnetic.

"Yeah. Be patient with me, though. I've … I've been through a lot." I know that's probably admitting too much, but I need him to know I have a reason for being so stand-offish before. When you go through something like I have, and then have to deal with the aftermath, it makes you skittish and untrusting of other people.

He winks. "Patience is my middle name."

"Of course it is." I laugh, bowing my head a little.

My dorm comes into view, and I start up the steps.

"Rae?" he calls.

I turn around and smile. "Yes?"

"This dinner on Sunday ... Are we really still going as acquaintances?"

My smile widens. "No, Cade. We're going as friends."

And then his smile lights my world on fire.

eight

. . .

"ARE YOU REEEAAAAADY FOR SOME FOOOOOOOOOTBALL?" Thea chants, coming out of the bathroom. She takes one look at me, wrinkles her face in disgust, and grunts, "You are *so* not ready for some football. What the hell are you wearing?"

"Uh ... jeans and a sweatshirt." I look down at my attire wondering what she finds so appalling about it.

"But it's all black! You can't go to the game like that! You'll stick out like a sore thumb! You need to wear our school colors!"

Since she looks like blue and gold have thrown up on her, I tend to disagree. Seriously, she has on little blue shorts with a fitted yellow short-sleeved top. Blue and yellow ribbons are wrapped around her ponytail. Even her eye makeup is blue and yellow.

She heads for the closet and starts rummaging around. It isn't long until she is throwing clothes at me that I somehow manage to catch. "Thea!" I groan. "I'm not wearing this!"

"Yes, you are!" She turns around, hands on her hips. "I am not letting you walk out that door looking like you're going to a funeral! This is a football game, and you're going to support your school! Team spirit, Rae! Team. Fucking. Spirit."

Jesus Christ, I am never going to win this argument.

"Fine." I strip off my shirt. "I'll wear that." I take the yellow shirt from her hands that is emblazoned with the school's mascot—a wolverine. "And I'll ditch the black jeans, but I'm wearing *blue* jeans, and not ... whatever that is." I wave a hand at the blue cotton shorts she holds that I'm sure are a twin of the ones she wears. No way am I leaving the dorm with my ass cheeks hanging out. That is *not* acceptable.

"Fine." She tosses the shorts back in her closet. "As long as you wear the shirt, I'll survive."

My lips quirk in amusement at her melodramatics.

Once I am changed and dressed to her satisfaction, it's time to leave.

I'm shocked by the flow of students when we step out of the dorm. Everyone seems to be heading to the game, and I have no idea how we'll even get seats.

"This is crazy." I hiss under my breath where only Thea can hear.

"No, this is football."

"Same thing," I mumble.

The walk to the stadium takes forever thanks to the crowd.

I have to admit that the energy is infectious.

"I don't have a ticket." I gasp when I realize they are checking slips of paper up ahead.

Thea turns her gaze my way. "Chillax, did you really think Cade wouldn't have us covered?" She holds up two tickets. "Best seats in the whole place. We'll be able to smell their sweat." She says the last part like it's the greatest thing in the world.

"I'm not sure I want to smell sweat," I tell her, wrinkling my nose.

"Oh—" she grins "—trust me, you do."

"Tickets?" a voice interrupts our conversation.

Thea hands them over and points to me so the man will know the second ticket is for me. He studies our seat numbers and gives her directions. She appears bored by his explanation, and I figure Thea has been to Cade's games often enough, even though she hasn't been a student here until this year.

Since Thea obviously knows where to go, I follow her.

At one point, we come close to being separated, and she grabs ahold of my arm, dragging me behind her.

Our seats are close to the front and in the middle of the field. The benches where the players sit are in front of us.

Thea sits down and claps her hands together, doing a little dance in her seat. "I'm so fucking excited!"

"I gathered that." I laugh, leaning away from her flailing her arms before she smacks me in the face.

"This is my first time attending a game as an actual student!" She grabs my arm and gives it a shake, like she's trying to force her excitement into me. "Aren't you excited, Rae?" Her eyes are large, ready to pop out of her skull. I'm pretty sure she's had too much sugar this morning.

"Ecstatic," I say, trying to force some enthusiasm into my voice.

Thea seems to buy it, or, at least, she pretends to. "God, I love football season." I swear her whole body is shaking with excitement at this point. I don't know how I am going to make it through the next few hours if she keeps this up. I wish I had a tranquilizer to give her—yeah, she's that bad.

"You really love football."

"Yep." She nods, threading her fingers together so they'll stop tap-dancing across her knees. "I've grown up with it."

A few minutes later, I ask, "When do they come out?"

She looks down at her phone. "Anytime now."

I want to ask her what number Cade is, but I figure she'll get the wrong idea, so I keep my mouth shut.

The stadium is large and packed. The sounds of that many voices all speaking at once sounds like a roar. The energy is contagious; I can feel it vibrating through my body.

"Here they come!" Thea grasps my arm, her fingernails digging in to the point that she draws blood.

Our team—and I only know that since they are wearing blue and yellow—runs out on the field. They're huge, all tall and muscular. It makes for an intimidating sight.

And then the atmosphere changes. Everything becomes hushed, and music—some rock song or something—starts to play through the speakers.

The last player slowly walks out onto the field, his shoulders straight. When the music picks up, he turns to face us as he walks sideways. He lifts his arms in the air and jumps up and down a bit, hyping the crowd up even more.

I *know* it's Cade. It sounds crazy, but I feel that it's him.

The antics he's pulling on the field with the crowd doesn't seem like the Cade I know, but what do I really know about him?

After he has the crowd worked into a frenzy, he runs over to his teammates. I make sure to memorize his jersey number.

Eighty-three.

"Isn't it incredible?" Thea asks me with wide eyes.

"Spectacular," I agree. And it is. I can't deny that even if I have no idea what the hell is going on.

The opposing team comes out without the pomp and circumstance ours had.

When they started playing, I watch with awe. For the first time ever, I'm not bored out of my mind watching football. My dad has been obsessed with it and every weekend during football season it was the only thing on our TV. I'd never cared about it then. But now I have someone to root for.

At one point, Cade is tackled to the ground, rather forcefully from what I can see, and I wince, hiding my face behind my hands. I don't like seeing him hurt.

During halftime when they are about to walk off the field, I watch Cade remove his helmet and turn to search the stands. His shaggy hair is damp with sweat, and he pushes his fingers through it, forcing it away from his eyes.

His gaze lands on me and his grin spreads. He slowly lifts an arm and points right at me.

Thea squeals, "I knew it!" She kicks her legs excitedly.

With a wink, Cade lowers his hand and runs off the field.

People in the stands look around wildly, trying to find who he'd been pointing to. I know it's impossible for them to figure out it was me, but I still find myself trying to blend in and not try to catch their attention.

"You are so dating my brother, you little liar," Thea says from beside me. I turn to her and let out a sigh. She isn't mad at the idea of me dating her brother, oh no, she is so dang excited, which makes it difficult to keep telling her that nothing is going on.

"I'm not, I swear," I tell her. "I know you're probably already planning our wedding and excited over the idea of us being sister-in-laws, but Cade and I are *not* dating." I slash my hands through the air. "We're just friends."

Thea sighs, her eyes growing sad, but she quickly brightens. "For now." She lets the subject drop and turns her attention to one of the people walking the stairs selling food. Once she's bought enough food for ten people, she shoves most of it at me and demands that I eat. Cade might be Cocky Cade, but Thea is Bossy Thea. It doesn't have quite the same ring to it, but it's the truth.

I can't believe that only a few weeks ago I told this girl I wasn't here to make friends, but yet I am sitting beside her at a football game, and it's safe to say that we're friends. My plans never seem to work out.

"So," I ask, munching on some popcorn, "where are Xander and Jace?"

"Xander plays football," she explains, "and Jace is ... Jace. This isn't his thing."

"He seems kind of ... odd. Nice," I assure her, "but odd."

"Like you?" Her eyes sparkle with laughter.

I laugh, tossing some popcorn at her. "Yes, like me."

"I don't really know how to explain Jace. We grew up with him too, but he didn't really become friends with Cade until high school. I don't know the story there."

"So ... what's going on with you and Xander?" I ask and watch her cheeks flame with color.

"Nothing."

"Nothing? Do you want there to be something?" No way am I letting her get off that easy. Not with the way she pestered me with questions about my nonexistent relationship with Cade.

"Yes. No. I don't know. It's weird, because we're friends, but he's Cade's *best* friend. We grew up together, and I don't think he sees me like that. I'm just Cade's sister to him."

I beg to differ. "I've seen the way he looks at you, and trust me, you're not just Cade's sister to him."

She turns her gaze to me, her eyes full of hope. "Really?"

I nod and let the subject drop.

We finished eating and wad up our trash when the players come back out onto the field.

Thea becomes even more energetic as the game progresses, which is saying something since she'd been bad enough before.

When the score is tied, Thea grasps my hand so tightly it goes numb.

In the final seconds of the game, Cade is sprinting across the field with the football cradled in his arm. His long legs almost seem to blur as he runs.

I find myself standing up and chanting, "Go! Go! Go!"

Thea grasps my hand and then we are both screaming as guys try to knock him down.

When Thea screams in my ear with excitement, I know Cade has made it. "He did it! Go, Cade! That's my brother!" She points, but no one can hear her. Everyone in the stadium seems to be screaming.

Cade's team runs over to him and the scoreboard flashes.

We've won.

I don't know why, but my blood roars at that. This football thing could be addicting and fun when I have someone to cheer for.

"Aren't you glad you came now?"

Yes. Yes, I was. "It was okay."

"Whatever, Rae." Thea rolls her eyes.

The stands began to slowly empty out, but the energy level is still high. I am sure there is bound to be lots of celebratory parties popping up along campus. People would want to draw out this win for as long as possible.

"Think you'll come to another game?" she asks, a knowing smile on her lips. I'm not fooling her. Not at all.

"Maybe." I shrug as we walked back to our dorm. I'm a little bummed that I won't see Cade, but I don't let that show. I know he probably has a lot of stuff to do with his team. "I'd love to bring my camera next time."

She grins. "So there will be a next time?"

I groan. I didn't mean for to let that slip out. "Yeah, there will probably be a next time."

She smiles, clasping her hands together as she dances ahead of me humming pleasantly under her breath.

For a moment, I'm envious of Thea. I wish I could see the world as beautiful and simple as she does. I used to. Now I just see the darkness and the pain that lurks around every corner.

nine
...

I DON'T KNOW what to wear.

Shocker.

But seriously, what does one wear on a non-date? I guess I should dress like I normally do, but that seems too easy.

I tap my fingers against my lips.

"What are you doing?" Thea asks, walking into our dorm. The door slams closed behind her—Thea never does anything quietly.

I'd hoped to be gone by the time she arrived. Of course, my luck isn't that good. Actually, I'm pretty sure my luck is nonexistent.

"Trying to find something to wear," I mumble, frustrated with myself for getting so worked up over this. What I wear shouldn't matter, but right now, I'm being a typical girl.

"Oh, yeah. That's right, you're going out with Cade."

"It's not a date," I spit.

She smirks. "I didn't say it was."

My cheeks flame. "It's really not."

"Hey—" she lifts her hands "—you don't need to defend yourself to me." She drops her bag on her bed. "Do you want any help?"

No. "Yes."

Thea walks over and peruses my closet. "Here." She shoves torn black jeans into my hands a loose gray sweater that hangs off my shoulders. "And these." She bends down, picking up a pair of chestnut-colored leather boots. "Cute and simple and not trying too hard."

"I don't want to try at all."

She huffs. "There is nothing wrong with that outfit. It's cute and something you'd wear around campus. It's not a skintight dress that has your boobs hanging out asking for some attention, so pull your panties out of that wad."

My lips twitch with the threat of laughter. "Okay," I agree.

I change into the outfit and look in the mirror. Thea's right; it's perfect.

Cade text me hours ago, telling me he'll pick me up at six. After arguing that I'd meet him at the restaurant instead of going with him, I finally gave in when he threatened to carry me out of the dorm and to his car if I didn't cooperate. I know he wasn't lying.

"Are you nervous?" Thea asks.

My head snaps in her direction. "Why would I be nervous?"

"No reason." She shrugs innocently. I'm going to throttle that beauty queen one of these days.

My phone vibrates in my pocket, and I pull it out to see a text from Cade telling me he's in the parking lot. Stupidly, my heart speeds up.

When I look up from my phone, Thea's watching me with a knowing smile.

"See you later," she sing-songs.

"Mhm," is my only reply, as I grab my bag and leave.

It isn't easy to miss Cade's black Jeep Wrangler sitting in the parking lot. The thing is huge.

He hops out of the truck and my breath falters.

Holy hell.

His hair is brushed back away from his forehead, which only serves to accentuate the curves of his cheekbones and the cut of his chiseled chin.

He's wearing a light-blue, button-down shirt that makes his eyes pop even more. His shirt is tucked into a nice pair of jeans and held up by a thin black belt.

Cade is good-looking. Period. But right now ... He's almost god-like.

When he chuckles, I realize I've stopped walking and stand there, staring at him. Such a great way to start off this *non*-date.

Shaking my head, I force my feet forward.

He opens the passenger door for me, and I climb inside. I can't help being reminded of my first date with Brett.

My heart raced in my chest.

Thump. Thump. Thump.

I'd had a crush on Brett for longer than I'd care to admit, and I'd been shocked when he asked me to go to the movies with him.

At first, I'd been excited, then scared, and finally, I was just plain worried.

Worried about what to wear.

Worried about how to fix my hair.

Worried about what to do or say.

The last thing I wanted to do was make a fool of myself. I'd been on dates before, and kissed guys, but none of them were Brett.

They didn't make my heart pound like he did.

Or a light sweat break out across my skin.

I took a deep breath and finished smoothing out the curls in my hair. I did my makeup, making sure not to do it too heavy. After all, we were going to the movies. This was meant to be casual, and I didn't want to get carried away.

"Stop freaking out, Rachael," I scolded myself. "You're being stupid."

And I was. I'd known Brett my whole life, but a part of me felt like that night was monumental—like my life might never be the same again.

I fluffed my hair one last time and went into my closet, trying on four different outfits before settling on a pair of skinny jeans, a flowered peplum top, and boots. It was nice, but not like I was trying too hard ... I'd hoped.

"Rachael!" my mom yelled up the stairs. "Brett is here!"

My heart jolted with excitement.

I took my time going downstairs, not wanting to appear too eager.

I couldn't help smiling when I saw Brett waiting for me in the foyer. His red hair was gelled back stylishly, and he was dressed in jeans and a green polo shirt that made his eyes appear even more green. He grinned when he saw me, and as his eyes perused my body I felt my cheeks heat.

I'd never been one to act so shy and girly before, but Brett made me nervous.

My mom and dad stood back aways, watching us. Finally, my dad cleared his throat and looked between the two of us. "Have her back by ten."

"Daaaaad," I whined. "I'm sixteen. I can stay out later than that!"

"Fine." He sighed, scrubbing a hand over his beard. "Eleven. But any later," he warned, "and I'm calling the police."

Brett chuckled. "Don't worry, Mr. Wilder. I'll have her back in time."

My dad narrowed his eyes and made a grunting sound that said: I'll believe it when I see it. I knew my dad was just messing with Brett, though.

"Come on," Brett said to me, "we don't want to be late for the movie."

My body hummed when he put his hand on my waist, guiding me to the door. My insides were a jumbled mess of excitement.

We walked to his car in silence, and he opened the door of his hand-me-down BMW for me to slip inside. "Thanks." I smiled.

He smiled back. Once he was seated, he admitted, "I didn't think you'd agree to go on a date with me."

"What? Why not?" I gasped, astonished.

He shrugged. "Look at you; you're beautiful, and smart, and amazing."

"You're all those things, too," I countered.

He grinned crookedly and lowered his head so that his hair brushed his forehead. "Not like you." He chuckled, starting the car.

It didn't take us long to get to the theater. He took me to the old one in town. Most people preferred the fancy new one attached to the mall, but not me, and Brett knew that. There was something so real about the old one, and it reminded me of a time when I believed people were happier—when life was simple.

"Is this okay?" Brett asked.

"It's perfect." I smiled. Our date had barely started, and it was already better than I imagined.

Inside, we ordered popcorn and soda.

The theater was pretty empty. Most people didn't come to this one. I liked that it allowed us to have a little more privacy.

We took our seats toward the back.

The lights dimmed, and I swore my heart sped up even more, if that was possible.

When Brett reached to hold my hand halfway through the movie, I thought I stopped breathing.

Once the movie ended and he still didn't let go of my hand, I thought I might burst from happiness.

We walked out of the theater, and Brett looked at his

watch. "We still have an hour before you have to go home; do you want to walk around town for a while?"

"Sure." I smiled. I wasn't ready to say goodbye.

We hadn't walked very far when Brett pointed to a diner lit up down the street. "They have the best pancakes I've ever had. Are you hungry?"

I wasn't, but I nodded, because if Brett wanted pancakes, then we were going to have pancakes.

He grinned and pulled me into the diner. His smile was wide as he looked at me across the table. We placed our order, and as soon as the waitress was gone, Brett started asking me questions.

We spent the next forty minutes laughing about random things that happened in school and stories from our past.

Brett paid for our meal and we headed back to his car.

On the drive home, he kept a tight hold on my hand. His was warm and soft. Comforting.

"I want to do this again ... if you'd like that." He bowed his head, as if he seemed unsure of what my reaction would be.

"I'd love it." I probably agreed a little too eagerly, but it was too late to take my words back.

He grinned. "Good." He parked in my driveway, and I started to get out of the car, but his hold on my hand tightened, and he wouldn't let go.

"Rachael?"

"Yeah?" I turned back around to face him and our faces were only inches apart. In the dim light, I could see his pupils dilate.

He tilted his head to the side and closed his eyes.

I did the same, and when our lips connected, I felt like a fireworks explosion had gone off in my body. Kissing a guy had never felt so ... magical. I melted against his touch. I grasped his shirt in my hand, moving my lips with his. When his tongue nudged my lips, they parted with a gasp.

He pulled away and placed a tender kiss on my cheek.

"See you later, Rachael."

"Bye." My voice came out sounding breathless.

I eased out of the car with shaking legs, looking at him over my shoulder. I knew that something had changed between us then and there was no going back—I didn't want to.

I shake my head, coming back to reality. I hope Cade didn't notice me zoning out, but since he's just easing into the car, I figure I'm safe.

He looks over at me and smiles. "You look beautiful, Rae."

"Thanks," I squeak.

Despite my demands that this not be a date, it's really starting to feel like a date.

Cade backs out of the parking space and heads off campus.

I don't bother asking him where we were going, because I doubt he'll tell me. I remember a mention of burgers.

Cade reaches over and fiddles with the radio. "What kind of music do you like?"

"This is fine," I tell him. "I'm not picky."

Cade nods and taps his long fingers against the steering wheel. He hums the song softly under his breath.

I sit back in the seat and look out the window. I haven't

gone exploring yet, but the town surrounding campus looks surprisingly quaint.

"Do you like it here?" Cade asks, breaking the silence between us. "College?"

I shrug and then nod. "Yeah, I do. It's nice being on my own." Not being judged. Having a real life.

"I probably shouldn't admit this—" those dimples pop out in his cheeks when he smiles "—but I had trouble my first year away. I *really* missed my mom's cooking."

"Yeah, the food on campus is a bit …" I wrinkle my nose.

"Lacking?" he supplies.

"That's a nicer word for it." I laugh, tucking a stray curl behind my ear. "I drive Thea crazy because I eat cereal for most of my meals. But the food looks so gross."

"It doesn't taste much better than it looks." He winks. That wink makes my stomach stir in ways it never has before. "Don't worry, though, where we're going, you won't be eating cereal. Get ready to feast upon the best burger of your life." Ducking his head slightly, he chuckles. Lifting his hands from the steering wheel, he holds them apart. "I swear they're this big. About the size of your head."

"Are you implying I have a large head?" I keep my face neutral so he won't know I'm joking.

"I didn't mean—wait, you're messing with me, aren't you?"

Of course my lips twitch, giving me away.

"Yeah."

"Wow."

"What?" I ask, tilting my head slightly in wonder at his statement.

"It's just ... I don't think I've heard you make a joke. It's refreshing." He gives me a serious look before returning his eyes to the road. "You're full of surprises, Rae."

"Something tells me you are too," I counter. "Everyone has secrets."

A muscle in Cade's jaw twitches. "Yes, yes they do."

"Marty!" Cade cries when we walk into the restaurant. I stand awkwardly behind him as he addresses the older man I assume is Marty. "Long time no see. I've missed you." Cade slings his arm around the man's shoulders and turns to introduce me. "Rae, this is Marty, the owner of this fine establishment. Marty, this is Rae."

"A girlfriend?" Marty's fuzzy gray brows shoot up so far they disappear beneath his bushy gray hair. "You've never brought a girl here before."

"I'm not his girlfriend," I growl.

Cade gives Marty a sad look. "Unfortunately, the lovely Rae here doesn't like me that way. Such a shame, right? We could be great together."

Marty chuckles and looks at me. "I can understand not liking this goon. He can be a bit much."

"He can," I agree.

"Go sit down," Marty orders. "I'll send someone over to get your drink order."

"Come on." Cade nods toward the corner of the restaurant that isn't as busy.

The place seems a bit shady from the outside ... and the inside too. The walls are crumbling and the floors look dirty. I have to admit, the food looks delicious—at least, what I've seen in passing.

Menus are already on the table, and I pick one up, looking it over.

"Everything is good," Cade tells me, not even bothering to look, "you can't go wrong."

I point to the menu and lean forward a bit. He leans in too, and there is barely any space between us. Up close, I can see flecks of gold in his blue eyes. "It looks like everything is not one of the items on the menu."

He bellows out a laugh. "Joke number two. This night is shaping up to be very interesting."

"If that's what you call interesting—" I sit back "—then you really need to look up the definition of the word."

He smiles, scratching his jaw. "You're not like other girls, Rae."

"No, I'm not," I agree. I'm not most like people. Not anymore. My innocence had been stolen a year ago when I ruined everything.

"So, where are you from, Rae?"

I squirm. Why did he have to ask that question? "Not anywhere near here," I answer vaguely. Vague is always good.

"I figured that." He stares at me, waiting for me to say something. I know I needed to give him some kind of information, but I don't want to lie. Lying only makes things worse, and my life is already fucked up enough as it is.

"What can I get you to drink?"

The sound of the waitress' voice is akin to angels singing. I'm thankful for the reprieve.

"Water for me," Cade says.

"Water for me as well." I smile at her.

"I'll give you a minute to look at the menu, and I'll be right back with your drinks." She taps her fingers lightly against the wood tabletop, and then she's gone.

Cade's eyes sear me when I look up. "Why don't you want to tell me where you're from?"

"Because it's not important."

He sighs, and I feel kind of bad for sounding like such a bitch. "Look ..." I place my hands on the table and leaned forward. "There are things that happened there, bad things, and I just don't want to talk about it. Okay?"

He absorbs my words, and I think for a minute he is going to protest. "Okay," he agrees.

I let out a sigh of relief.

"What *can* I ask you?"

"I don't know." I laugh. "Something easy."

"What's your middle name?" he asks.

"Madison. Yours?"

"Paul. Favorite color?"

"Purple. Yours?" I smile at our back and forth. This, right here, is simple and easy. I need more of this in my life.

"Gray, I guess. I don't really have a favorite. Favorite movie?"

I have to think about that one. "Titanic. It's romantic and heartbreaking. What's yours?"

"Ghostbusters. Favorite band?"

"One Republic. Yours?" I rest my chin on my hand, fighting another smile.

"Fall Out Boy. Favorite—"

"Here's your water. Are you ready to order?"

I jump at the sound of the waitress' voice. I hadn't realized, it but while we were talking, Cade and I had leaned closer and closer together. I sit back, tucking my hands onto my lap.

Cade orders, and I mutter, "I'll have the same." I didn't even really bother to scrutinize the menu.

"Good choice." Cade grins.

"Of course you'd say that." I squeeze the lemon into my glass of water just to have something to do.

"Well, I mean you did order the same thing as me, and I have *excellent* taste in everything."

"Is that so?" I ask, raising a brow.

"I mean, I am sitting here having dinner with you. I think that proves I make good choices."

I bite my lip and look down. My fingers find the paper napkin on the table, and I begin to pick it apart. "What is it about me that makes you think I'm a good choice?"

His eyes narrow. "You really don't see yourself the way others see you, do you?"

"I don't know what you mean," I mutter, not meeting his gaze.

"When I say certain things you act like you're a monster."

I *am* a monster; Cade just doesn't know it yet. "I don't understand it."

"You don't understand *it* or *me*?"

"You. I don't fucking understand you." His jaw tightens.

I lower my head and realize that I am ruining our whole evening. "Look," my voice cracked, "you don't know what I've been through. The things people have said to me. The names I've been called. It's been horrible."

"Then tell me," he pleads.

"I can't. I barely know you."

"Don't you see?" he snaps, waving his hand between us. "I'm trying to get to know you, but you're making it impossible." He lets out a heavy, pent-up breath. "I'm sorry. I shouldn't have snapped at you." He lays his hands on his table. "But I promise you right now, Rae, I *will* get you to trust me, and one day, when you're ready, you're going to tell me everything."

I doubt it, but I don't tell him that.

Our food arrives, and I decide to change the subject. I don't want there to be any more awkwardness between us because of me. And, frankly, I actually want both of us to enjoy tonight.

"I had fun at your game," I tell him, squirting some ketchup on my plate.

"You did?" He perks up, smiling.

"Yeah. It was cool seeing you play. I've never been into the sport before." I shrug.

"And now you are?" he questions, his smile turning into

a full-blown grin. The dimples aren't quite showing, but I feel like the tension has dissipated fairly well.

I hold my thumb and index finger up with a tiny bit of space between them. "Just a little bit."

"Only a little bit?"

"Okay, maybe this much." I widen the space.

"That's better." He chuckles, taking a bite of his burger.

I do the same. "You know, Thea is extra crazy at football games. I thought she might pull my arm off with the way she kept yanking on it, or maybe bust my ear drum."

Cade chuckles. "Thea is highly enthusiastic."

"Yeah, kind of like a puppy."

Cade snorts and then laughs so hard I fear he can't breathe. "Did you just compare my sister to a puppy?"

"Hey—" I raise my hands "—don't tell me you haven't thought the same thing. She's a ball of energy. Except in the mornings. That's when she's dreadful."

Cade continues to laugh. "I'm sure it must be interesting living with Thea."

"You have no idea. I'm really tempted to throw everything she owns that's pink out the window. It's just too much. No one should ever own that much pink." Yeah, I *really* hate pink.

"You should see her room at home if you think your dorm room is bad," Cade chortles.

"Oh, God." I slap my hands over my eyes, like the thought alone is too much to handle.

"In her defense, that's mostly our mom's doing. She

always thought Thea should be a princess," he explains, grabbing a fry.

"Like with the pageants?" I question, raising a brow.

"She told you about that?" Cade's eyes widen with surprise.

"I guessed. She confirmed," I reply.

"Ah, I see. She doesn't tell most people about that. She finds it embarrassing. Our mom's a bit ... zany."

"That's a kind word for crazy." *Shit. I shouldn't have said that out loud.*

Cade chuckles. "That's true."

We finish eating while chatting about more random things. It surprises me how easy it is being with Cade. Even when it's rough—like our conversation earlier—I still found myself comfortable in his presence. I might've tried to stay away from him, but that is for his protection. He can't see that I would ruin him, but I am growing too weak to stay away. I need Cade Montgomery in my life any way he'll give me.

The waitress lays the receipt on the table, and before I can react, Cade has already grabbed it with a credit card in his hand.

"Cade," I groan, "you said this dinner was as friends. Please let me pay my half."

"No can do, Sunshine."

"Caaaaade," I draw out his name.

He stares at me, and I stare right back.

The waitress comes back by, and he hands her his credit card.

"You didn't need to do that," I tell him.

"I know." He grins. "Now just sit back and say thank you."

I sigh, fighting the urge to kick him beneath the table. "Thank you, Cade. The meal was delicious, and I enjoyed spending time with you." I mean it, too.

His grin spreads. "I enjoyed spending time with you too."

My fingers tangle together, and I look away, unable to handle another second of his stare.

The waitress returns with his credit card, and after signing the slip, we head out to his Jeep.

"So," he starts, shoving his hands in the pockets of his jeans, "does this mean I might get to take you on a real date?"

I stop walking and level him with a glare. "Don't push your luck." I like Cade way more than I should already—anything that might lead to *more* has to be avoided at all costs.

He chuckles and lifts his arms in mock defense. "Hey, I had to ask." He reaches out and opens the passenger door for me. I climb inside and swear I feel his eyes on my butt.

Once he gets in, he turns the heat up and rests his elbow on the armrest. His hand is dangerously close to mine. If I was a different girl—one who hadn't been through what I had—Cade would be the perfect guy, and instead of running from him at every turn, I'd open my arms and embrace him. I'm scared, though—terrified, really—of what he will think of me if he knew the truth. The best course of action is to distance myself from him, but I know it will be impossible.

Not only because Cade is unavoidable, but because I've actually come to like him.

The drive back to campus is peaceful.

He parks the Jeep and unbuckles his seatbelt. "I'll walk you to the door so I know you get in safe." He climbs out of the car and meets me on the other side. Together, we head toward the dorm in the distance.

At the door, I stop. "Thanks." I smile, looking up at him. "For walking me to the door and for dinner. I ... I had a good time."

"Good." He leaned his solid shoulder against the glass door so I can't open it.

I stand still, waiting for whatever he might do or say next, because with Cade, you never know.

Only a few seconds pass before he lifts his fingers to my cheek. My eyes close and my lips part with a breath as his fingers ghost against my skin. His touch feels like the most delicious kind of torture.

"Goodnight, Rae."

I blink my eyes open slowly and see him already walking back to his Jeep.

"Goodnight, Cade," I whisper, lifting my fingers to my cheek. I never knew a simple caress could make your whole body soar with feelings, but Cade apparently has a magic touch.

ten

...

"I HATE YOUR BROTHER, and he needs to crawl in a hole and die before I kill him myself," I snap at Thea as I hunch over the toilet. I spent all night sick with stupid food poisoning, and I still am not feeling better.

Thea stands in the doorway frowning. "I'll give him the memo."

"You do that," I assure her. I flush the toilet and brush my teeth for at least the twentieth time since I got sick. "I'm going back to bed."

"And I'm going to class." She pulls on a jacket and grabs her backpack. "I'll check on you at lunch and see if you want anything to eat."

I gag at the mention of food. "That's unlikely." I plan to never eat again.

I burrow my way into the fort of blankets on my bed and roll around until they are wrapped so tightly around me that I'll have to cut my way out. Sleep had been pretty much nonexistent last night, and there is no way I'd make it through class today. I am just going to have to suck it up and miss. That's upsetting, but I don't have a choice.

I'm close to drifting asleep when someone knocks on the door.

I hold my breath, hoping they'll go away, but then they knock again.

Dammit. I am going to have to get out of my cozy nest, and that is *so* not cool.

I figure it's probably the RA, wondering why it sounds like someone is dying in here.

I roll out of bed and pull on a sweatshirt, trying to tame my wild mane of hair when the person knocks again.

I swing it open and wouldn't you know, there stands Cade. Apparently, he got the memo and wasn't afraid of what I wanted to do to him. I might feel like shit right now and too weak to do anything, but the minute I feel better, he is going to suffer for this.

"Thea said you were sick."

"No—" I hold up a hand "—not *sick*. I have food poisoning."

He winces. "Shit."

"Yeah." I lean against the doorway for support. "So, if you wouldn't mind, I'm going back to bed now." I start to close the door, but he pushes his way inside. "God, you're fucking annoying," I groan. "Can't you just go away? I'm not in the mood, Cade."

"You're sick. It's my fault." He puts his hands on his hips, nodding at his words. "So I'm going to do the right thing and take care of you."

"No, the right thing would be to get out of my fucking room and leave me alone."

He chuckles. "I'm glad to know that even when you're sick you're still the same, Rae."

"Get out," I plead.

"No, I'm staying."

I sigh heavily. I'm never going to win this argument. Cade is too stubborn for his own good.

"Fine," I climb into bed once more. "Then be a good lad and fetch me a Sprite."

He snorts. "Did you just use the words *lad* and *fetch* in one sentence?"

"I did," I declare.

"I feel used."

"Hey," I scold, cracking an eye open, "you're the one that said you weren't going to leave. Now make yourself useful."

His lips turn up into a smirk. "I'll be right back."

By the time he gets back, I've already dozed off and he has to wake me. "Here—" he slides a straw into the can and holds it to my lips "—drink. I'm sure you're dehydrated."

"That's why I asked for the Sprite."

"Such a smart ass. Now drink."

I do, and the cool liquid soothes my parched throat. "That's enough," I tell him when I've had my fill. He sits the can on the table beside my bed.

"Scoot over," he demands.

"What? You're not getting in bed with me," I guffaw.

"Yes, I am." He pushes gently at my body, trying to coax me over. "I need to be close in case you need anything."

"Thea's bed is plenty close!" I squeak.

"Yeah, but if there's an emergency, I think it's imperative that I be within touching distance," he argues.

"Where do you come up with this stuff?" I gape. Before he can answer, I say, "Listen, I don't even want you here, so don't push your luck. Be a good boy and sit on Thea's bed. I'm going to take a nap. Frankly, I'm exhausted and don't feel like dealing with any bullshit."

"Okay." He raises his hands in surrender. "You win." He sits on Thea's bed. "I'll sit here and be a good boy." He waves his hands in the air with a grin as he mimes my words.

"Thank you," I croak, and I mean it. In fact, I'm kind of glad someone is here with me, but I'm not going to tell Cade that.

"Go to sleep, Rae," he whispers.

The way he looks at me has my throat closing up. It reminds me of a time I've tried to erase from my memory—of a boy that stole my heart and died with it.

"You like him, don't you?" Sarah teased, swinging on the swing set in my backyard.

I tore my gaze away from where Brett was mowing the grass in his yard.

"What? No, of course not," I scoffed. "We're only friends."

"Leave her alone," Hannah defended me. *"If she likes him that's her business, not ours."*

Sarah and Hannah might've been my best friends, but Sarah was one person I couldn't share everything with. She was a gossiper, and if I admitted to having a crush on Brett, it would be all over the middle school halls come Monday morning.

"It's pretty obvious." Sarah snorted. *"But if you don't like him—"* she hopped off the swing set *"—then I think I'll go talk to him."* She tossed a smirk over her shoulder and sauntered through the field that separated my house from Brett's.

I knew she was only doing it to get a reaction from me, but my feelings were uncontrollable. When Brett turned off the lawnmower to talk to her she put her hand on his arm, looking back at me. I saw red.

"Rachael—" Hannah warned, but it was too late.

I was already marching across the field, ready to drag Sarah back by her shiny platinum blonde hair.

"Sarah, what are you doing?" I hissed, leveling her with a glare. I'd never had the desire to claw a girl's eyes out, but right then, I was ready to pounce on her.

"I was just asking Brett if he'd like to hang out tomorrow." She batted her eyes innocently.

"He can't. He's busy. We have plans," I spat.

"Plans?" Brett piped in.

"Yes." I maneuvered so I was in front of him. *"Very important plans that can't be canceled."*

"Oh, well forget I said anything." Sarah smiled victoriously and headed back to my house.

"What was that about, Rachael?" Brett asked, closing his hand around my arm so I couldn't leave.

I turned around and glanced sheepishly at my feet. I'd always been able to tell him everything, but this was different. I refused to jeopardize our friendship by telling him I liked him.

"I don't know," I mumbled.

His fingers grasped my chin, forcing me to look at him. His stare was intense, and I squirmed, trying to get away.

"I really better get back to them." I tossed a thumb over my shoulder.

He stared for a moment longer and released me. "Yeah, I guess so."

I turned and started walking away, pushing the tall grass out of my way.

"Rachael!" he called.

I glanced at him over my shoulder. "Yeah?"

"I'll see you tomorrow, since we have plans and all." He winked, turning my world upside down.

"Y-yeah, tomorrow," I stuttered.

He chuckled and the lawnmower started up once more.

I shook my head and went back to the swing set in my yard.

"I knew it," Sarah chimed, clapping her hands together.

I made no comment. Instead, I looked over at the boy next door and let myself dream of what a future with him might be like.

I can't move when I wake up. At first, I figure that it's because of the way I wrapped the blankets around me, but I quickly realize that I'm wrong.

Cade hadn't listened to me at all.

That little liar waited until I fell asleep and got into bed with me. He isn't under the covers, but he still managed to wrap his arms around me and put one of his legs between mine. His breath tickles my neck as he sleeps.

I should wake him up, but I don't.

Instead, I stare at him like a complete weirdo. I've never really allowed myself to study his face, but now that I have my chance, I'm not going to miss this opportunity.

Since he's sleeping, the cut of his chin and the angles of his cheekbones seem softer.

A lock of hair falls over his eyes, and I wiggle my hand out to brush it away. His hair is surprisingly smooth between my fingers. Unable to help myself, I brush my finger down the straight line of his nose and over the curve of his lips.

"Rae?"

I jump, pulling my hand back.

"What are you doing?" He cracks an eye open.

"Uh ..." I have no explanation for what I was doing, and he knows it.

He smirks. "Speechless? That's a new one."

I guess it is.

"At least you didn't push me out of bed. I was expecting that." He chuckles, raising up to peer down at me.

"There's still time." My voice sounds breathless with want, and it pisses me off. I'm sick, and regardless, I shouldn't want Cade. But I do. Oh, God, I do. How could I not? He's nice, and funny, and hot, and a million other things wrapped into one. I'd have to be a fucking nun *not* to be attracted to him. It doesn't mean I'm going to act on it, though.

Cade eases out of bed, careful not to kick me with his long legs. He pulls on his boots, and my heart freezes. He's leaving. Why does that thought fill me with such sadness?

"I'm going to get you some soup. I won't be gone long." He starts toward the door.

I sit up, pulling my hair over my shoulder. "Okay." I force a smile. "Thanks, Cade."

He taps his fingers against the half-open door, his eyes oddly serious as he looks at me. "It's no trouble at all."

He ducks his head, and the door clicks closed behind him.

While he's gone, I decide to shower. No way am I doing that with him around.

I take an extra-long time washing my hair and scrubbing my body. After being sick all night, I don't smell pleasant. I wonder how Cade had been able to ignore it.

I watch the white soapsuds swirl down the drain before turning off the water. I pull a towel around my body and brush my hair so that it doesn't tangle and end up looking like Medusa. That's something no one wants to see. I pad into my room and change into a pair of sweatpants and a baggy shirt. I had just climbed back into bed when Cade returns. Thank God I'm dressed. I can't imagine how mortified I'd feel if he saw me naked.

He sits down on the end of my bed and shoves a Styrofoam cup with a lid on it into my hands. "Eat," he demands, and this time hands me a spoon.

I pluck the lid off and set it aside. I have to admit, the aroma of the chicken noodle soup makes my stomach rumble.

"You're not going to feed me?" I joke, dipping the spoon into the liquid.

He chuckles, brushing his hair out of his eyes. "I figured you'd hurt me if I tried. I'm kind of afraid of you."

"You, the big bad star football player, are afraid of me?" I laugh.

"Hey, you can be scary," he defends.

"I feel like I should be offended." I lift the spoon to my lips.

"Nah, I like the way you are. If I didn't I wouldn't be here right now." His face grows serious, and I know he means it.

"Thanks," I whisper, lowering my head so he can't see my eyes.

"Thanks? For what?" He's puzzled.

I slowly lift my head and force myself to look at him. "For staying with me today. I know I was kind of a bitch this morning but I'm glad you're here."

His smile widens and his eyes light up. "Anything for you, Sunshine."

"Why do you like me?" I ask. I can't seem to stop the words from spilling from my mouth. I want to know. I'm not the nicest person, not anymore, and Cade ... He's amazing.

He chuckles and leans his head against the wall. "Because I see more than you think I do, and I like what I see." He turns his head toward me. "One day you'll tell me what weighs so heavily on your shoulders. And you know what, Rae?"

"What?" I whisper.

"It won't change anything for me."

My hands shake and a little bit of soup sloshes over the side. "You don't know me."

"I beg to differ." His blue eyes flick up to mine. "I think we've done a mighty fine job of getting to know each other the past few weeks. We're friends, Rae, and yeah, I want more with you. I'm not going to hide that fact."

"But why?" I gasp. "Y-you could have any girl you wanted, why me?"

He shrugs. "Those girls don't want me for me. Things are different with you."

"How can you be so sure?" I counter. "What if I'm just like those other girls?"

"Are you?" he asks, his lips twitching with the threat of a smile.

"No," I answer, staring down at the soup that is rapidly growing cold.

"Exactly." He nods. "Being around you, it's refreshing. Even if you never wanted an actual relationship with me I think I could be content with this ... With being your friend."

"Really?" I raise a brow in disbelief.

He chuckles, rubbing his jaw. "I could try."

"I-I would like more with you," I admit, and my heart lurches when his face lights up, "but I'm not ready for that."

His face falls, and he nods. "I understand."

"Do you?" I ask.

"Not really," he admits, "but I can respect that you have a reason."

"You're something else, Cade Montgomery," I state, staring at him in awe.

He chuckles. "What's that supposed to mean?"

"Just that most guys in your position—being a superstar football player—would be a major asshole, but you're not. You're unlike any guy I've ever met." It's in that moment that I realize Cade is an old soul. I'd often heard my mom use the term to describe people who seemed wise beyond their years, and that's Cade. Yeah, he could be cocky at times, but he'd never, not once, been a jerk to me.

He shrugs. "I never asked for popularity, and I didn't want it anyway. At the end of the day, I'm really a dork." He winks.

I laugh, smiling. "You're not a dork, you're just ..."

"I'm just what, Rae?" His voice grows husky, and desire swirls in the air between us. My rapidly growing feelings for Cade scare me and make me feel like I am betraying my first love. But he's gone, and Cade is here, and can I really suffer alone for the rest of my life? My mom always told me one day I'd have to accept the harsh facts and move on from the past. I used to think that was impossible, but

Cade, and even Thea, have shown me that I could let go. I am still holding on tight to the past, though, but one finger is slipping, and it won't be long until I am forced to release it.

"You," I finally answer. "You're just you."

He grins, his whole face lighting up. "I take it that's a good thing?"

"Yeah." I crack a smile. "Because even when I want to hate you, I like you."

He chuckles. "You want to hate me?"

I finish the soup—or at least what I can manage to get down—and set it aside. "Yes," I answer honestly. "Because hating you would be so much easier than wanting you."

"So ..." he starts, "you know I want you, and now you've admitted to wanting me too, but we're going to do nothing about it?"

I frown, snuggling beneath the covers—more for a silly sense of protection than actual need for the warmth. "I can't, Cade. You said you could try being my friend, and that's what I need from you right now."

"I did say that—" he nods "—and I meant it." He sighs, pinching the bridge of his nose. "This won't be easy for me, but I'll be damned if I can't have you in my life in some way. I'm sick and tired of isolating myself because of fear."

"What do you have to be afraid of?" I ask, suddenly grasping that there is more to Cade than I've ever realized. Lately, I've become too blinded by own thoughts and feelings to see other people's problems. But now it's clear—things aren't dandy for Cade.

He slowly raises his eyes to meet mine. The normally bright-blue has become a stormy gray. "Monsters."

I make no comment, because I understand his meaning.

With a sigh, he kicks off his shoes. "Roll over. It's cuddle time."

"Uh ... I don't think friends cuddle." My words fall flat since I am already scooting over to make room for him.

He brushes my hair away from my neck and his breath tickles my skin. "We're special friends, Rae."

If special is code for fucked up, then that's exactly what we are, because I know now that we are two people haunted by very real demons.

eleven

. . .

WEEKS PASS and life seems to be … not good, but okay.

Cade and I are working on being friends, and Thea is … well, Thea.

Cade joins us now for lunch most days, unless he has something else he has to do. Since he's a senior, he doesn't have many classes, which leaves him with a lot of free time.

He's already sitting at the lunch table when I arrive. His long legs are kicked up on the table and he has his hands crossed behind his head. People, guys and girls, tend to stare at Cade when he's around. I can't blame them. There's something about the sight of him that's mesmerizing. Lord knows he makes my brain and body do funny things.

"Hey, Rae of Sunshine," he greets me. "How's your day been?"

"Boring," I supply with a shrug, setting my bag and food down.

"Boring?" His brows rise. "We can't have that."

"Some days just are." I unwrap my sandwich and look it over carefully for any mysterious discoloration or oozing—school food can be gross. Since it looks okay, I take a bite.

His feet drop to the ground with a thump. He leans toward me, flicking his shaggy hair out of his eyes. "What can I do to make this boring day exciting?"

I can think of a million and one ways he could make this day more exciting. Most of those ideas include him naked and sweaty—God, my hormones are in overdrive lately.

I don't tell him that, though.

"You could let me take your picture," I supply. I've wanted to photograph Cade for a while now, but I haven't wanted to tell him that—he's already cocky enough as it is.

His eyes widen in surprise. "You want to take my picture?" He grins slowly. "Oh, this could be interesting."

A lump forms in my throat. Something tells me my suggestion is going to earn me nothing but trouble. I knew I should've kept my mouth shut.

Thea appears at the table and sits down. She's breathless, with her hair blown back. "God, it's windy out there."

"Rae wants to take my picture," Cade announces, not acknowledging her comment.

Thea gives me a sly smile and turns to her brother, her face sobering. "I didn't realize Rae was doing nudes now."

I choke on my sandwich.

Thea reaches over and beats my back as I struggle for air. "Thea!" I groan when I have enough air.

"What?" She shrugs innocently. "It was a good joke. Admit it."

Cade seems to think so; he's laughing so hard I'm surprised tears aren't streaming down his face.

"It wasn't even remotely funny," I huff.

"Aw, come on, Rae," Cade chortles. "It was funny."

I pick at my sandwich, suddenly not hungry. Nope, I'm mortified, because what Thea said had reflected my previous thoughts.

As my humiliation subsides, I grudgingly admit, "It was a little funny."

"See?" Cade grins. "That wasn't so hard now was it?" Without waiting for me to answer, he asks, "So, when are we going to do this?" He tips the chair back on two legs and waits for me to answer.

"After my last class, I guess." I shrug, finishing my sandwich. While my appetite might have vanished moments ago, I know if I don't eat now I'll be starving in an hour. "Around three?"

"Sounds good." He drums his knuckles against the top of the table. "What do you think?" He over-exaggerates a pout. "Will I make a good model?"

"If you don't do that, I think you'll be fine." I find myself cracking a smile.

"Oh, man," he groans, "I thought that was going to be my signature pose."

"Not even close."

"I love it when you get bossy." He smirks.

Thea gags. "You guys are the most sickeningly sweet couple ever and you're not even a couple. Just do it already so I don't have to continue to watch your nasty foreplay."

Cade chuckles. "The fact that you think this is foreplay is hysterical, but also a good thing, because it means I don't have to kill anyone on this campus for touching you." Oh, no. Cade's protective big brother side is coming out. I know Thea hates it.

She wrinkles her nose. "You realize I'm not a nun, right?"

Cade's face screws up with distaste. "Let's end this conversation before I do something stupid."

My phone starts vibrating in my pocket. I sigh. I know who it is and the last thing I want to do is talk to her.

"I'll see you guys later," I tell them, answering my phone as I gather up my stuff. "Hi, Mom." I try to keep phone calls with my mom to a maximum of once a week. It isn't that I don't want to talk to my mom—I've always been close with her and tell her everything—but after last year, things changed. She couldn't protect me anymore, and she became yet another reminder of everything I lost, because she was so closely tied to all my memories.

"Rachael, you haven't called in a while, and I was getting worried. Is everything okay?"

"It's great," I say honestly, throwing my trash away before heading for the glass double doors. As I leave, I can feel Cade's gaze on my back like a brand marking me. "I've been really busy."

"Oh, of course." She sighs. "I miss you, Rachael. I wish you'd call us more. You've only spoken to your dad once since you left. It's not easy for us having our only baby away at school. Will we see you at Thanksgiving at least?"

I haven't thought once about the holidays, but the

thought of going home is nearly crippling. I stop and lean against the wall of one of the buildings, needing the support.

"I'm not sure, Mom. The break is only a few days, and as busy as I've been, I doubt I'll have the time to drive home." I pinch the bridge of my nose, feeling terrible for the lie, but now that I am away from that God-awful town, I never want to go back.

"Oh, well if anything changes, you let me know. I'm sure your dad would be happy to drive down there and get you. It's only three hours from us."

"Mom, we'll see, okay?"

"Okay," she agreed, but she knows I'm not coming home. I think she's beginning to realize that I may never come home again. "I'll talk to you soon, sweetie."

"Yep."

"Love you."

"Love you too, Mom." I hang up, and tears prick my eyes. I wish so much that I could go back to the days where my mom and dad could chase all the monsters away. But now they lived inside me, where no one but me can see.

"Rae?"

I look up and see Cade jogging toward me.

I blink my eyes to clear them of moisture. "Yeah?"

"I just wanted to check on you," he explains, stopping in front of me. "You seemed upset when you left."

"I'm fine," I assure him.

"Who were you talking to?" He winces. "Shit, never mind, that sounds like a nosy question so don't answer."

"It was my mom," I supply, suppressing a laugh at his words.

"Oh." He frowns. "Are things ... rough with you guys?"

I shrug, not sure how much I should tell him. "We're close, or we used to be. Then shit happened and ... I lost who I was. I couldn't confide in my mom anymore. Nothing was really the same."

"Couldn't or wouldn't?" he questions.

"Huh?"

"You couldn't or wouldn't confide in your mom?" he clarifies.

I sigh, glancing down at the ground and away from his penetrating gaze. "Wouldn't."

"That's hard." He reaches up and grasps one of the curls blowing in my face.

"W-what?" I suddenly can't think, not with him standing so close. It's like my brain has lost all sense of function.

He chuckles, seeming to know what he did to me. "It's hard having no one to talk to."

"You speak from experience." It isn't a question; I caught the meaning in his words.

He nods, tucking the curl he'd been playing with behind my ear. "I do."

"You have secrets," I state, my eyes flicking up to his.

He nods and leans forward. I stop breathing as his lips brush my ear. "I'll tell you mine if you tell me yours."

Before I can react, he's gone, striding across campus.

twelve

...

I REGRET MAKING the suggestion to take Cade's picture. This gives me free rein to stare at him, and oh Lord, my stomach is doing somersaults. After a few pictures, he stripped off his shirt—despite the fact that it's fifty degrees and windy—and revealed his lickable abs. Yes, lickable, because I'm standing here looking through the lens of the camera thinking about how I want to run my tongue over all the dents and curves of his stomach.

I need to get a grip and tell my hormones to calm the fuck down.

Cade closes his eyes, lying in the grass as multi-colored leaves swirl around him. It makes for an amazing picture, but I am still tempted to tell him to put his shirt on. But then he'd know it's bothering me, and I can't have that. I guess I'll just have to tolerate it. As if it is such a hardship to look at his chest.

"How's the picture taking going?" he asks, cracking one eye open.

I jump at the sound of his voice. It's been quiet between us for a while and he scared me.

"Good," I say. It seems to be the only word my mouth can formulate at the moment.

"Can I see?" he asks, sitting up and sweeping his hair away from his face—but not before I snap another photo.

I sit down beside him, and he scoots over so there is no distance between our bodies.

His scent is magnetic, and I find myself leaning even closer.

My hands shake slightly as I hold the camera where he can see. His lips quirk, and I know he noticed.

"These are good," he comments, as I scroll through the different photos.

I snort. "Did you think they'd be bad?"

He chuckles. "If you're implying that I might've doubted your abilities, that's a no. I knew you'd be good. I wasn't sure I'd be the best subject."

"Why? You're hot."

Oh. My. God. Crap on a cracker, I said that out loud. *No, no, no.* I want to take it back. Why doesn't life come with a rewind button?

My cheeks turn an unflattering shade of red, and I want to crawl away, find the nearest hole, and die in it.

"You think I'm hot?" He grins, his smile stretching his whole face.

I set the camera in my lap and bury my face in my hands. "You know you're hot," I finally mumble.

"I very much like the fact that *you* think I'm hot." I look up to find him nodding with a cocky smile.

"Can we stop talking about this?" I plead.

"Why? I think my hotness is an interesting topic. Don't you?" He winks.

I grab his shirt and throw it at him. I stand up, gather my stuff, and try to get away from him as quickly as possible. I have to get away before I say something even more embarrassing that I can't take back.

"Rae! Where are you going? Rae!" he calls after me.

I hear his feet thumping against the ground as he runs to catch up with me.

"I'm sorry." He grasps my wrist and no doubt feels my pulse jump. "I didn't mean to make you feel uncomfortable." He releases his hold on me and shoves his fingers through his hair, almost like he's frustrated. "Sometimes I forget how sensitive you are. I was only joking around with you."

Shit, now I feel like crap. Rachael would have never overreacted like this.

I hang my head in shame. "No, don't apologize. You're right, you were only joking, and I shouldn't have reacted like that." I let out a pent-up breath and admit, "Sometimes I forget."

"Forget what?" He tilts his head, his brows furrowing together.

"How to be normal," I mumble. I *wish* I could be a normal girl—like Rachael again. I want nothing more than to joke and laugh with Cade and not be so ... so *sensitive*, like he said. But I can't help myself. It's an automatic reaction, and it makes me angry with myself.

He chuckles, and the sound is rich, warm and husky. "Rae ..." He skates his fingers down my cheek, and my eyes flutter closed. "There's no such thing as normal." My eyes open when his thumb circles over my bottom lip. He makes that simple touch feel like so much more, and I have to suppress the urge to moan. "Come with me." He nods his head in the other direction. "I want to show you something."

I open my mouth, unsure of what to say.

"Please, don't say no," he plead.

The smart thing to do would have been to refuse him and go back to my dorm. But I haven't done the smart thing from the moment I set foot on campus, so why change now?

I nod. "Okay."

He grins boyishly, and I can't help smiling in return.

I follow him across campus, and the amount of times he is stopped by someone wanting to talk to him is insane. I'm starting to understand why he normally stays hidden. And I know Cade well enough to tell from his body language that he doesn't like the attention. Yeah, Cade can be arrogant at times and cocky, but what guy couldn't? Most of the time, he's rather shy. I find it endearing.

"Finally," Cade breathes when we reach a set of doors.

"Where are we going?" I hiss, looking over my shoulder. "I get the impression that we're not supposed to be here."

He chuckles. "Relax, I've got a key." He pulls a key out of his pocket and holds it up for my inspection.

"For some reason that isn't providing me comfort right now."

"Oh, Rae—" he shakes his head, his hair falling forward to hide his eyes "—you need to get out more."

It's true, so I don't argue with him.

He twists the key in the lock and reaches inside, turning on a light switch.

I step inside and look around. Tile floor. Tile walls. And lockers. Lots and lots of lockers.

"Why are we in the locker room?" I ask as he closes the door.

"This isn't what I wanted to show you, if that's what you're thinking. This is just a shortcut."

"A shortcut?"

"Shortcut. Pitstop. Does it matter?" He quirks a brow and stops beside a basket. He picks up a football from inside and cradles it in his arm.

"Are we playing football?" I ask, following him once more.

He tosses the ball in the air and catches it. "I suppose, if catch was considered football."

"Catch? Trying to make it easy on me?" I laugh as he unlocks another set of doors. This time, we step into what appears to be a tunnel. I can feel the cool evening breeze flowing around us and see the stadium ahead. A rush flits through my body. If this is even an ounce of the high Cade feels before a game ... Wow.

"Aw, Sunshine, I'd never make it easy for you. Then you

might win and my pride can't handle that." He winks, bumping my shoulder playfully with his.

Feeling mischievous, I reach up and snatch the ball from his hands and start running.

"Cade," I call over my shoulder with a laugh, "I always win."

Our laughter echoes in the tunnel, and then I am on the field, still running.

A scream tears out of my throat as Cade catches me around the waist and starts spinning me through the air. "Cade!"

We come crashing to the ground in a tangle of limbs.

He rolls so he takes the brunt of the fall, but he is quick to roll again and pin me to the ground.

His hair hangs in his eyes, and we both breathe heavily.

The air crackles between us with electricity.

He reaches down, smoothing the hair off my forehead. My breath falters as his hand then trails down over my lips.

Things are changing between us; that much is obvious, and I am too weak to fight it anymore.

The distance between us begins to close, becoming smaller and smaller. My heart beats like a drum, my blood roaring through my veins.

This is it.

He's going to kiss me.

And this moment, it's going to change everything.

My eyes close, and I wait, feeling his lips so close to mine. It's an effort to stay still. I know the smart thing to do would be to move, to stop this, but I can't.

I am helpless when it comes to Cade. I've been running and running, and he finally caught me. Literally and figuratively.

But then, his weight is gone from my body and he stands above me, holding out a hand for me.

The electricity is gone too, carried away by the wind.

I'm stunned. I thought ...

What I thought doesn't matter.

I don't accept his hand as I stand.

"Rae," he starts, reaching for me.

I take several steps back. "I'm okay." I force a smile. I'm not sure whether I mean I am okay from the fall or okay because he didn't kiss me. I guess it doesn't matter. Honestly, I can't blame him for not kissing me. I'm constantly sending him mixed signals. I'm surprised he isn't suffering from whiplash.

Besides, a kiss between us still won't change anything. We can't be together. He did the right thing.

I take a deep breath, sorting through my feelings and storing them away once more in carefully labeled boxes.

Putting on a playful smile, I point at the ball. "So, are we going to play or what?"

He tosses the ball from hand to hand. He seems to be contemplating something, but finally throws it toward me. "Yeah, let's see what you've got, Sunshine."

I roll my eyes and catch the ball. "What would you call me if my name was Mary?" I ask rhetorically.

He chuckles. "Gary?"

I throw the ball at him, aiming for his head, but he

catches it. "That wasn't nice." He wags his finger like he's scolding a child. "A Rae of Sunshine isn't supposed to be so naughty."

"I never said I was a Rae of Sunshine. You're the one that made it up," I counter.

He chuckles, furthering the distance between us. "Good point. Are you ready?" he asks, lifting the ball.

"Yeah," I answer, holding up my hands.

He launches the ball at me and I catch it, but the force sends me falling to the ground while the football lodges itself in my stomach. I choke on air.

"Rae!" He runs toward me and falls to his knees beside me. "I'm so sorry, I didn't think I threw it that hard."

When I manage to get enough air into my lungs, I say, "Do you enjoy knocking me down?"

He laughs at that while looking me over for injuries. "You do seem to fall a lot around me."

"Fall?" I raise a brow, my hand cradling my stomach where I know I'll end up with a massive bruise. "Falling would mean that I'm just a klutz and trip over things."

He chuckles and starts lifting my shirt.

"Hey!" I swat his hands away. "Stop that!"

"What?" He looks at me with innocent blue eyes. "I was just looking you over."

"Well, can you not?" I grasp the end of my shirt tightly in my fists.

"I've seen you in a bra before, what's the big deal?" He shrugs. "Besides, I wasn't going to take it off. I was only lifting it," he defends. Suddenly, his eyes widen with understanding. "Is this about the scar?"

"No," I lie, looking away from his eyes that always see too much.

"I've already seen the scar, Rae. It's not that bad."

"Not that bad?" I repeat. The scar on my abdomen is large, raised, jagged, and a disgusting shade of pink. There is nothing *not that bad* about it.

Cade sighs, and his eyes darken. "Everyone has scars. *Everyone.* Sometimes, you can't see them and those can be the worst."

I close my eyes and breathe out. "You're right. I'm sorry," I apologize. "The scar is ... It's a touchy subject for me."

Cade looks at me and his lips twist—almost like he wants to laugh at me. "Most subjects are touchy for you."

It's true.

Since our game of catch had turned into a failed kiss, and now this, I thought it might be best if we headed back to the dorms. "I think we should head back." I point toward the entrance we'd come through.

"No way." He shakes his head. "It's just starting to get dark."

"That's precisely why we should go back." I sit up, picking grass off my jeans.

He shakes his head. "There's something else I want you to see. Please, stay with me a little longer?"

If this "something else" turns out like everything else has in the past twenty minutes, then I am sure it will end in disaster. But, I agree anyway. "Okay."

He grins like a little boy, his eyes lighting up, and my heart soars. *I* make him smile like that—and that smile of his always makes my heart speed up.

"Come on." He helps me up and doesn't let go of my hand as he guides me to the center of the field. He sits down and then stretches out on his back, so I do the same. Our hands stay connected, making my body warm. "Do you feel it?" he whispers. "The energy? Even when there's not a crowd here I still get a buzz in my veins."

"Yeah, I feel it," I whispered back. A few minutes pass. "Why are we laying here?" I mean, this is nice and all, but I don't understand why he begged me to stay for this.

He chuckle and turns his head so that his breath tickles my skin. Even in the dimming light, I can still see his eyes sparkling. "You don't have a patient bone in your body, do you?"

"No." I laugh, smiling at him.

"Coach gave me a key to the stadium so I could practice whenever I want," Cade explains, even though I hadn't asked him about that. "I don't think I've actually come in here once to practice on my own." He chuckles. "Instead, I come here when I need to think. I need to think a lot," he mutters the last part under his breath. "I especially like to come here at night, when I can look up at the stars. It makes me feel like a kid again, camping in the backyard. It reminds me of a time when things were simple and there wasn't this ... this ... *pressure*. When everyone was happy."

"Who's everyone?" I whisper, rolling onto my side to face him.

"My dad. My mom. My whole family," he answers after a moment. His face darkens, and an immeasurable sadness reflects in his eyes. Something bad happened to Cade, I can feel it. You don't get that kind of look in your eyes because your ice cream fell on the ground. No, Cade has suffered some sort of tragedy and that makes me wonder if maybe he will understand what I've been through—but I'm not willing to risk telling him the truth.

I see that he doesn't want to elaborate, and since he hasn't pushed me to reveal my secrets, I will respect his boundaries.

"I like it out here," I say instead, changing the subject.

"You do?"

"Mhm," I hum. "I can see why you come here to think."

I shiver from the cold, and he murmurs, "Come here," as he pulls me into his arms. I lay my head on his chest, cradled below his neck. It doesn't feel stiff or awkward being in his arms. It feels *right*. More right than anything ever has before and that scares me. I don't try to move, though.

He rubs a hand up and down my arm, trying to create friction.

It doesn't take long for the whole sky to grow dark and for the stars to twinkle above us.

If I'm honest with myself, I don't care about the stars or the moon or any of that.

I am here for one reason and one reason only—because Cade asked me to stay.

thirteen

. . .

"WHAT THE HELL is going on here?" A gruff voice invades my sleep.

I blink my eyes open, and the world comes into focus—and the world is not my dorm room like it should've been.

Instead, I am curled against Cade asleep on the football field.

And the man looming above us has to be the coach.

I look beyond him and sigh in relief when I see that it's only him. I'd been afraid the whole team might be looming behind him.

Cade sits up and rubs his eyes. "Hey, Coach."

"Don't 'hey, Coach' me, Montgomery," he scolds. "What the hell do you think you're doing out here? And with a girlfriend, no less?" The man plucks a toothpick from between his teeth.

"Sorry, Coach." Cade shrugs, seemingly unaffected at being caught. "We were looking at the stars and fell asleep."

"Well, how romantic," the coach drones. "That key is for practice use only. Not wooing this little lady here." He waves a hand in my direction.

"It won't happen again, Coach." Cade chuckles. I think he should be more worried about us being caught, but he is completely at ease. I feel like running away.

"Like I believe that one, Montgomery." The coach turns to walk away. "Walk that one back to her dorm and get ready for practice."

"Yes, sir," Cade calls.

"Oh, my God," I clutch at my shirt, because I needed something to hold on to. "I can't believe that just happened."

"It's okay. Coach was cool."

"Cool? *Cool?* He did not seem cool with this to me," I babble, pushing my sleep mused hair off of my forehead.

"Trust me, he was fine, and he didn't really care. Coach likes to act tough but he's really a softy." Cade stands and stretches his arms above his head.

"I am mortified," I continue, still sitting on the ground. At this point, I'm not sure if I can even walk. "This is the most embarrassing thing to ever happen to me."

"Oh, I doubt that, sweetheart."

I level him with a glare which only makes him laugh harder.

I slowly pick myself up off the ground, and together, we head back to the tunnel and through the locker rooms. I silently thank whichever god is listening that the room had been empty. I don't think I could handle any more humiliation.

The campus is clear of students as Cade walks me to the dorm. It's still early in the morning and people haven't started roaming around yet. I'm glad that no one is around to witness the two of us together at this time of the morning. If someone caught us, the rumor mill would start up.

Cade stops beside the doors of my dorm and glides his fingers over my cheek. He does that a lot. "Thank you for last night." Leaning forward, he whispers, "For the record, I really wanted to kiss you."

―――

The dorm room is dark, and I ease inside, making sure the door closes silently. I'm still reeling from Cade's admission, and I don't know what to make of my feelings. They're all over the place. A raging storm.

"Where have you been all night?"

Fuck.

I never imagined I'd have to worry about waking Thea since she usually slept like the dead until her alarm went off.

"Tell me everything." She claps giddily with a grin. Suddenly, she frowns. "On second thought, maybe you shouldn't tell me. You were probably with my brother and that would be gross."

I lean against the door and sigh. I know there is no way I am getting out of this. "Yes, I was with your brother."

"And did anything happen?" she prompts.

I frown, thinking of the almost kiss. "No."

"Did you want something to happen?"

"Thea," I snap, "would you please stop prying? I have no idea what all these feelings inside me mean and talking about them with you only makes them get even more jumbled." I start to pant from lack of oxygen.

"Oh." Her eyes widen in surprise. "I'm sorry I asked."

"Please, don't be mad," I plead, "but I hardly understand what I feel and when you ask me questions it only makes it more confusing." I press a hand to my head, feeling a headache coming on. "God, this is confusing."

"Have you ever been in love before? Sorry—" she slaps a hand over her mouth "—that was another question."

I sit down on my bed and decide to open up and share a little bit of myself with Thea. "Yes, I've been in love. I thought he was my forever."

"So ... what happened? Did he turn out to be a jerk?"

I close my eyes and swallow thickly, tears pricking my eyes. "He died." *And it was my fault.*

"Oh." Her mouth parts. "Rae, I'm so sorry."

I look away, not wanting to see the pity in her eyes. The people that don't know the whole story are always so sympathetic. I don't deserve it. Not when I am the one responsible. Sometimes, I feel like the hate is easier to deal with than the pity. At least the hate I can understand. I feel it too, because I hate myself. That doesn't mean I want to surround myself by those people, though.

"Some things just aren't meant to be." I shrug like it's no big deal. I don't want her to know how much I am still affected by Brett's death. Forcing my eyes to hers, I plead, "Could you do me a favor and not tell your brother about this?" It was hard enough telling Thea; I don't want Cade to know too. I don't want to become that girl, the one where whispers are heard behind her back as people point and speculate. I've gotten enough of that back home, and the last thing I want is Cade asking questions, because he will.

Thea nods slowly. "If you don't want me to, I won't, but I don't see what difference it makes if he knows or not."

"You wouldn't understand," I mutter.

She sighs. "Maybe I would if you'd actually trust me." With a sigh, she lies back down and rolled over with her back to me, effectively ending the conversation.

I pinch the bridge of my nose.

I can see now that if I don't open up to Thea, and Cade too, about everything, I will inevitably lose them.

I'm not sure which pain would be worse—having them know the truth, or not having them in my life?

fourteen

. . .

"WHAT THE HELL SHOULD I WEAR?" I ask Thea as she primps in front of the mirror in the bathroom. "I don't think I've ever been to a club before."

She peeks around the doorway of the bathroom. "I can tell you right now that I know for a fact there is nothing remotely club related in your closet."

"I don't even want to go to a club," I whine.

I'd been talked into going, because Thea was desperate to go to this new club and I refused to let her go by herself. Stranger danger and all that jazz.

"Then you don't have to go," she counters, putting on a necklace.

I sigh. "And let you go by yourself? I don't think so."

"Then stop complaining," she chides, heading to her closet.

She grabs a slinky black dress and throws it at me. "Wear that."

I eye the short dress with strategic cutouts. "I think a nipple might pop out."

She snorts. "Rae, you'll be fine. Have I ever steered you wrong?"

So far, she hasn't, but there is a first time for everything.

I slip into the dress and feel extremely naked in it. "I'm going to freeze to death."

"Oh, please." She rolls her eyes. "You're such a baby. I know you have that super cool leather jacket with the studs on it in your closet somewhere. That'll work just fine and keep you warm."

"That might keep the top half warm, but what about all of this." I wave a hand at my bare legs.

"Sometimes you have to suffer for fashion. It's a fact of life."

I don't really think one should have to suffer, but I know there is no arguing with Thea.

I pull a pair of combat boots on and say, "Okay, I'm ready."

"You're not going to do anything with your hair?" she asks.

I tug on a curly strand. "Nope. I'm leaving it down."

She smiles and grabs her clutch. "Well, if you're ready, let's get out of here."

I follow her out the door feeling like this is a very bad idea.

"It's so nice to get out on the weekends!" Thea yells over the music, taking a sip from some fruity concoction.

"It is," I agree, because it seems like the right thing to say. I would've rather been at the dorm editing photos, but I know Thea wouldn't understand.

"Ah!" Thea sets her glass down on the bar roughly so that some of her drink sloshes over the sides. "I *love* this song! Let's dance!"

I wrinkle my nose. *Dance? Um, no thanks.*

But the girl will not take no for an answer and whatever she's drinking must've been strong because she's definitely not in control of herself.

She drags me onto the dance floor and starts dancing in a way that would make other clubbers think we were lesbian lovers. Not cool. Not that there is anything wrong with lesbians, but I don't want anyone getting the wrong idea or to think we are going to put on a show.

"Thea, stop," I groan when she starts getting touchy feely. "This is weird."

"You're no fun, Rae." She pouts. "I need fun!"

I groan. We've barely been here thirty minutes, and I can already tell I am going to have to drag my drunk roommate home, which is going to be so much fun. We took a cab here, so I'll have to call one to come get us and I'm sure they'll be thrilled if she throws up in there.

But I don't need to be thinking about that. Instead, I need to focus on what she's doing now, which is—

"Thea! Did you just grab my ass?" I gasp.

She giggles and hiccups before sashaying her hips. "Maybe! You need to lighten up!"

"Thea," I groan when she put her hands on my hips trying to get me to move to the beat of the song, "stop it."

"Fine," she pouted. "You're no fun."

"Thea!" I call when she melts into the crowd of dancers and disappears.

I should've just kept my mouth shut, because now I've lost a drunk girl in the middle of an insanely large crowd. Not good.

"Thea!" I call again, pushing my way around people. I even elbow some dude in the gut when he tries to grope me. Honestly, can't people keep their hands to themselves?

I look and look, moving through the crowd, but Thea is gone.

Fabulous.

I make my way back the bar, figuring it will give me the best vantage point to try to find her.

I grab an empty stool and sit down, craning my neck.

"Looking for someone?"

I jump at the male voice.

I turn around to face the man. He isn't much older than me, maybe twenty-two. He has light gray eyes—they almost seem white, like they were leached of color. His brown hair falls in messy waves over his forehead. "Uh, yeah," I mutter, feeling a bit creeped out. I scoot the stool a smidge away and pray he doesn't notice. "My boyfriend." The lie slips out of my mouth easily. Something about the guy is just ... off. I hope that if he thinks a guy is going to appear any second he'll stop looking at me like … like he wants to lick me.

"A boyfriend? Really?" He raises the glass of whatever he's drinking to his lips. "You came in with another girl, and I haven't seen you with a guy."

My pulse jumps, and a sweat breaks out across my skin.

This is not good, and my gut tells me I need to get away.

"He's meeting me here," I mumble. "Excuse me." I slide off the stool, scurrying away from Icky Guy.

I'm going to find Thea and we are getting the fuck out of here whether she likes it or not. I am also never ever letting her talk me into this ever again.

When I still can't find her, I head to the back where the bathrooms are, figuring she went there.

I haven't made it far when my body is slammed roughly into the wall, causing my teeth to clank together and blood to blossom on my tongue.

Before I can scream, a hand slams against my mouth.

My eyes connect with Icky Guy's. I am so screwed.

Panic begins to choke me, but I try to talk myself down. If I panic, I won't be able to think straight, and since I can't count on someone coming along and helping, I have to rely on myself.

His other hand gropes my side where there is one of the cutouts. "You have beautiful skin," he whispers, lowering his head to mine. "It's soft. Like velvet."

I whimper when his nose grazes mine. I don't want any part of him touching me.

"I love your hair." His fingers move to grasp one of the

long curly strands. "There's something exotic and hypnotizing about your eyes," his voice lowers. "They tell a story."

I wonder if they tell the story of how I am going to kick his ass, because if he thinks he is taking advantage of me, then he's insane. I am not going down without a fight. He isn't the biggest guy on the planet, and I am fairly certain I could get him off me and have time to run away.

The question is, how far will this go before I find the opportunity to get away?

He lowers his hand from my mouth, but before I can suck in oxygen to scream, his mouth is on mine in a bruising kiss. I bite down on his lip and the fucker bites me back like he enjoyed it.

Stay calm, Rae. Stay calm and think.

Brushing off my rising panic, I try to relax my body. Maybe if he thinks I'm giving in, he won't hold me so tight. With the way he holds me now, I know I'll have bruises on my arm and hip from his hold.

I hate the taste of his lips on mine—ashy like cigarettes mixed with alcohol. It is enough to stir my stomach. I'm sure he won't be thrilled if I throw up in his mouth, but it would be sure to get him away.

I feel tears prick my eyes, and about that time, his hold lessens.

Now is my chance.

I maneuver my legs so that one is between his.

And then I kick.

With a yelp, he falls to the ground.

I stand for a few seconds, stunned that it actually worked.

Then my mind screams at me to run, so I do.

My legs can't carry me away fast enough. Panic still chokes me, and I am terrified that at any second, he will grab ahold of me and drag me back to that dark corner.

My hands slam into the exit doors and I run outside.

Breathless, I sit down on the sidewalk, trying to calm my racing heart. I am in shock, and my body shakes uncontrollably. Did that really just happen? The tracks of my tears on my cheeks tell me that it did.

I expect the guy to bust out the door any second and I wish I had driven here instead of taking a taxi, because now I am stranded here.

I hear footsteps and jump up, ready to run, but when I turn, it's Thea.

Seeing Thea does nothing to calm me, though.

"Rae!" she cries, all but falling in her heels. "I saw what happened! Oh, my God, I couldn't believe that! Are you okay?"

I back away from her with my hands held up and my lower lip trembling. "Stay away from me," my voice cracks. I'm livid with Thea. This was her idea. Then she'd run away, and because of her, I ended up having Icky Guy try to ... I won't let my thoughts go there.

"Rae?" She stops, looking at me with a hurt expression.

"This is your fault," I accuse. "Stay away from me." I cross my arms over my chest and start to walk away.

"Rae! You can't just leave!"

"Watch me," I growl.

"Rae! I called Cade, he'll be here any minute!"

I whip around and scream, "I don't care! He can pick you up then, which is great since I really don't even want to look at you right now!"

I feel like if I am stuck in her presence for a minute longer, I might end up strangling her.

"Rae, please be sensible," she pleads.

Oh, she's gone and done it now.

"*Sensible?*" I scream. "Sensible would've been staying in the fucking dorm like we're supposed to! Not going to a fucking club in the middle of fucking nowhere!"

"You didn't have to come with me," she defends.

"Yeah, well guess what, Thea? I came because I was scared something like *that*—" I pointed toward the building "—would happen to *you*! I was looking out for you, but where were you when I needed you? Huh? He could've hurt me, Thea!"

She starts to cry. "You're right. I'm so, so sorry. This is all my fault." She buries her face in her hands.

Wrapping my arms around my body, I sit down on the sidewalk once more. When I hear her heels clack toward me, I snap, "Thea, seriously, back off." She cries harder, but my own tears seemed to have dried up. Now I am angry and am taking it out on her. At least this time the person I am angry with actually deserves my wrath.

A few minutes later, headlights light up the parking lot and Cade's black Jeep screeches to a halt in front of us. He gets out of the car and slams the door shut, making me flinch.

"What the fuck were you two thinking?" he shouts.

"I'm sorry." Thea sniffles. "I'm so sorry."

Cade storms over to her and speaks in a hushed voice. Thea's head lowers and she nods, muttering something back.

He opens the back passenger door and helps her into the Jeep like she's a small child.

Then he stalks over to me. His body towers above me, and for the first time in a long time, I feel small. Fragile. Like I could break apart into a million pieces too small to be put back together.

"Rae." He crouches in front of me and reaches a tentative hand out to my face. I recoil against his touch, but he is unfazed. "Rae, please let me take you home."

Home. What is home? Certainly not the place I'd grown up and not where I am now. I don't have a home. I belong nowhere.

Now that my anger is fading, sadness is taking its place.

I slowly bring my head up, and my eyes connect with Cade's. He looks worried, his brows drawn tight.

A million different emotions swim through my body, and I'm not sure if I can wade through them.

"Take my hand, Rae." He holds his hand out for me. "Take my hand, and let me get you away from here. Please."

With my fingers trembling, I place my hand in his. It closes around mine and he hauls me up into his sturdy arms.

Suddenly, my tears come back in full force, and I am helpless to stop them.

He wraps his large arms around me, and I cry against his solid chest. If it wasn't for him, I'm pretty sure I would've crumbled to the ground.

"Shh," he hushes, rubbing his hand up and down my back. "I'm here now. You're safe."

I cling to him, my hands grasping the fabric of his sweatshirt so tightly in my fist I'm sure it will be wrinkled later.

"Let it out, Rae," he coos, laying his head on top of mine. "I've got you." I feel his warm lips press against my cool forehead. My eyes close, and I inhale his scent—clean, woodsy. *Cade.*

"I'm so sorry this happened to you," he continued, "but it's over, and I'm here, and I'm not going to let anything hurt you ever again."

It's a promise he can't keep, but I appreciate the gesture nonetheless.

He pulls back a little, holding onto my arms with his hands, and lowers his head so he can peer into my eyes. "Are you okay now?"

I nod slowly. "I'm okay," I echo. *Now that you're here.*

"Come on." He wraps an arm around my shoulders and guides me to the Jeep. My body still seems numb, and when he sees that I don't possess the energy to climb into the vehicle, he helps me inside.

I feel like I am disconnected from my body. Here, but not. I keep replaying what happened over and over in my mind—but the outcome is always different as I imagine the various ways Icky Guy could've hurt me. Things could've been so much worse than they are. I could've become one of those stories you hear about on the news.

Once in the vehicle, Cade cranks up the heat and reaches over, giving my knee a reassuring squeeze.

"I'll deal with you later," he hisses at Thea. He sounds like a father scolding his child, and disappointment laced his tone.

Thea doesn't reply. I'm glad. I don't want to hear her voice.

Cade starts to pull out of the parking lot, but his headlights flash over a man leaning against the side of the building smoking a cigarette. It's him. My body stiffens and I whimper. Cade notices and slams his foot on the brake, which shoves all of us forward.

"Is that him?" he asks. "That's him, isn't it?"

He doesn't wait for me or Thea to reply. He's out of the vehicle in one lightning fast move. I watch, frozen, as he runs up to the guy. He must yell something, because Icky Guy looks up and then Cade's fist slams into the side of his face.

The guy falls to the ground, his cigarette forgotten, as he clutches the side of his face.

Cade bears down on him and hits him again and again.

"Oh, my God," Thea gasps from the backseat, "he's going to kill him." I hear the seatbelt click and then she slips out of the car after Cade.

She grasps her brother's arm, pulling as hard as she can. She finally gets his attention and points at the vehicle. No, not at the vehicle, at me.

Cade shoves his fingers through his hair and nods.

They get back in the car and Cade speeds out of the parking lot, his jaw clenched tightly.

I lean my head against the cool glass of the window and close my eyes.

I want to pretend that tonight didn't happen—to erase it from my memory with one swipe of my fingers over the delete button.

I tried that once before, but memories have a way of haunting you for the rest of your life. They don't just go away. They become a part of you—an essential element of your make up.

fifteen

...

I CRACK my eyes open on Sunday morning to find Thea standing above me with a tray of breakfast food. After last night, I hadn't bothered to get up and run this morning. When I woke up at five, I promptly went back to sleep, muttering, "Screw it."

"What are you doing?" I rub my eyes free of sleep and glare at Thea.

"Well ..." She frowns. "I'm trying to apologize for last night."

"I think you did that with the thousand and one times you told me you were sorry." I sit up, stretching my arms above my head.

Thea sits the tray in my lap and then proceeds to perch on the end of my bed.

"Yeah—" she frowned, looking forlorn "—but I didn't think you forgave me."

She has that right. "No, I didn't."

Tears prick her eyes. "You have no idea how sorry I am, Rae. I was selfish by running off and leaving you alone. It was stupid of me. I can't take back what I did, but I want you to know that I feel awful." She swipes at a tear coursing down her cheek.

I swallow thickly. I don't want to fight with Thea. "You're forgiven." She brightens at my words. "But don't you dare try to get me to go out some place like that ever again."

"Deal," she agrees, reaching forward to hug me.

I stiffen at first, but then return the gesture.

Thea's sweet and she has good intentions. I also feel that Thea could be a bit naïve to the ways of the world. She has an almost childlike innocence that I'm envious of. I walked face first into the harsher facts of life, and there was no coming back from it.

I finally look down at the tray of food. She'd gotten three to-go boxes full of food from the diner. "Do you really think I'm going to eat all this?" I laugh.

"Well, I was kinda hoping you'd forgive me and we could share."

This time it's my turn to say, "Deal."

While we eat, Thea does a good job of getting my mind off last night. She tells me stories about being a kid and all the trouble Cade, Xander, and she used to get into. Apparently, they were quite the troublemakers. Especially the boys.

Hearing Thea talk about her childhood makes memories of mine spring to mind. I miss my friends. I miss Brett. I miss the future I could've had.

Brett and I were always close. We'd known each other

since we were in diapers, thanks to our parents being friends. Not having him in my life anymore … At times his loss is crippling. I loved him.

I startle.

I *loved* him.

I'm thinking of him in the past tense. *Loved*. I loved him once. No more. Well, that isn't exactly true. A part of me will always belong to Brett, but I'm … I'm no longer tied down by my feelings. And that … Yeah, that's sort of freeing.

After we finish eating, I get dressed for the day. Nova and I have plans to meet up around lunchtime to work on our project some more. It's coming together nicely, and I can even see myself becoming friends with the purple-haired girl.

"What are your plans for the day?" I ask Thea as I wiggle into a pair of jeans.

She sits cross-legged on her bed with a magazine in her lap. "Don't know. I might go get my nails done. They're looking shitty." She holds her hands out and wrinkles her nose at the chipping polish. I can't help but look down at my own nails and the purple polish that adorns them. "Yeah, nails it is." She nods her head. "You're welcome to come if you want."

"Uh …" Rachael loved getting her nails done. Rae, not so much. Rae does her own nails and a crappy job at that. "I'm supposed to meet up with Novalee to work on our project."

"Invite her!" Thea chirps. "We can make it a girls' day! Go to the mall! Come on! It'll be fun!" she pleads.

Sometimes, I feel bad for Thea. In instances like this, I can tell just how lonely she really is.

"I can ask her, but I doubt it's really her thing."

"You can let me know then." Thea smiles, but I don't miss how her shoulders sag.

I sigh, guilt eating away at me. "I'll text her, and if she's not into it, I'll ask her if we can reschedule."

"Really?" Thea brightens, her eyes wide and happy like a puppys.

"Yeah." I nod. "Plus, I think you owe me after last night's disaster," I tease.

"I really do."

"I was only kidding, Thea," I tell her, grabbing my phone off the bed.

"I know, but you're right. I don't know how I'll ever make it up to you." She looks at me forlornly.

"You don't need to make it up to me." I wish now I hadn't said anything, even if I had only been joking.

She gives me a look that says she clearly does. I ignore it and text Nova.

Not even a minute passes when she responds.

I look up at Thea and grin. "She's in."

"Thea," I groan, "so help me *God* if you put that hot pink polish on your nails I will beat you within an inch of your life."

She giggles and places the bottle back on the shelf. "What would you suggest then?"

"Black," Nova speaks up.

Thea wrinkles her nose. "Um, no."

"Do you really like pink that much?" I ask, suddenly feeling bad for what I said.

"Not really," she admits.

"What's your favorite color?" I ask.

"Green," she answers immediately.

"Then go with green." I pick up a deep hunter-green color. "Try this one."

She grabs the bottle from my hand and looks at it. "Okay. I'm going to do it."

Something tells me this is a big step for Thea. The color of nail polish probably seems like such a little thing, but from the little Cade said, I got the impression their mom is controlling when it comes to Thea. She wants her daughter to be a pink glamour princess.

Thea hands her nail polish over to one of the ladies working there. Now that Thea is taken care of, it's my turn to pick something. I settle on a dark purple with glitter that appears nearly black unless the light shines on it. Nova chooses a deep red.

They seat us so the three of us are in a row and could talk.

We're all quiet at first. I think Nova and Thea don't quite know what to make of each other.

Nova is the first to break the silence. "If you like green, why were you choosing pink?"

Thea shrugs, and the nail lady scolds her for moving. "My mom—" *I knew it* "—likes me to look a certain way."

Nova eyes the designer jeans and pale yellow blouse

Thea's wearing. "So I'm guessing this uppity nun garb you're wearing isn't quite your style."

I snort. Nova is blunt, and I kind of like that about her.

"No." Thea laughs. "It's not."

Nova nods and seems to be pondering something. Finally, she says, "I find that pleasing other people in turn makes ourselves miserable." Pain flashes in her eyes, and she hastily looks away. I study the side of her face wondering what that look means.

"Yeah …" Thea sighs. "I feel pretty miserable a lot of times."

My spine straightens. What? I didn't know that? Thea … She's always so *happy*. I would never guess that she felt that way. I'm shocked to say the least. I guess it shows that I don't know as much about her as I thought I did. Just like she doesn't know the truth about me.

Some friends we are.

Nova turns back to Thea. "I think after we're done here, we should go shopping and get some clothes that *you* like."

Thea ponders her words. "I'm not even sure I know what I like."

Nova smiles sympathetically. "We'll figure it out."

Right then, my gut clenches. This is so familiar. I used to do things like this with my best friends, Sarah and Hannah, but they we are gone now, and I'm … I'm here. I'm here with Nova and Thea, and I feel like, maybe, the three of us could be best friends—if I find it in my heart to let them in.

When our nails are done, we stroll through the mall,

going into practically every store we come across. I'm glad I wore my Converse, otherwise my feet would be killing me.

Nova and Thea seem to have instantly bonded which I find funny, since they seem so opposite. Thea's obsessed with Nova's purple hair, and I wouldn't be surprised if in a few days hers was purple.

Exhausted, we stop to eat at one of the restaurants in the mall.

We've just placed our order when two guys I recognize strolled in. Nova and Thea are sitting on the opposite side of the booth so they don't see them.

Cade smiles when he sees me watching him and saunters over with Xander close on his heels.

"Hello, ladies." Cade slides into the booth beside me. Xander squeezes in next to Thea and lowers his head to quickly whisper something in her ear.

"What are you doing here?" I ask.

Cade holds up a shopping bag from the sporting goods store. "Shopping." After giving the bag a shake, he drops it on the floor. "I hope you don't mind if we join you."

"Not at all." I smile. I shouldn't be happy to see Cade, but I am. My body hums pleasantly anytime he's near, and I've become addicted to the feeling.

Cade finally swivels his gaze to Thea and glares at her.

I may have forgiven her for last night, but it's clear Cade hasn't. "I can't believe you dragged her out again."

Thea frowns and seems to close in on herself at his words. "I thought it would be nice to get out. She didn't have to come. I would've come by myself," she defends.

"Cade—" I put a hand on his forearm "—I wanted to come. It's okay."

"No, it's not okay." His muscles flex beneath my touch. "Last night could've been a whole lot worse, and I don't think Thea grasps that."

Thea's face grows red, and she slams a hand on the table. "I do understand that, and I feel *awful*. I don't need my douchebag brother making me feel worse."

Whoa. I think that's the first time I've ever seen the siblings argue. It's weird. And ... and they're arguing because of me.

"As long as you understand, I might forgive you ... one day," Cade mutters. He picks up my glass of Sprite, takes a sip, and slides it back my way. At my look, he shrugs. "I was thirsty."

Of course he is.

The waitress comes by and startles at our new guests. "I'll get you guys a menu," she mutters before walking off.

She returns a moment later with the menus and grabs their drink order. Cade insists that we share. "Rae doesn't mind." He winks at me.

The waitress nods and walks away.

"You should've gotten your own," I mutter, feeling Thea's eyes on us.

He shrugs. "And miss the chance to share straws with you, I think not. Especially since—" His voice lowers and he whispers in my ear, "I haven't kissed you yet. And trust me, Rae, when you're ready I'm going to kiss you like you've never been kissed before."

My breath catches, and something tells me he's right. Kissing Cade would be unlike anything else I have ever experienced. Even with Brett. Cade is different. I see that clearly now, and it scares me. I want to run, but I want to stay even more.

When the waitress returns with Xander's glass of water, the two guys place their order.

I realize then that poor Nova is completely out of the loop.

"Nova, this is Cade. Cade, this is Nova. We have class together. She's a photographer too. Cade is also Thea's brother," I add.

"Nice to meet you."

"Likewise." Cade reaches for my drink again. I'm about to ask the waitress to just bring me my own, but I know Cade will only drink from that one too.

"And this is Xander, Cade's best friend." I point to the guy seated beside Thea.

Nova has to lean forward to see him. "Hi." She gives a small wave and he returns it. I don't miss the way his hand grazes lightly over Thea's shoulder before dropping below the table.

Thea catches my gaze and hastily looks away. Clearing her throat, Thea turns back to me. "What are you doing for Thanksgiving?"

I shrug, taking my Sprite from Cade before he drinks it all. "Just staying on campus."

Cade swivels in the booth to look at me while Thea's jaw

drops. "You can't spend Thanksgiving by yourself! That's just ... wrong!"

"I don't want to go home," I mutter. I feel bad because I know my parents want to see me, but I can't do it. I won't subject myself to that town's ridicule anymore. I can't bear to run into Brett's parent's—and they're nearly impossible to avoid since they live next door.

"Why don't you spend Thanksgiving with us?" Thea pleads. "I'll ask my mom, but I know they won't care. She always makes too much food anyway. Please, Rae?" she begs. "You can't be alone on Thanksgiving."

"It'll be fun." Cade waggles his eyebrows with a grin. "We can have a Harry Potter marathon."

I feel unsure of what to do. A part of me is ecstatic that they'd offer, but I'm also scared. A whole four days at their house—sleeping near Cade? Something tells me this could be dangerous. But I find myself saying, "If it's okay with your parents, then I'm in."

"Yay!" Thea claps her hands together. "This is going to be so much fun!"

Fun? Or a disaster?

sixteen

...

THE HOUSE IS modest in size, smaller than I expected. The front is gray stone with large windows. The wood front door has orange and yellow leaves hanging around it with a wreath in the center. It has a cozy, lived-in look to it.

"Home sweet home," Cade mumbles, sliding out of the Jeep. He doesn't sound all that thrilled to be home.

I'd step onto the driveway when the front door opens and a short woman with hair the same color as Thea's comes running toward us. "You're home! You're home!" she chants. She acts as if she hasn't seen them since they left for school, which I find odd since it only took us thirty minutes to get here. Surely, she'd come to one of Cade's football games.

She hugs Cade and then Thea. She doesn't appear to want to let either of them go.

"I've missed you." She holds Thea at arm's length as her eyes narrow. "What are you wearing?"

Thea looked down at the leggings, brown boots, and jean shirt she wore with a coat. "Um ... clothes."

"You look like you're homeless." With that, her mom turns to me. "You must be Rae." She envelopes me in a motherly hug. She seems nice enough, but her previous words to Thea had been rather rude.

"I made lunch. I thought you guys might be hungry. Get your bags, eat, and then you can get settled." She pats my cheek. "You're a pretty girl."

I'm not sure if I should say thank you, so instead, I stand there. She seems to take that as an answer.

Once she's gone, I say, "Your mom seems ... nice."

Cade laughs, getting all of our bags from the trunk. "Yeah, if nice is a code word for crazy."

"Hey." Thea slaps his arm lightly. "She's our mom. Be nice."

Cade sighs and looks at me. "She tries, but she can be very judgmental. Our mom, I mean," he adds as if I hasn't figured out who he's talking about. "Like I told you before, she's zany."

"But we love her," Thea adds, like it needs to be said.

"Where's your dad?" I ask, looking around like he might pop out from behind a bush.

"Probably inside spying on us," Cade grumbles.

Thea picks up her duffel bag. "I'm starving." She heads toward the house, leaving Cade and me alone.

"Wish you'd stayed on campus yet?" he asks, peering down at me with a sad look on his eyes.

"No."

With a sigh, he turns his face toward the sky. "There's still time."

After we eat, their mom, whose name is Lauren, leads me to the guest room. It's across from Thea's room and down the hall from Cade's. I'm thankful that they were near.

The room is decorated in soft blues and purples. It's peaceful and nicer than most hotels. It even has a bathroom attached.

I sit my duffel bag on the chair in the corner and look around.

I'm startled when there's a knock on the door.

Opening the door, I find Cade standing there. He pushes his way inside and sits on the bed. I close the door once more, wondering why he's here, since I've literally just been with him.

"Is everything okay?" I ask quizzically and sit down beside him.

He sighs and lies back on the bed, looking up at the ceiling. "Nothing is okay when I'm here."

"What do you mean?" I lie beside him.

He turns his head away from the ceiling to face me. "You'll see soon enough," he mutters. "I hated the thought of you staying on campus by yourself," he adds, "but now that you're here ... I'm sorry. I'm going to try to make this weekend good for you, but ..." he trails off.

I wonder what happened to the Cade who had joked

about a Harry Potter marathon. He clearly doesn't want to be here.

"Don't worry about me," I assure him. "This weekend will be fine."

"I hope so." He sighs. "My dad called me before we left campus—" I figure that's where this sudden mood of his has come from "—and he was being an asshole. I almost told you to stay behind so that you wouldn't have to deal with this shit." He reaches up and swipes his fingers over my cheek and into my hair. "But then, because I'm a selfish prick, I decided that I could get through the next four days so much easier if you were by my side."

"Cade." I sit up, and my long hair falls forward, tickling his chest. "I'm glad I'm here. Especially if I can make things easier for you."

"You're too good for me." His voice is soft, and his fingers brush over my lips. That familiar hum invades my body.

I laugh self-deprecatingly. "Cade, I think it's *you* that's too good for *me*." It's the truth too. He's ... He's real. Genuine. He's one of the few guys in the world that isn't afraid to express who he is. There are no false pretenses with Cade. It's surprising, really, considering his "type". I stereotyped him at first, Thea too, so shame on me. They are two of the most kind and giving people I've ever met.

He sits up, leaning over me. The movement causes his long-sleeved black T-shirt to pull taut over his chest. "I guess we'll have to agree to disagree." His head lowers and my heart stops.

He's going to kiss me.

This time it's really going to happen.

I close my eyes, startling when I feel the lightest of touches, and my heart thumps madly, but when I open my eyes, it's his fingers I felt.

Without a word, he eases off the bed and slips out the door, leaving me alone to sort out my now muddled thoughts.

Hours later, I'm seated in the family room of the house with Thea and Cade. I have yet to meet their dad, and their mom is in the kitchen making dinner—as well as getting a head start on making dishes for tomorrow's Thanksgiving dinner.

I offered to help, but she insisted that the three of us relax. I feel bad watching her bustle around her kitchen alone, muttering under her breath about this and that.

Cade turns the TV on and flips through the channels. He doesn't appear to be paying attention, and I have the feeling he wants to fill the silent space with noise as well as occupy his restless fingers.

I keep eyeing the large framed photo of the family hanging above the mantle of the fireplace.

Mom. Dad. Three children.

Three.

But I only knew of two.

Cade sits beside me on the couch with a modest amount of space between us. Thea sits in the leather armchair with her legs thrown over the arm, flipping through the pages of a magazine.

"Cade?" I question, my voice hushed.

"Yeah." He doesn't look at me.

I'm seeing a whole new side of Cade today—one who's distant and unhappy, except when he came into the guestroom earlier. I don't like seeing him like this, but it gives me an idea of what he deals with from me. It makes me wonder why he bothers with me at all.

"That picture—"

"What about it?" he growls, brows drawn tight.

I'm tempted to let it drop, because he clearly doesn't want to talk about it, but something makes me persist.

"Who's the little boy?" I ask, bracing myself for his reaction. I know how much I hate it when people pry into my business, so I'm prepared for him to tell me to fuck off. I wouldn't be angry if he did. I'd understand.

His eyes close, and his face screws up as if he's in pain.

"Come with me." When he looks at me, my throat closes up at the sadness I see in his eyes.

He takes my hand and drags me upstairs, down the hall, and into the room I know is his.

I take a moment to look around at the décor—trying to get to know Cade a little more.

The walls are painted green and the furniture is a dark cherry color. Bookcases line one wall, and they're indeed covered in books with the odd trophy sitting on a shelf here and there. A desk sits in the corner with a Macbook. It's clean. Sparse. Almost like Cade had cleared most of his possessions out—at least the ones he could easily take to college.

"I should've explained to you about Gabe sooner, but ... it's not something I like to talk about." He sits down on the end of his bed, scrubbing the palms of his hands on his jeans.

"I'm sorry, you don't have to tell me." I start to back out of the room, my hand on the knob of the closed door.

He shakes his head. "No, you deserve to know. It's why my mom's so ... Well, you know, and why my dad's an ass. Sit." He nods his head toward a chair in the corner. "Get comfortable."

It doesn't escape my notice that he's putting space between us.

He runs his fingers through his hair, making it stick up in random directions.

He looks to the ceiling and lest out a breath. "We were on vacation, and Thea wanted all of us to go horseback riding. I was fifteen, Thea was eleven, and Gabe was eight. My parents arranged for us to go on this trail ride, all five of us. My dad and I were up front with the guide, while the others hung back. Gabe was nervous and didn't really like it so my mom had to keep coaxing him along." Cade paused, clenching his jaw. "The horse got spooked, reared back, and sent Gabe flying." I watched with shock on my face as a tear coursed down Cade's cheek, getting lost in the stubble. "When he landed, he broke his neck and fractured his skull on a rock. He was paralyzed instantly and then bled out." He swallowed thickly. "He was just ... gone."

Cade looks away and out the window. His shoulders are

slumped, like the burden of his memories is too much to bear.

"Nothing was ever the same after that," he whispers, his voice gruff with barely contained tears.

My eyes close, and my body shudders. How often have I said the exact same thing?

I know all about how one moment could haunt you for the rest of your life. How it consumes you and every facet of your life.

Cade isn't paying attention as I ease from the chair and come to sit down beside him. I place my shaking hand on his forearm and feel how taut the muscle is pulled. For once, I'm more concerned about someone else's pain than my own.

He slowly moves his gaze from the window to me. Strands of hair fall forward to hide his eyes. As if it's second nature to me, I reach up and push the hair away, but leave my fingers tangled in it.

"I know exactly how you feel," I whisper, the confession falling off my lips easily.

"Do you?" He doesn't say the words harshly like someone else might would. His voice is soft, curious.

"Yes," I nod, my body shuddering with a breath.

"Tell me," he pleads, his hand seeking mine.

"I ... I don't know if I can." I squish my eyes closed from the onslaught of memories. The squeal of tires. The blood. It was all so horrible.

"Please, Rae." He reaches up, cupping my neck in one hand. My breath falters at his touch. It shouldn't feel so good to have him touching me. It should be wrong, but it's so undeniably right. "Tell me." His lips graze my chin. "Let me in. You can trust me."

I pull away from his touch like it burned me. I pace his room restlessly, my hands wringing together. Can I do this? Can I really tell him the truth? My stomach rolls at the thought. I'm terrified of what the truth might do to us—as if there is actually an *us*.

He sits quietly, waiting for me to sort out my racing thoughts.

My hands fist at my sides. "I don't know if I can." I wipe a hand over my forehead.

Cade doesn't reply. He just sits watching me. Waiting.

Finally, I sit down once more in the chair I previously occupied.

If Cade can tell me about his brother—and I'd witnessed how painful that was for him—then I can do this. I'm not going to tell him because I feel like I *owe* him. No, I'm telling him because he deserves to know the truth. I can't keep dragging out this strange, twisted relationship between us if he doesn't know the truth about me.

I take a deep breath and brace myself. "It happened last summer, a few days before my senior year of high school started ..." I tap my fingers against my jean-clad knees. The words are hard to push out of my throat. I know Cade won't want anything to do with me after I tell him. Hell, *I* don't want anything to do with me. But it's kind of hard to abandon yourself.

"The top was down on my car and the breeze tickled my face." I close my eyes, and it's like I'm back there in that car with Brett, Hannah, and Sarah. "The sun was warm and we were laughing. We were on our way home from the mall. Brett was grumbling about all the time us girls had wasted at the mall when we could've been at the lake. But I knew he was only joking. Brett loved me and he was more than happy to tagalong." I wring my hands together. "I remember hearing Sarah say she loved the song playing on the radio, so I turned it up and we all started singing along. We were just ... having fun."

Tears course down my cheeks now as I get to the bad part. The part where I made one decision that forever changed my life and took the lives of three others.

"I got a text message, and like a fucking idiot I picked up my phone to read it. You know what it said?" I don't bother to wait for his response. "It said, 'Hey, is this Bill?'" I laugh humorlessly. "They had the wrong fucking number. It was nothing important. Although, no text is important enough to take your eyes off the road, because a second ... That's all it took for me to lose control of the car. I was going around a turn and the car flipped twice before hitting a tree."

I shudder at my re-telling. I've never told anyone everything. I didn't want to talk about it. But I want Cade to know. He deserves to know the truth. That I'm a monster.

I squeeze my eyes shut as I'm transported back to that day in the car.

I looked down at the text message on my phone. It was clearly a wrong number and not worth my time.

I went to put it back in the cup holder where it had been

sitting before, when I heard Sarah scream, "Rachael! Look out!"

I looked up to see that I'd drifted off the road. I jerked the wheel, trying to get back in my lane. But I turned the wheel too hard and lost control.

Everything happened so fast.

Screaming.

The tearing of metal.

The burnt oily smell of tires.

My body jolted roughly and something slammed into my abdomen. I tasted blood on my tongue like old pennies.

I tried to move, but everything hurt.

"B-Brett?" I choked on the blood coating my mouth.

Nothing.

I closed my eyes, wiggling my fingers and toes just to see if I could. When they moved, I breathed a sigh of relief.

Despite the pain, I forced myself to turn and look.

"Brett?" My voice caught on a scream. "Oh, my God!" Blood coated his face and his body was dotted with shards of glass from the windshield. His eyes stared blankly at me.

I was going to be sick.

"Brett," I sobbed, praying that he'd blink or move his fingers. Something. *But there was nothing. He was gone.*

"S-Sarah? Hannah?" I couldn't turn around to see them, and I was starting to panic. I looked into the rearview mirror, hoping I would find them alive.

I saw Hannah slumped over and bloody. She wasn't moving.

And Sarah... it was like she wasn't in the car at all.

Despite the searing pain in my abdomen, I leaned over the door and looked out toward the road. Maybe I'd passed out and she was okay. Maybe she'd gotten out to get help. Maybe, maybe, maybe.

I couldn't see her anywhere, but I saw something behind the car lying on the ground. I squinted my eyes, hoping to see more clearly.

My hand shot to my mouth as I sobbed.

Sarah lay on the road behind the car, broken, mangled, and bloody. Her neck lay at an unnatural angle—as did her arms and legs. She reminded me of a broken doll. So ... shattered.

"Oh, God," I choked, trying to force air into my lungs. She must not have worn her seatbelt and I hadn't noticed.

Tears coursed down my cheeks.

I'd done this.

I'd killed them.

I glanced down then and noticed the chunk of glass lodged into my abdomen. Blood coated my shirt and legs. I'd never seen so much blood before.

My adrenaline was fading, and my eyes drifted closed.

I knew I wasn't strong enough to live through this.

Sirens rang in the distance, but I knew—I hoped*—they'd be too late.*

My body shuddered all over as I relived those horrible moments in the car.

"I-I never told my mom and dad, but I woke up in the car. When I realized what had happened, I tried to check on the others. Brett ... oh, God," I sobbed, "there was so much blood and his eyes were blank and I knew he was gone. I tried to check on Hannah and Sarah. I saw Sarah lying on the side of the road. Her body ... it was so mangled. It was horrible. And Hannah, she was gone too. I passed out at that point, from blood loss." My hand absentmindedly strokes the gash on my abdomen. "They said I was lucky, but there's nothing lucky about living when you kill your friends."

"You didn't kill them, Rae." He speaks softly, like he's afraid if he raises his voice to a normal level I'll be scared away.

I snort. "Um, I'm pretty sure they're dead and I was driving so that makes it my fault. I killed them just as surely as if I held a knife to their throat. They're never going to graduate high school, college, get married, have kids. Their lives are over." I slash my hands through the air. "And I'm still living mine. It isn't right."

Cade stands and stalks toward me slowly.

He reaches up and cups my cheek. I flinch, ready to back away, but he grasps my neck to hold me in place.

"Don't you dare try to run from me," he growls lowly.

"I'm a monster."

I try to hide my face from him, but then the fingers of his free hand are on my chin forcing my head up.

"You're not a monster, Rachael."

I swallow thickly. Rachael. He called me Rachael. It's the first time he's ever said my whole name.

"Things like that happen. It's awful, and it was wrong, I'm not denying that, but you can't beat yourself up for the rest of your life." The hand at the nape of my neck curls into my long hair. His forehead lowers so that it's pressed against mine. "You have to move on and live your life for the people that can't. Your friends would want that for you."

"Why would they?" I counter.

"If you were the one that had died, would you want one of them or all of them to feel as guilty as you do? To weigh themselves down with this unnecessary burden?"

No one had ever asked me that before. I ponder over his words. "No, I wouldn't want that."

"See, that wasn't so hard to admit now was it?" He smiles, and butterflies assault my stomach. I used to think that Brett's smile left me breathless. But Cade's? It twists my world around so that I'm not sure which way is right side up. "Thank you for sharing that with me, Rae." His eyes flicked to my lips and back up. "I know that was hard for you."

It had been. In fact, I'm sort of still in a daze that I actually told him—that he knew, and ... and he wasn't looking at me differently.

"It was," I confirm, my pulse jumping in my throat.

"And Rae?" He lowers his head so his lips graze my ear. My breath falters, and he chuckles. "This changes nothing."

seventeen

...

IT ISN'T until the next evening when we sit down for dinner that I finally meet Cade's father.

He stayed mysteriously hidden.

Sitting at the head of the table, he glowers at all of us.

I keep my head ducked to avoid his searing gaze. His eyes are blue like Cade's, but lighter like they're leached of color. Of happiness. Something about him reminds me of the creep who cornered me at the club. I know, without this man saying a word, that I don't like him.

One word keeps echoing through my skull whenever I spare a glance in the man's direction.

Danger.

Malcolm Montgomery is not a nice man. That much is obvious.

I wonder now if the siblings truly wanted me to spend Thanksgiving with them because they didn't want me to be alone, or if they'd invited me along as a buffer.

As things are now, it's tense.

Food's passed around, but no one speaks.

This is nothing like the warm and happy home I'd grown up in.

The silence continues as we eat. I'm the one to break it, unable to stand it for a moment longer.

"Lauren, the meal is delicious." I smile pleasantly.

"Thank you," she replies.

Forks clank against the glass plates.

"Have you been to one of Cade's games?" I ask her.

"No." She wipes her mouth daintily with the fabric napkin. "I'm very busy."

I want to ask what she's so busy doing, but I don't want to sound rude, so I keep my mouth shut.

"Cade's been playing very poorly this year," Malcolm pipes in. "So you haven't missed anything."

Cade sighs and his head lowers. He uses his fork to shuffle his food around the plate, not eating.

I don't want to look at Malcolm, but I force my gaze in his direction. "Really? I thought he'd been playing very well. Granted, I've only been to a few games."

"Believe me—" Malcolm smiles, and there's nothing friendly about the expression "—he's been a shitty player this year."

Cade stiffens at my side, his hands balling into fists.

I don't know what makes me do it, but I reach over and place my hand on top of his. Instantly, his body relaxes, as if my touch soothes him.

"You know it's true," Malcolm sneers at his son.

Cade says nothing in response.

On and on, Malcolm drones through the rest of our very unpleasant Thanksgiving dinner. I feel horrible that I brought up the subject. I should've kept quiet, but I had no idea it would lead to that.

Once dinner is finished, Thea and I are told to wash the dishes. I don't mind; I'm happy to have something to do. I hate standing around feeling as if I'm in the way.

"I'm sorry," I tell Thea, since I haven't had a chance to apologize to Cade yet. "I didn't know bringing up football would lead to that."

She sighs. "It's okay. That's ... that's just my dad. He expects a lot from Cade."

"I can tell," I snort.

"He's still a good dad," she mumbles, more like it's something she's *supposed* to say rather than the actual truth. "My dad always wished he'd done more with football, so he's been pushing Cade to do it professionally for years."

I eye her, and she looks away, wiping the plate dry. My parents never forced me to do anything I didn't like, and I can't imagine being in Cade's situation. I'm sure a part of him wants to please his dad, and that has to be difficult when he knows football isn't what he wants for the rest of his life.

Once we're done, I go in search of Cade. I don't find him in his room, so I'm left to explore the house as I look for him.

When I can't find him anywhere, I step out onto the deck for some fresh air.

It's cold, and I wish I would've thought to put shoes on and grab a jacket.

I'm about to head inside to get them when I hear voices coming from below the deck.

I creep over to the railing and see Cade arguing with his dad.

Half of what is said makes no sense to me. It's all football garble—a language I am not fluent in.

I know if I was smart I'd turn around and go back in the house.

But something compels me to stay.

"I don't want to go pro!" Cade yells, gesturing wildly with his hands, his back against the siding of the house.

"This is all you've wanted since you were a kid! Why would you throw that all away?" Malcolm poked him harshly in chest.

Cade shakes his head vehemently. "No, Dad. This is what *you* want. Not me. I've never wanted this. Do I love football? Yes, but it's not my life."

"This is about that girl, isn't it? She's got you all messed up in the head and now you're off track!" his dad yells and I see spittle fly from his mouth, landing on Cade's jacket.

"Dad!" Cade roars, his teeth clenching. He reaches up and tugs on his hair, like he's losing patience. "She has absolutely nothing to do with this! I've told you for years that this isn't for me, but you refuse to listen!"

Malcolm's fist cocks back, connecting with Cade's cheek.

Cade's head swivels to the side. He spits out blood and glares at his father. Both of the mens' chests rise and fall sharply.

Something tells me this is a common occurrence for

Cade. He could've moved and avoided his father's fist, but instead, he let him hit him.

"Think about what you're throwing away," Malcolm hisses before starting for the deck steps.

I scurry back inside and close the door as quickly and quietly as I can.

I sit down on the couch and pretend to have been watching TV when Malcolm steps inside.

He doesn't look at me or acknowledge my presence in any way as he heads down to the basement.

Cade doesn't return immediately, and I don't want to go look for him if he needs a moment to compose himself.

I pad into the kitchen and look in the freezer for an icepack. When I don't see one, I grab a bag of frozen peas instead.

I jump when I hear the glass door of the deck slide open.

Cade sees me and keeps his face turned, so that I won't see where his dad hit him.

"I saw, Cade," I whisper, my voice soft. "I know."

He doesn't move his head, but his shoulders sag—from relief or despair, I don't know.

"Come here," I coax.

Head downcast, he slowly makes his way over to me.

I point to one of the stools in front of the bar. "Sit," I command.

His lips tip up. "I didn't know you could be so bossy."

"I don't like seeing you hurt." My hand shakes as I lift the bag to press it to the tender skin beneath his eye. His hand clasps around my wrist, steadying it.

"Why don't you like seeing me hurt?" His eyes are dark, and his voice becomes husky. In the dim kitchen, his face is etched in shadow.

My lips part with a breath. "Why do you think?"

"Say it, Rachael."

My eyes close.

Rachael. He called me Rachael again. After the accident, I hated being called Rachael, but hearing Cade say my name ... Yeah, I like that.

"Say it," he prods when I don't immediately speak up.

"Because I care about you," I snap. "I care about you more than I should and I don't want you hurt."

"You care about me?" He smiles. The hand on my wrist drops to my waist, and I squeak when he pulls me into the space between his legs. "That's good to hear, because I care about you a lot." His other hand tangles in my hair.

"How can you still like me after what I did?" I ask, and the tears threaten to fall once more. After our confessions yesterday, neither of us discussed it again—which left my mind free to run wildly with thoughts of how disgusted he was by me.

"You didn't do anything, not on purpose, anyway. I'm not saying what you did was right, you shouldn't have looked at your phone, but you didn't set out to kill them, Rae. There was no intent there. You're not a murderer like you think."

"How'd you know I think that?" I bite my lip to stifle a sob.

His eyes soften and he rubs his thumb against my cheek. "Because I see more than you give me credit for."

I back away and grab the other stool. Being that close to Cade is making my brain fuzzy. Once I'm seated, I hold the frozen peas against his cheek again.

"You know, you're nothing like the guy I thought you were during our first few encounters," I admit with a soft laugh.

He chuckles with a small smile. "And what did you think of me, Sunshine?"

"Well, I thought you were hot—" he grins at that "—but an arrogant, egotistical, jerk."

He laughs. "A jerk, huh?"

"Well, you were really laying it on thick and you did drink my coffee. That was rude."

"Hey, I gave you mouth to mouth, sharing a drink was no big deal," he counters, grinning so his dimple showed.

"I actually hated how much I was attracted to you. I didn't want to like you," I admit. "I didn't want to like anyone."

"But you do."

"But I do," I confirm, even though it wasn't a question.

"How much do you like me?" he asks with a boyish smile.

I snort. "What is this, kindergarten?"

"Hey, I'm just trying to gauge my chances here." He chuckles warmly. "I don't want to push you too far, too fast. Something tells me *you* might punch me in the face."

I frown. This brings us back to the reason we're sitting here in the first place.

"How long has he hit you?" I ask hesitantly, afraid to pry too deeply. After all, he hasn't told me about this. I found out by accident—which made me wonder, if I hadn't walked out there, would Cade have told me on his own?

"Since Gabe died," he answers immediately. "Neither of my parents has handled their grief well ... or at all. I'm actually surprised they didn't end up divorcing. For a long time, my mom just cried all the time, then she started putting Thea in pageants again, because that stopped for a while after the accident, and she got a little better. But she was very controlling. She wanted us all to appear as the perfect family. My dad turned to alcohol, and when he drinks, which is all the time, he gets angry." Cade's hand comes up to mine, pulling the bag away from his face. He lays it on the counter and wraps his hands around mine. "Regardless of all the shitty things that have happened in my life, I still think I turned out okay. The bad things don't define us, it's what we make of them that does. Turn a negative into a positive, that kind of thing." He winks. "You know—" he reaches up and cups my cheek, then tucks my hair behind my ear so he can see my face "—I think you turned out okay too."

I laugh. "Okay? If this is what you call okay I don't want to know what you think is bad."

"You're too hard on yourself, Rae." He stands and puts the bag of peas back in the freezer. He leans against the refrigerator's stainless steel surface and crosses his arms over his chest. "You're a good person that had to deal with a tragedy."

"A tragedy that I caused," I counter. I want to shout, but I can't risk his parents or Thea overhearing our conversation. "Everyone back home blames me for what happened, and they're right to. It was my fault."

His jaw tenses and his eyes narrow. "Did I ask my dad to punch me?"

"No," I answer immediately, wondering where he's going with this.

"You didn't ask to kill your friends." He stares at me, waiting for me to react to his words.

I sigh heavily, like the weight of the world is on my shoulders. "That's different, and you know it."

"It was a fucking accident, Rae. An *accident*," he repeats, like he's trying to drill the word into my head. "It shouldn't have happened, but it did, and now you have to find a way to stop blaming yourself."

I look away. He's right. But how do you stop blaming yourself for something that you did?

"You said earlier that you wouldn't want them feeling guilty if the situation had been reversed. It's good that you could acknowledge that, it's part of healing," he continues. "And I'm not going to lie, healing is hard. It's painful. It isn't the easiest thing in the world, but you have to do it. I couldn't have prevented Gabe's death any more than you could have stopped theirs."

"I didn't have to look at my fucking phone!" I scream and slap a hand over my mouth.

Cade's face softens as I begin to cry. He steps forward, pulling me off the stool, and wraps his arms around me.

I cry into the wall of his chest. "Some things ... they just happen. There's no explanation and no justice in them, but it happens anyway, because sometimes it's just a person's time. Gabe, he was only a little boy, but he died because it was his time. I had to get older before I saw that, but it's the truth."

"You're saying that it was their time to die?" I cry, clinging to the fabric of his shirt. "I don't know if I can believe that."

"I believe it for you." His lips brush against the top of my head.

He pulls my face away from his chest and uses his thumb to wipe away the wetness clinging to my cheeks. "Despite what you believe, you are a Rae of Sunshine, and I'm going to make you see that. I swear it."

eighteen

. . .

I LIE AWAKE IN BED, staring at the ceiling of the Montgomery's guest bedroom.

After our talk in the kitchen, Cade and I sat down on the couch and indulged in that Harry Potter marathon he'd talked about.

It had been nice . ...something a normal couple would do—although, we were far from normal and definitely not a couple. I'd enjoyed myself nonetheless.

I'd fallen asleep against his shoulder, and when I woke, his head was on top of mine. It had been sweet, and I'd liked it more than I should have.

Now that I am alone in bed, my thoughts are free to run wild.

Is Cade right? Was it their time to die and nothing could've prevented the accident?

I *want* to believe that, but I can't.

I am a logical thinking person, and the facts are glaringly obvious.

If I hadn't looked down at my phone they'd still be alive.

Just like if Cade's family hadn't gone horseback riding, Gabe would still be alive.

But "if" doesn't matter. There is no such thing as a do-over. And we can't allow ourselves to question every single little detail, but that's exactly what I have done for the last fifteen months. Cade's right; I have to stop beating myself up over this. It's going to take time for me to get beyond this, though. I can't snap my fingers and magically become Rachael again.

I jump when the door to my room creaks open.

I sit up as a tall, dark figure steps inside.

"Cade," I hiss, "what are you doing?"

"I couldn't sleep." He tiptoes across the room, and let me, tell you it's funny watching a guy as burly as him try to be quiet. "I thought maybe you couldn't, either."

Without asking for permission, because let's face it, this is Cade, he pulls back the covers and slides into bed beside me.

"So ... you thought you'd sleep in here?" I whisper into the dark room.

His chest is bare. I can tell because he wraps his arms around me and pulls my body against his.

"Well, I think that's pretty obvious. Should I tell you a bedtime story?" He smooths the hair away from my neck and kisses the spot where my pulse races.

"Um ... no." I wiggle around, trying to get comfortable.

"If you keep that up, we'll have a problem," he warns in a low voice. "Now, it's story time."

"I didn't ask for a—"

"Once upon a time, there was a girl. She was beautiful, like a ray of light, but when she looked in the mirror, she saw nothing but darkness."

I squish my eyes closed, wishing I could block out his words.

"She thought she was an evil, soul-sucking creature ... like a vampire." He chuckles. "But to everyone else, she was an angel. A beautiful soul. But she was sad, and that made her prince sad."

"Her prince?" I ask, my voice sounding squeaky.

"Yeah, her prince. He was a nice guy. And very handsome."

"Of course." I snort.

"He saw how beautiful, smart, amazing, and kind she was. He wanted to banish the darkness she clung to so desperately—the darkness that didn't even exist. But he knew that the only way to do that was to win her heart ..." he trailed off.

Minutes pass in silence. Finally, I speak. "Did he?"

"Hmm? Did he what?" he asks, his voice sounding sleepy now.

"Did he win her heart?" I whisper, afraid to push the words past my lips.

"Not yet—" he rubs his thumb lazily against my stomach "—but he will."

And I believe him.

"Do you really have to go back?" Lauren cries, hugging her daughter goodbye.

I stand by Cade's Jeep, feeling like an awkward bystander. Our four-day break has been anything but a break. The secrets revealed between Cade and me had been enough to rid me of all energy. And while his mom is nice enough, his dad gives me the creeps, even more so after I saw him hit his own son. The man is just ... odd. Even now; he isn't present to say goodbye to his kids ... and yet, I can see him lurking by the front windows. Watching. Always watching.

"Mom," Cade groans, "let her go, we need to leave."

Lauren releases her daughter and levels her son with a glare. "The University is only thirty minutes away. It's just silly to leave before you've even eaten breakfast."

Cade looks at me, and I see his eyes flick to the window where his father lurks like a ghost. "I think it's time for us to leave, don't you?" he asks his mom.

She sighs, seeming to know what he's talking about.

Could she know that her husband hit her son and let it happen? My God.

She hugs Cade, stretching up on her toes to reach his shoulders. "I love you."

"Love you too, Mom." He closes his eyes, squeezing her tight.

I turn away and climb into the vehicle. Thea is already seated in the back.

"I don't know about you, but I'm ready to get back to

campus. Man, I never thought I'd say that." Thea laughs and I hear her rummaging through her purse. A moment later, I can hear her chewing on gum. I wonder if Thea knows about her dad hitting Cade. I get the impression that she doesn't. But watching their mom, and the way she now keeps looking over her shoulder at the house, she knows. Yep, she definitely knows.

I can't help thinking of a fifteen-year-old Cade, dealing with the grief of losing his little brother, and having his father smack him around.

And now he's twenty-two and it's still happening.

It's awful—but sadly, stuff like this happens all the time. People either don't notice or look the other way.

I begin to think of how painful the last year of my life has been and how Cade has been dealing with this for seven years. I suddenly feel selfish for how I dealt with things. Yes, what I did was wrong, there was no denying that, and I knew it would *always* haunt me. But there are other people out there suffering, it isn't just me. I've overlooked everyone else's pain, because I selfishly believed that my pain was greater than others—as if suffering was some kind of competition to be won.

Cade slips into the vehicle and reaches over to squeeze my knee. I can't help the small smile that graces my lips in response.

"Ready?" he asks, glancing back at Thea.

"Yep." She nods.

"Let's get out of here." He sighs, and his words are heavy with meaning.

He looks at the house one last time and then backs out of the driveway.

Instead of going straight to the dorms, the three of us stop at the diner for breakfast.

Cade sits beside me, his hand resting on my leg where Thea can't see. I feel like this weekend has changed something. There are no more secrets between us. It feels good having him know. I thought once he knew he would hate me, or look at me like everyone else did—with disgust and pity—but he doesn't. Cade never ceases to amaze me.

I know I still have a long way to go until I am healed and ready to truly move on with my life, but I feel like with Cade's help I am going to get there. It doesn't seem like this insurmountable feat anymore.

Thea stretches out in the booth and looks over at the two of us. She seems to be trying to figure out exactly what's going on. I know once we're alone in our dorm I will end up assaulted with a billion questions—none of which I'll have any answers for. I'm clueless as to exactly what Cade and I are to each other, and that's fine. I don't see the point in rushing things.

Cade looks down at his phone and then at us. "Hey, I got a text from Jace. He's playing a bar tonight. You want to go?" He looks at me when he asks the question.

"Sure. Sounds good." I smile. It's better than staying in the dorm all evening—which is funny since when I arrived on campus my plan had been to lie low all year. So much for that.

"I'm in." Thea shrugs, taking a sip of water.

The waitress brings our food and my stomach rumbles. I didn't realize how hungry I was.

"So, Jace is a musician?" I ask.

"He plays guitar and sings, but he's really an artist."

"Really?" My eyes widen in surprise as I think of the blond-haired, tattooed guy. "An artist?"

"Yeah," Thea pipes in, "he does these amazing pen and ink drawings. He's really talented. He even does sculptures."

"Wow," I gasp in awe. "I had no idea."

"He does tattoos too—draws them, I mean," she adds. "All the ones he has he designed himself."

"That's really cool." I mean it, too. While I'm into photography—which is obviously creative—I've never known someone that is an artist the way Jace is.

"Yeah," she agrees. "I'm thinking of having him design a tattoo for me. I haven't decided what I want yet, though."

"It should be something important."

"Do you have any?" she asks me.

"No." I laugh, shaking my head.

"Cade does." She grins. "Jace designed that one too, and our parents were livid when they saw it."

"You have a tattoo?" I gasped. "Can I see it?" The words tumble from my mouth and my cheeks color when I realize what I asked.

He appears sheepish. "It's not that big of a deal. And—" his voice lowers "—I'd have to take my shirt off for you to see it."

"I've seen you shirtless before, and I never noticed a tattoo."

Shit. I said that in front of Thea. Now she's really going to ask me questions.

Cade chuckles, ducking his head so strands of dark hair fall forward to hide his face. "It's on my shoulder."

"Oh." That explains it.

Leaning toward me, he whispers in my ear, "It's a sun. Ironic, huh?"

"A sun?" I choke.

He nods, nuzzling his head closer to the crook of my neck. My pulse jumps. "Yeah, because I always wanted to carry a little ray of light with me—so even when things got bad I'd be reminded that the sun will always shine again."

I swallow thickly. I don't know what to say.

He brushes his lips against my ear, and my body jumps in response, which makes him chuckle. "So jumpy," he murmurs and pulls away.

I relax, but instantly miss the warmth of his body.

Cade starts talking to Thea about something, but I'm not paying attention. I'm lost in my thoughts and still reeling from the fact that his tattoo is of a sun. What are the odds?

We finish our meal and Cade drops us off at our dorm before departing.

"Did you enjoy your weekend?" Thea asks while unpacking her bag.

I nod. "Yeah, I did." Despite the weirdness with their mom and dad, I did enjoy myself. Even more important was the fact that I'd shared my secret with Cade and he was okay with it. I'd never expected that reaction from him—or anyone. I hated myself for what happened, so naturally I assumed that everyone else would too. Telling Cade the truth had been freeing. I wondered if I should consider seeing a therapist again. Maybe now would be a better time, because the last one hadn't been able to do much good.

I know in my heart that I am finally ready to heal and restore myself to the Rachael I once was. She didn't have to die because her friends did. Instead, she had to live because they couldn't.

nineteen

. . .

I BUBBLE WITH EXCITEMENT—AND I'm not sure if it's because we're going out, or because I am going to see Cade again. Probably because I am going to see him. We only parted this morning, and I am already desperate to see him. That's scary and exciting all at the same time.

I change into a ratty pair of jeans and a loose, cream-colored sweater that drapes over one shoulder. My long, brown hair hangs in curls down my back. Thea opted to leave her hair curly as well. I smile when I see she's wearing some of her new clothes from our shopping excursion with Nova. She looks killer in a leather skirt, black boots, a white shirt, and studded leather jacket. Yeah, I can totally get used to this new badass Thea. The pink had been overwhelming.

"Are you ready?" she asks, twirling in front of the mirror. She smiles at her reflection. I get the impression she's glad to be rid of the pink too—although, her pink bedspread stayed.

"Yeah," I tell her, grabbing my own army green jacket.

She looks me up and down and grins. "It's like we did a role reversal."

I have to laugh. It's kind of true. I'm wearing less black; Thea's wearing more.

"It is," I agree.

"You know," she sobers, "I think we needed each other."

I mull over her words. In a way, I needed Thea. She managed to start breaking down my walls and weaseled her way into my heart—becoming my best friend. "Yeah, you're right. We did." I pause, unsure if I should continue. "Thank you."

"Thank you?" she repeats with a mystified look on her face. "What are you thanking me for?"

"For being my friend."

"Oh." Her face softens. "You don't need to thank me for that. Besides, I feel like I've been a pretty shitty friend. I'm still sorry for that night at the club."

I laughs. "Thea, I forgave you, and I meant it."

She shrugs, a sad look on her face. "I haven't forgiven myself."

"Well, you should." I pull my hair over one shoulder. "We should go. Cade said he was here like five minutes ago."

Thea giggles. "Yeah, if we take much longer he'll bat his eyes and sweet talk some poor defenseless girl into letting him into the dorm."

"He definitely could ..." I pause and tilt my head. "Has Cade ever had a girlfriend?" I can't imagine a twenty-two-year-old guy never having a girlfriend, but stranger things have happened.

Thea's face screws up. "That's not my story to tell. You'll have to ask him."

"Did he get screwed over?"

She purses her lips. "Something like that."

I let it drop, because I know Thea won't say anything else. She might be the younger sibling, but she is as protective of Cade as he is of her.

When we reach the stairway to head down to lobby, I'm not surprised to see Cade coming up the steps. I start laughing and can't seem to stop.

"What's so funny?" he asks his sister.

She shrugs. "We just had a conversation about how we were taking too long and you'd find a way into the building."

He smirks. "I'm glad you both know me so well."

My eyes slither up and down his body. Jeans hang low on his hips, and he wears a dark green sweater. His hair is still damp from a shower, making it appear nearly black instead of its normal brown. Stubble dots his cheeks, and his eyes are bright and happy.

"Like what you see?"

I blush at having been caught staring. "Only a little."

He chuckles at my reply. "Only a little? Should I take my shirt off to bump that statement up to a lot?"

Several girls stop on the stairs at his words and swivel to look at him.

"Keep your shirt on," I warn. There's no reason to give the whole dorm a show.

"I'm thinking I should." He smiles playfully and begins to ease up his shirt, exposing his toned stomach with those drool-worthy indents that disappear into his jeans. A trail of hair starts beneath his belly button and disappears just like the indents. Before he raises it anymore, he shrugs and lets it drop back into place. "Never mind. It's cold. I might get frostbite."

I'm pretty sure one of the girls behind me whimpers.

I quirk a brow. "I don't think you can get frostbite in a dorm."

"Hey, you never know, and I like to err on the side of caution." He looks around at the leering girls still occupying the steps. "On second thought, it looks like being eaten is more likely than frostbite. It's like I'm man-meat or something." Taking a dramatic bow, he jogs down the steps. "Have a wonderful evening, ladies!" When neither Thea nor I move, Cade huffs, "Don't make me show my abs again. We're going to be late."

Thea and I rush down the stairs.

Cade grins proudly. "Now I know how to get you guys to do what I want."

"Oh, shut up." Thea pushes his shoulder.

Cade bows his head, laughing. I love watching the two of them interact. Cade slings his arm over her shoulder and they start for the door. Suddenly, he looks back, and his eyes connect with mine. He grins slowly. "Are you coming, Sunshine?"

Always.

The bar is packed when we arrived, but Xander and Jace have snagged a booth for all of us. Cade slides in first across the black vinyl, beside Xander, and grabs my hand so that I am forced to sit beside him—as if it is such a burden to be close to Cade.

"Hey, guys," I say to the other two.

Xander smiles, and Jace gives me a head nod. They both seem like guys of few words.

"I didn't know you were a musician, Jace."

He looks up at my words and shrugs. "I'm not."

Thea rolls her eyes. "He's amazing."

"No, I'm not," he mumbles, looking around the bar broodily. "I'm going to smoke."

He slips out of the booth and disappears.

Thea sighs and looks at me sympathetically. "That's just Jace. Don't take it personally."

Cade nudges my shoulder. "He's kind of like you. Bristly like a porcupine, but once you get to know him he's a fluffy teddy bear on the inside."

I snort. "I doubt that, and are you comparing me to a porcupine and teddy bear?"

He grins, squeezing my knee. "You know it's true."

It is true. I am feeling less and less like that prickly porcupine and more like the squishy teddy bear. I don't have to hate myself. I don't have to hate the fact that I am alive. I've been punishing myself for too long, and it can't continue. It doesn't mean I have to forget my friends, just that I have to forgive myself. And forgiving? That's hard.

"You guys!" We all look up to see a winded Jace sliding

back into the booth. I've never seen him so exuberant before. His green eyes are bright with excitement. "I just saw the hottest chick I've ever seen in my fucking life. Like ... damn." He whistles. "She was driving a fucking motorcycle. It was the sexiest thing ever."

Could it be ...?

"Did she have purple hair?" I pipe in.

Jace turns to look at me, his mouth falling open in surprise. "Yeah, do you know her?"

"She's my friend. We have some classes together."

Jace grins. I'm pretty sure it's the first time I've ever seen him smile. He has a nice smile. It transforms his whole face. "Would you introduce me?"

"Sure." I shrug. I don't see the harm in that.

I look around, and when I see her step inside, I wave her over. She smiles and pushes her way through the crowd around the bar.

"Hey." She stops at the table. "This place is packed. I didn't think I was going to get a seat at the bar. You're a life saver."

I slide closer to Cade and Thea slides closer to me so we could make room for the new addition.

"Nova, this is Jace. You didn't get to meet him the other day. He's another friend of Cade's."

"Jace." She seems to be mulling over the name. "You wouldn't happen to be Jacen Andrews, would you?"

"Yeah." Jace's eyes widen in surprise and he sits up straighter.

"Oh my God," Nova gushes. "I've seen some of your

drawings. You're amazing." She suddenly blushes. "Sorry, I sound like a gushing fangirl, but I've always wanted to draw like that."

Jace cracks a half smile and smooths his hair out of his eyes. The look he gives her could only be described as a smolder. Oh, yeah, Jace is putting the moves on Nova. This is funny to watch. I kind of want to lean back and munch on popcorn while it all plays out.

"Really?" He leans forward, like he's trying to bridge the gap the table provided. "Maybe I could give you lessons sometime?"

"That would be awesome," Nova chimes.

"Excellent." Jace grins and slips from the booth. "If you'll excuse me, it's time for me to play."

"Play?" Nova asks, looking around at the four of us as Jace disappears.

"You'll see." Cade chuckles, reaching over to play with a strand of my hair. Leaning into me, he rubs his nose against my cheek. "You have the softest hair."

"And you seem to like playing with it," I comment.

He grins, tucking the piece behind my ear. He makes sure to sweep his thumb over my cheek. "I like to see your face. That's why I play with your hair. You tend to hide behind it." Brushing his lips against my ear, his voice lowers so no one can hear. "You don't need to hide, Rachael. Not ever. And definitely not from me."

When he says stuff like that, it does make me want to hide, because I don't want him to see just how much those words meant to me.

His hand falls away, and he returns to his previous position, as if none of that had happened.

I take several deep, steadying breaths.

One person should not turn your whole body into a fluttering mass of butterflies, but Cade does that. It's a good feeling too. One I could get used to. I could get used to *him* —having him in my life as more than a friend.

Cade glances down at me and grins, his dimples popping out. "What?" he asks. "Why are you looking at me like that?"

"Sorry." I shake my head. "I didn't know I was."

His smile softens, and his eyes twinkle. "It's okay, I like that you were looking."

"Why?" I ask, not caring that Thea is beside me, listening to every word we say.

"Because it gives me hope that you have feelings for me too."

"I do have feelings for you," I admit, the words falling from my mouth before I can stop them. A part of me wishes that I can bend down and pick them up and pretend I'd never said it—but word vomit is a mess that can't be wiped away.

Despite my embarrassment, my words are true. I do have feelings for Cade. Strong feelings. I'm not sure when they first surfaced, but they're there, and growing stronger every day. The fact that I've spent the afternoon missing him proved that. And now that he knows what I've done, there really is nothing holding me back except my own hang-ups— that I might cause someone else I care about to die, like I am some kind of grim reaper or something.

"These feelings you have, are they good feelings?"

I laugh. Only Cade. "Yes, very good." There is no point in lying now. Besides, I am sick and tired of denying my feelings to him and myself. I don't have to be ashamed. Not anymore.

He grins like a little boy who'd just been given the best Christmas present ever.

He's cut off from saying anything further as Jace's voice rings out around us.

Jace doesn't bother to introduce himself to the patrons. His voice is soft, almost hesitant as he starts, but as the song picks up so does his voice. He closes his eyes and I know he *feels* the words he's singing.

"Holy shit," Nova mutters. "I think I just fell in love."

I snort at that. Cade turns to me at the sound, the same grin still on his face. I love his smile, and maybe if given a little more time, I could fall in love with him.

Then again, maybe I am already there and too stupid to see it.

Jace's voice might be incredible, but I find myself unable to take my eyes off the man beside me.

"You want to get out of here?" Cade asks, his eyes heated.

"Yes," I breathe. I want that more than I want anything else in the world.

Cade turns to Xander and says, "Excuse us."

Xander smiles knowingly and slides out of the booth so we can follow.

"Can you take Thea back to the dorms?" Cade asks him, grabbing ahold of his arm before he can sit back down.

"Yeah, that's not a problem."

Cade released him, and Xander sat down.

We shrug into our coats, and he reaches for my hand, entwining our fingers together. His eyes crinkle as he smiles. "Let's go."

The chaos of the bar melts away along with the soulful sound of Jace's voice.

Cade pushes open the door, and we step outside. In the short time we've been inside, the world has been covered in a thin sheet of white snow. It falls down around us in tiny white puffs like the feathers of an angel.

Our collective breaths fog the air, and I can't help smiling.

The moment is perfect, and Cade is about to make it even more perfect.

"Rae?" he asks, his voice thick with emotion. Little flakes of snow stick in his hair.

"Yeah?" The one word sounds like a gasp.

"I really want to kiss you right now, but I don't want to scare you."

I close my eyes, a smile on my lips. If only he knew how many times I had wanted him to kiss me and he hadn't.

"Kissing me would be more than okay. If you don't, I might never speak to you again." I open my eyes so he can see that I'm serious.

"Really?" He smiles cockily, stepping forward. "You'd give me the silent treatment?" He cups my cheeks in his large hands, and his touch manages to heat my whole body.

"Oh, shut up." And then I do something that completely shocks Cade.

I take charge.

Yep, that's right. I take what I want, and that's a kiss from Cade.

I wrap my arms around his neck, and even though I am tall, he's even taller, so I stand on my tiptoes and press my lips to his.

Softly, at first, almost hesitant.

I've only ever kissed one boy, and for all I knew, I sucked. So, I'm a bit scared to try out something crazy. I figure Cade could take the lead.

His body is rigid against mine with surprise, but once he realizes that I kissed him, he relaxes, and his mouth moves against mine.

It's like we're dancing.

But with our lips.

A dance only the two of us know.

He tilts my head back and deepens the kiss. I can't stop the moan that passes between my lips and into his. He growls in response as his teeth lightly nip my bottom lip. Then he's soothing the spot with a flick of his tongue.

Kissing had never been this soul shattering.

It's like with one kiss, Cade is tearing me apart and putting me back together.

I swear, with the heat we're generating, the snow has to be melting around us.

The passion with which he kisses me is intoxicating.

This is the kiss of a man staking claim. He wants to make

a point, to show me that I belong to him. But if I dig deep enough into the recesses of my mind, I know that he'd staked his claim the very first time we met.

I haven't been looking for love.

Or friendship.

Or a lot of things.

But the things you think you don't need can turn out to be *exactly* what you didn't know you were searching for.

Cade Montgomery crashed into my life, literally, and now I never want him to leave.

He's my salvation.

My hands move from around his neck to fist the fabric of his jacket.

I want closer to him—to sink inside him so that his light and goodness can clear away all the dark shadows around my soul.

I know it doesn't work that way, but for a moment, I want to pretend that I am worthy of him—that I am healthy and whole and not this fractured and splintered girl I've become.

For a moment, I want to be enough.

And I am.

twenty

...

CADE PULLS AWAY and places a light kiss on the end of my nose.

"I feel like I've been waiting forever to do that," he breathes.

"Not quite forever," I joke, "but close enough."

He grins crookedly and entwines our hands together, heading back to his Jeep. "Wanna go to the football field?"

I wave my hand at the swirling snow. "Isn't a bit cold for that?" Not to mention his coach might bust us again.

He chuckles and lowers his head to nuzzle my neck. "Don't worry, Sunshine. I'll keep you warm."

My body hums at his words. Oh, I have no doubt he could keep me warm, and my cheeks flame with thoughts of just how he'd go about it.

"Sounds good," I agree as he opens the passenger door of the Jeep for me.

When Cade slips into the driver's seat, he takes my hand

once more. I can't help staring at how our fingers wrap around one another's, like neither of us ever want to let go.

Things have been changing between us for a while, slowly at first, and now all at once. I don't think there is any coming back from this.

"What are you thinking about?" Cade asks, rubbing his thumb in soothing circles on my hand.

I shrug, wiggling in the seat. I pretend my restlessness comes from a need to adjust the seatbelt.

"Come on, Rae, tell me," he pleads, glancing over at me.

"It's embarrassing," I mumble.

The glow from a set of headlights brighten his face for a moment before he is bathed in darkness once more.

"Do you really think I'll laugh at you?" His gaze flicks in my direction. "You should know me better by now. I won't laugh. I promise."

I knew he isn't going to leave it alone. "I was just thinking that I don't believe there's any coming back from this. Not for me anyway. It's different with you," I admit, biting down on my bottom lip before anymore truths could come tumbling out of its depths.

He doesn't say anything. Or smile. Or give me any sort of indication of what he's thinking, and that scares me. Maybe I said the wrong thing and admitted too much. The only thing that keeps me from completely freaking out is the fact that he still clasps my hand in his.

One heartbeat ...

Two ...

Three ...

I wait. Counting until a full minute has passed.

"I agree completely," he finally replies. I let out the breath I hadn't realized I was holding—the sound of my exhale seeming to echo around the car. "I've never felt anything like this before." Grinning now, he adds, "That's why I was so relentless in my pursuit of you."

Relaxing, I joke, "Really? I thought it was because you were a cocky jock that couldn't take no for an answer."

His smile sweetens. "Rae, you should know by now that I'm not a cocky jock."

He definitely isn't. Cade Montgomery is unlike anyone I've ever met before.

He parks near the stadium, and we head inside the locker room and out onto the field.

Instead of leading me onto the field, Cade surprises me by turning and jogging up the steps to the bleachers.

When he turns and sees me still standing below, he says, "Come on. I never get to experience it from up here. Let's sit here for a while." He's already making his way down one of the aisles.

"Sure," I agree, hurrying up the steps after him.

The stadium is open on top so the snow still swirls around us, coming down more frequently now. The whole field is a sheet of white. Maybe it's a good thing we hadn't gone out there. Our tracks would show a disturbance, and his coach would no doubt figure out it was us.

Cade sits down and stretches his feet out in front of him. Lifting his arm, he waves me over to curl my body against his. It's all the invitation I need.

His warmth wraps around me as I snuggle close.

After losing Brett and my friends, I never thought I'd have this closeness with another human being. I've never been happier to be proven wrong in my life.

Cade looks around and chuckles softly under his breath. "You know, it's funny, when this place is empty it kind of reminds me a skeleton. Just a shell of what it can be."

I look around and shrug. "Yeah, I can see that."

"You think I'm crazy." He chuckles, his fingers tangling in my hair.

"No, not crazy—" I snuggle closer, resisting the urge to purr like a kitten at his touch "—just passionate."

"Passionate," he muses. "I don't think I've ever had anyone call me passionate before."

"Really?" I ask, sliding down and stretching out my legs on the bleachers so that I can lie down. I rest my head on his thigh, and he resumes stroking my hair.

"Yeah." He nods, looking out at the field. Smiling down at me, he adds, "I think I like being called passionate." He reaches out and traces the shape of my lips. "I also really like kissing you."

My cheeks warm despite the cold. "I like kissing you too." My heart flutters, and I feel like a little girl again, falling in love for the first time, where everything is still sweet and innocent and there are no complications. Clearing my throat, I ask, "How many girlfriends have you had?"

Cade's jaw clench and his eyes darken.

"I'm sorry," I mumble hastily, "I shouldn't have asked that."

"No, it's fine." He sighs, his breath fogging the air with a thick cloud. "I just didn't expect you to ask that." He looks away and seems to be gathering his thoughts.

"You know there was only Brett for me and I just ... I was curious," I ramble, feeling the need to explain myself.

He smiles down at me then. "Don't feel bad, Sunshine. Just give me a minute." He looks out toward the field and takes a deep breath. "There was a girl in high school. We dated from the time we were sophomores until it was time to leave for college. That's when it all fell apart ..." he trails off. "She wasn't happy when I told her I wasn't planning to go pro. She argued that I ruining *our* lives. Throwing everything we could have away. She didn't understand that I'm not that kind of person. I'm in it for the love of the game, not the fame."

I sit up, leaning my head on his shoulder, and reach for his hand, giving it a small squeeze for reassurance.

"She said some things that were hard to swallow, and I kept trying to get her to see where I was coming from. But it became clear that she was only with me for the future I could possibly provide for her. She didn't love *me.* She loved the *idea* of me." He sighs, pinching the bridge of his nose. "I was hurt for a long time after that. She was my first love—" he smiles at me "—and I was a lovesick fool. For a long time, I kept hoping she would change her mind. I heard from someone that she'd moved on to a guy that was due to inherit his dad's millions. That confirmed to me that it was all about the money for her. After that, I dated here and there, but most girls were just like her. And the ones that weren't didn't hold my interest. To be completely honest with you, I fucked a few of them," he mumbles, and I can see the shame etched on his face. "I hated myself for that, for using those girls for selfish needs. My dad might be an asshole, but neither of my parents raised me to act like that. So, I started keeping to myself." He begins to play with my fingers. "I hated the cocky jerk I'd become, so I changed."

I lift my head to look at him. "You changed? Just like that? I find that hard to believe and you acted very cocky with me," I jest.

He chuckles and scratches at his stubbled jaw. "Do not mistake my confidence for cockiness. Big difference. *Huge.*"

I narrow my eyes. "That sounds suspiciously like an euphemism."

"Sunshine—" he winks "—I'm not one to be coy."

I shiver and he moves to wrap his arms around me, bringing me close to his body. I inhale the scent that is uniquely Cade and let it comfort me.

"I still don't know what you see in me," I whisper, my words carried away by the wind.

He lowers his head and tenderly kisses my forehead. "I knew from the moment I saw you that there was something different about you. I had to get to know you." He pauses, seeming to contemplate his next words. "I could tell that you were sad, and I wanted to know why, and frankly I wanted to make you smile." Wrapping a strand of my hair around his finger, he says, "But I really wish you could see how amazing you are, because then you'd never ask me that question. You'd know."

I close my eyes, exhaling softly.

Me, amazing?

I'm not amazing. Not even before the accident.

I was boring Rachael Wilder. My life was average. *I* was average.

"Do you ever think of them?" he asks suddenly, changing the subject.

"Who?" I ask, although I'm sure I already know.

"Your friends. Your boyfriend." He clears his throat and wiggles a bit, like he's afraid the question might set me off.

I look up at him. "I try not to, but I think of them all the time. How could I not?" I babble. "Sometimes I swear I can feel them around me." I fear I might start crying. Talking about them is nearly unbearable. "I feel so horrible for what happened. I wish I could forget it—have some miraculous loss of memory, but I know that's never going to happen. Getting away from home was the best thing that ever happened to me, because when I was there, I definitely couldn't escape their presence. Their families made sure of that."

I didn't tell Cade, but Brett's parents are the worst of them all. Since they lived beside my parents, Brett's mom made it a point to come around and let me know that she thought I was a murderer. Maybe that's when I started believing it too. Hearing someone, especially an adult, say such horrid things about you can make you crack.

He smooths his fingers through my hair and is quiet for a moment. "You know it wasn't your fault, right?"

I laugh, but there is no humor in the sound. "Cade, it

was my fault. Nothing you say can make me see it differently. If I hadn't looked at my phone, three people would still be alive. But I'm learning that I can't blame myself forever," I admit, "and that's all thanks to you."

He smiles, rubbing his hand up and down my arm to keep me warm. The snow isn't falling as frequently now, but it still dots our hair and sticks to our lashes.

"You know it's not your fault that your dad hits you, right?" I mimic his words.

He chuckles. "Yeah, I know. Didn't used to, though. For a while, he had me convinced that I was a horrible brat that needed to be punished. By the time I got old enough to see that he was just a miserable human being, I ..." He pauses and looks at me, suddenly uncomfortable. "This is going to sound so stupid, but I pitied him."

My eyes widen in surprise. "What? Why?"

He shrugs, clasping my hands in both of his. I'm thankful for the added warmth.

"He lost his son, and that would crush anybody. Once I put myself in his shoes, I felt bad. I'm not saying if I lost a kid I'd hit my other one, but ... I get it, I guess. Besides—" he shrugs "—hitting him back wouldn't solve the problem. It would only make more."

I look up at Cade with awe in my eyes. In many ways, he has things worse than I did and he thinks of everything so sensibly. That's rare, and I wish I could be that way too.

Before I can speak, I shiver again.

Cade stands up. "We should go. You're going to get sick again, and I don't want it to be my fault this time."

I bow my head, a smile on my lips as I remember being locked in my dorm all day with Cade. I'd been so mad at first, but then I became thankful for his presence.

He leads me down the bleachers and through the tunnel and locker room.

Once in his car, he turns to me. His eyes are serious. "I'm not ready for tonight to end."

"Me either," I confess, holding my hands out where the heat can warm them.

"Not to sound presumptuous, but would you want to come back to my dorm? I'm in a single, so we don't have to worry about disturbing a roommate." He winks. "Not that I expect anything to happen," he hastens to add.

I shake my head, a smile on my lips. "You are one strange guy."

"Strange?" he repeats. "How?"

I laugh. "Most guys *would* expect something, but I know you mean it when you say you don't."

He chuckles, backing out of the parking space. "Are you saying I'm weird?"

"That's one word for it." I laugh again.

"Would you rather me be like other guys?"

"No," I answer without any hesitation, "I like you just the way you are."

"And I like you the way you are."

I smile. "Even though I'm an incredibly fucked up head case?"

He laughs and reaches for my hand. "We're both fucked

up, Rae." His face darkens from the shadows in the parking lot. "But that doesn't have to define you."

"It doesn't?"

He shakes his head. "No, it doesn't. You had no idea what I'd been through with my dad and brother. You thought I was 'normal', didn't you?"

"Yes," I admit reluctantly.

"Exactly, that's because those things don't define who I am as a person, they're one of the many pieces that make up who I am. A *piece* is not a *whole*. Remember that, Rae."

"But is there really such a thing as normal?" I counter.

He ponders my words. "I guess not, but I think we all have our own idea of what normal is." He parks his car in front of his dorm building. A grin lights his entire face. "Ready to see my room?" He waggles his brows. "The bed is small, so we'll have to snuggle."

I snort. "Of course we will."

He grin, and it's so infectious that I can't help smiling back. "I'm a master snuggler."

"I'm aware." I laugh, undoing my seatbelt. "Remember when I was sick?"

"Oh, I can snuggle way better than that. There's even a special kind of cuddling where we don't wear any clothes."

I laugh at his comment, but then it has me picturing Cade naked and that is no laughing matter. I wonder what he'd say if I told him I was a virgin. Brett and I had been serious, but I'd never been ready to make that leap.

And now my brain is picturing Cade and me rolling around in his bed.

He'd told me he wasn't going to push me for more, but now his joke has me thinking all kinds of naughty things. My hormones need to take a hike before I do something stupid.

Cade hops out of the Jeep and jogs around to get my door.

It's late, nearing midnight, but on a college campus that's still considered early.

The people milling about don't bother to hide their stares as the two of us make our way to the building holding hands.

I'm not sure I'll ever get used to the fact that Cade is considered a celebrity on campus. Hell, I don't think Cade is even used to it, and he's been going to school here for four years.

"Ignore them," Cade whispers, releasing my hand and moving his to the small of my back. "I do."

I wish I could ignore them, but I can't help wondering what they see when they look at us. Probably the school's football star slumming it with the freak. Yeah, I am probably way off base, but ever since the accident, I feel like an outsider. I think a huge part of me is convinced that everyone could know what I've done just by looking at me—as if I'd stuck a Post-It note to my forehead declaring my transgressions.

When we finally enter, the building I breathe a sigh of relief.

Rachael had been fine being the center of attention, but Rae doesn't like it.

Luckily, the dorm is empty as Cade leads me to his room.

I'm thankful that no one caught me going into his room. I'm sure if someone had, it would've been the talk around campus for the next week.

His room is dark, and he fumbles around to turn on a light.

The room is a little smaller than the one I share with Thea, but large enough not to induce claustrophobia.

He doesn't have anything decorating the walls, which I think is weird.

His bed is made and the room is clean. I wonder if Cade has some sort of issue with tidiness, since his room at home had also been impeccably neat.

I sit down on the edge of the bed and close my eyes, letting myself pretend for a moment that I am just a normal girl unscarred by her past.

I know telling Cade had helped me heal, but only a little bit.

It's going to take far more than a confession to a man I am falling for for me to get better.

I feel like I'd only put a Band-Aid on the situation, and if I don't do more to rectify this, I'll be right back to where I was before.

"It's not much." Cade shrugs. "I didn't feel like decorating."

"I like it," I tell him, and it's the truth. While it's sparse, it's still his. And the stacks of books in the corner, mostly fantasy, more than make up for the lack of decoration. Besides, he's a college senior, and a guy. I figured most guys with decorations hadn't put them up themselves—it was either done by a girlfriend or mom.

"You look really uncomfortable sitting like that." He waves a hand where I sit on the end of his bed. My hands are clasped in my lap, and my back is ramrod straight.

With a laugh, I kick off my shoes and remove my jacket. I stretch out on his bed, wiggling around until I'm comfortable. Propping my head on my hand, I eye him. "Is this better?"

His blue eyes turn a stormy gray as he looks at me. His tongue flicks out the tiniest bit to moisten his lips.

"Much better." His voice comes out as a low throaty growl.

He removes his own shoes and jacket before fitting himself onto the empty bed space beside me. He lies down on his back and wraps his arm around me so that I am fitted against his chest.

Cade clears his throat and puts a finger beneath my chin to raise my face to his. "I never knew it could be like this, that something as simple as lying in bed with someone could feel this good." His fingers skim gently up my arm, and even through the fabric of my sweater, his touch is searing.

I want to open my mouth and tell him that I agree. I'd loved Brett, in whatever way a seventeen-year-old girl could possibly love a boy—like as if at eighteen I had so much more life experience—but I guess in a way I did since life's events had changed me so much. But for whatever reason, I couldn't make myself say the words. A part of me was terrified to acknowledge the presence of something *more* between

Cade and me. It felt like an insult to Brett's memory, like he didn't matter, when he always would. He might've been gone, as well as Sarah and Hannah, but that didn't mean I forgot them and the relationships we had.

Realistically, I knew I wasn't replacing Brett with Cade—it was me moving on, but it didn't feel that way in my warped mind.

I startle when Cade tapped his fingers against my forehead. "What are you thinking about? I know something has you upset. Talk to me," he pleads.

Instead of lying or saying "nothing", I decide to be honest. "I'm scared I'm replacing Brett with you, but I know that's wrong. And what I feel for you is so much stronger, and that ..." I pause. "That scares me and makes me sad at the same time, because I worry that maybe I didn't care about Brett enough." I sit up a bit so my hair swoops down between us.

Cade's fingers curl into my hair, his hand resting at the nape of my neck.

"You know that isn't true. If you didn't care for him so much you wouldn't be worrying about this." He moves his hand to my face, rubbing his thumb over my bottom lip. "It's okay to let go of the past," he whispers, "letting go doesn't mean forgetting."

Deep down, I know that, but it's hard to accept.

I lower my head once more, to burrow into the space where his head meets his neck.

Protected.

That's what I feel when I'm in Cade's arms.

I squeak when he moves suddenly, causing me to sprawl on my back with him hovering above me.

He lowers his head so strands of his hair fall forward to tickle my face. "I'm thinking I should kiss you now."

I reach up, my fingers grasping his shirt. All thought of our previous conversation is gone.

With one declaration, Cade turned me into a normal girl, at least for a moment, and all I can think about is how his lips will feel against mine again.

"Don't tease me," I warn, my mind emptying of all worries. Right now, all that exists is Cade and Rachael. Yes, Rachael, because right now, I feel like her again, and it feels good to know she isn't entirely lost.

He chuckles, his lips turning up into a playful smirk. "Never, Sunshine, especially when kissing is involved."

And then he closes the space between us and kisses me hard and fierce. It's a burning kind of kiss, one that shatters worlds and leaves you striving for another breath because all of yours has been stolen.

With a brush of his tongue, he has me gasping beneath him, ready to beg for more.

My legs wrap around his waist, and I pull him down so that we are touching in the most dangerous of places.

My fingers move from his shirt to fist his hair. His stubble scratches my skin but I don't mind.

"Rae," he gasps between our lips.

A moan escapes me at the sound of my name.

Kissing has never been like this before.

I want more, so much more, and that's scary.

If I let myself think that far ahead, I see a future with Cade, a life I stopped letting myself imagine when I lost Brett. But now I see it all, and beyond that, I *want* it.

His fingers skim beneath my sweater, ghosting along my skin like he's afraid if he truly touched me I'll run screaming.

"Cade?" I gasp, pulling away from his lips.

His hand stills and he starts to pull away, but I tighten my hold on him. "If you don't really touch me I'm going to lose my mind, and don't you dare stop kiss—" He silences my following words by doing exactly what I want him to do.

With every brush of his lips to mine, I feel as if the shackles binding me to my past begin to weaken and crumble.

His fingers press more firmly against the skin of my stomach, easing my shirt up slowly. I finally grab the garment and rip it off. I know he didn't expect me to go that far, not tonight, but I need to feel him against me.

Once my shirt is gone, his lips ghost down my neck, lingering against the spot where my pulse races.

My body arches against his, and a breathy sigh passes between my lips.

"I want you so bad," he confesses. "But I want all of you, before we go that far."

I close my eyes, knowing what he means. He wants *Rachael*. The real me. The whole me. Not this shell that's grasping onto life with weak fingers.

I know I have to change, not for him, but for me. I need to take ahold of my life and move on. I have to get better before I live my whole life being miserable, because let's face it, that would be no life at all.

I feel like a baby fawn, trembling on new legs—terrified at what may lie ahead of me, but knowing that I have to do it.

I *want* to be able to tell Cade that he does have all of me, but we would both know thatves a lie.

I had to hope that by the time I'm ready to give him everything, he hasn't given up on me.

"Stop thinking, just feel," Cade growls, nipping my chin.

Suddenly, he pulls away, grasping me by the waist so I go with him. I end up straddling him with my arms around his neck so we're face to face.

He stares at me for a moment. I notice that his lips are slightly swollen from our kisses.

His fingers tangle in the curls of my hair. "I wasn't looking for anyone to care about like this, but now that I have you ... I wouldn't trade this moment for anything."

And then his lips are on mine again and the night, the room, everything ceases to exist.

twenty-one
...

I WAKE UP, stretching my arms above my head—and promptly smack Cade in the face.

"Oh, shit." I roll out of his bed and onto the floor, probably bruising my ass in the process.

I'd fallen asleep in his bed. Lovely.

Cade groans and rolls over. He lazily peeks his eyes open to spy me on the floor. "Why the fuck are you down there? That doesn't look the least bit comfortable."

"I fell," I defend.

He cracks a smile. "That's funny."

It kind of is, but then the enormity of the situation hit me. "Cade," I groan, "we fell asleep."

"I'm aware of that." He rubs his eyes sleepily and stifles a yawn. "Best night of sleep I've ever had ... and it doesn't have to end. Get back in bed, Sunshine."

"What will Thea think?" I hiss, looking down and realizing that I am only clothed in a bra and panties. Where the hell are my pants?

Cade notices what I'm looking for and chuckles. Propping his head on his hand, he says, "You got hot in the night and kicked them off."

I groan and use my hands to hide my face.

"I promise I had nothing to do with it," he continues.

"I believe you," I mutter, but his words do nothing to alleviate the embarrassment I feel. "How am I going to walk out of here?"

"Easy." Cade grins. "You stand up, put your clothes on, and walk out the door." He uses his fingers to mime a person walking.

"Don't be a smartass," I groan. "You know what I mean."

"So what? There's nothing to be embarrassed about." He shrugs then rolls onto his back. "What time is it anyway?"

I locate my phone. "Seven," I answer. "And you know it isn't that simple. You're, well, *you*." I wave my hand at him. "People pay attention to what you do, and I don't want to become some story for gossips."

Cade rises up once more, leveling me with a glare. "You act like we had a fucking one-night stand and that if you walk out the door everyone will think you're a slut. Maybe I didn't make my intentions clear enough, but after last night, I very much thought you were my girlfriend."

My eyes widen in surprise. I didn't expect him to say that. Not at all. In fact, I am pretty sure all the air leaves my lungs and the room, because I suddenly can't breathe.

"Girlfriend?" I repeat, my voice no more than a squeak.

"Yeah." He looks at me like I've lost my mind. "Did you really think I would fuck you and kick you out? And, might I add, there was no sex involved last night. Besides, I would *never* fuck you, Rae. A girl like you deserves so much more than that."

I clasp my hands over my eyes. This is too much. *He* is too much.

"I don't mean to embarrass you, Rae," he rattles on, "but it's the truth. I'm no saint, but with you, things are different."

I hear the bed squeak as he sits up. Then he's crouched in front of me, prying my hands from my face.

"I don't know if it's because I'm technically a jock that you find me hard to believe, but I would never lie to you, Rae. I'm not a player, never was. Yes, I fooled around, but it was random hook-ups that were *rare*. I was hurt by what my first girlfriend did to me." It doesn't escape my notice that he still didn't reveal her name. "But I'm not like these other guys that have a different girl in their bed every night. I'm not like that and I don't want to be."

"I don't need an explanation," I tell him, "you just caught me off guard."

"I know, but I wanted to explain myself. You should know by now that this isn't me wanting to get in your pants." He chuckles. "Although, I am a guy, so I want that too," he says with a wink. "But I've told you stuff I've never told anyone else. Most people don't know about my brother and the shit with my dad? No one knows that." He reaches out, smoothing a finger down my cheek. "Now, Rae," his voice drops low and his eyes bore into mine, "are you my girlfriend or not?"

I take several deep breaths, trying not to think about the day when Brett asked me to be his girlfriend.

"I guess so."

"You guess so?" He chuckles. "It's kind of a yes or no question."

I think about how much I care about him already, so really there is only one answer. "Yes."

He grins, his eyes crinkling at the corners. Instead of saying anything, he takes my face in both his hands and kisses me deeply, stealing my breath and maybe even a bit of my soul.

"Now, can we *please* go back to sleep?" he asks, pulling away.

I laugh as all my fear at what people will think falls from my shoulders and drifts away. "Sleep would be good."

"Why am I not surprised?" Thea slides into the seat across from me in the dining hall. Her gaze swivels from me to her brother who sits beside me. "You know, you could've at least told me you weren't coming home last night. I was worried."

"I'm sorry." I frown. I'd been horrible not to consider that Thea might worry when I didn't come back to the dorm. If it had been her out all night, I would've been worried sick like a protective mama bear. I probably would've torn the whole campus apart looking for her.

"You better be sorry," she scolds. Smiling slowly, she says, "Now that that's out of the way, I have to say, it's about fucking time." With that said, she picks up her yogurt and peels back the top.

I look at Cade and both of us are trying not to laugh.

"Glad you approve, sis," Cade chuckles, giving my hand a squeeze.

She sticks the spoon in her mouth, licking away the yogurt, and then points it at us. "Hey, I've been gunning for this from the moment I found out you two knew each other. My best friend and brother together forever? I mean, that's just awesome. But I better be the maid of honor at your wedding or I'll cut a bitch."

I snort. "Um, it's a bit too soon to be talking about weddings. And, we weren't even friends when you found out that Cade and I knew each other."

"Logistics." She waves her hands wildly through the air. "I knew we'd be best friends one day, and guess what? It happened." Grinning, she adds, "It's like I can see the future or something."

Cade snorts. "Or something, sounds right."

She narrows her eyes on her brother. "Do not make me flick yogurt at you. You know I will."

Cade chuckles, raising his hands in surrender. "This is my favorite shirt. No yogurt please."

"For that reason alone, I should flick it at you."

Cade looks at me and sighs dramatically. "Little sisters are so annoying."

"And big brothers are a pain in the ass," Thea adds. "Do

you know that a guy from one of my classes was going to ask me out and this oaf comes along and scares the poor guy away? He'll probably never speak to me again."

"As it should be. Besides, what could you possibly see in a guy that wears skinny jeans? I mean, I don't see how he even has any balls in pants that tight." Cade picks up his bottle of water, spinning the lid around before taking a sip.

I snort at his words, and Thea looks mortified.

"They were not that tight!" she hisses.

Cade eyes her. "They were. I've never understood guys that think that looks cool. It's just weird. Your balls need room to breathe."

Thea claps her hands over her ears. "Shut up! I don't need to hear you talk about balls. It's gross."

Cade laughs, lowering the water bottle to the table. "Okay, okay. No more talk about balls of any type. Not bouncy balls, or hairy balls, or footballs."

Thea picks up her tray, glaring at her brother. "I'm out of here. Enjoy your breakfast."

With that declaration, she moves to another table.

I swivel to look at Cade. "You did that on purpose to get her to leave."

"Maybe I did." He shrugs, picking up the apple from his tray and taking a bite. "I wanted to enjoy breakfast with my girlfriend."

Girlfriend.

Cade has said that word a lot this morning. It's like he enjoys saying it, which blows my mind. Isn't the guy supposed to be the hesitant one in the relationship, not the girl?

As if he can't control himself, he leans over and kisses my forehead. My eyes close and a soft breath passes between my lips at the gesture.

"Oh, I wanted to talk to you about something," he starts, taking another bite of apple. Once he swallows, he continues. "Some of the guys on the football team are throwing a party. They share a house off campus, and I'm supposed to go, and I want you to come with me."

"Uh ..." A party at a bunch of football players' house doesn't sound like my cup of tea, but Cade is giving me that puppy-eyed look, and it's hard to resist. "When is it?"

"Friday," he answers.

I don't want to go, but I know I need to. Rachael wouldn't have hesitated to go. Besides, I'll be with Cade, and that will make it worth it.

"I'll go," I reply, hoping I don't regret this decision.

Cade smiles like I've given him the best present ever. "Thank you."

"Do I need to dress up?" I ask.

"No, it's a casual thing, but I'm sure there will be some ... barely dressed women there seeking attention."

"Oh, so I'm not an attention seeker?"

"Definitely not," he replies, leaning in close and nuzzling his face against my neck, "and that's a good thing."

I pull away reluctantly and look at my phone, sighing. "I've got to head to class, and I need to call my mom. I'll see you later." I lean over to kiss his cheek, but he moves his head at the last second so my lips collide with his. He deepens the kiss, drawing me close, and I am pretty sure someone whistles in the dining hall.

Breathless, he pulls away. "See you later."

Damn him. My legs are shaking now, and he knows it. I grab my bag and toss my trash. When I reach the door to exit, I can't help turning back and peeking at him. Cade watches me with his arm slung over the chair I just vacated. He smiles when he catches my gaze, and my stomach fluttered.

I finally tear my eyes away from his, knowing my cheeks are now colored a light shade of pink, and push the door open.

The air is cold, and I immediately zip up my jacket. I pull my phone from the pocket and ring my mom.

She answers on the first ring, and that makes me feel bad. How often does the woman sit around hoping I'll be a good daughter and call home?

"Rachael? How are you?" she rattles.

"I'm good." I reach up, catching a strand of hair that wants to blow into my mouth. "School keeps me busy."

"Of course," she agrees. "I'm glad you called. We miss you. I really wish you had come home for Thanksgiving. Surely you'll be home for Christmas?"

I wince, scrubbing my free hand over my face. "Um, I'm not sure yet, Mom. I'll keep you posted," I lie.

"Your dad and I were thinking about driving down there one weekend. A few hours in the car won't kill us, and we want to see you. We could stay for a weekend ..."

I don't know what to say, so I settle on, "Whatever you

want." Before she can continue, I interrupt with, "So, I called because ..." My throat closes up, and I'm not sure I can get the next words past my lips. I've contemplated this a lot, and I'm sure of my decision, but that doesn't make it any easier to confess.

"What is it?" she asks, sounding hesitant. "You're not pregnant, are you?"

I snort. "No, Mom."

"Sorry, I had to ask. These things happen, and you're a good girl, but even good girls do stupid things."

Yeah, I guess she's right about that. And I'd already made one stupid decision by looking at that text message instead of driving my car like I was supposed to.

I sigh, knowing I need to get back to the reason I called in the first place. "I called you because I've decided that it's time I saw a therapist again. I know Dr. Snyder gave you a list of recommendations for people in the area. I was hoping you could email it to me." Dr. Snyder had been my therapist at home. I'd never thought he did me much good, but I thought it was worth trying again, especially since he'd been so disappointed that I refused to continue treatment with a new doctor when I went to college. He'd said I needed more time to talk to someone and work out my issues. I'm thinking he was right.

My mom is quiet on the other end. So quiet that I think maybe the call had been disconnected.

"Mom?" I ask.

"Sorry," she replies, "you surprised me."

It's pretty sad that the fact that I want to see a therapist again surprises my mom. Had she come to the conclusion that I'd always be fucked up? Had my own mom given up on me?

"I think it's great that you're ready to talk to someone again," she continues. "How about I call the people he recommended and see if I can find a good fit for you? I know you're busy with class, and I'd like to do something for you."

I reach the building where my class was located and lean against the stone exterior. Nova passes me and smiles, throwing up her hand in acknowledgement before disappearing into the building.

"That would be great, Mom," I tell her. "Thank you."

"Anything for you, Rachael." She begins to sniffle, the sound of my mom's tears breaking my heart. "I just want to see you happy again."

I lean my head back and close my eyes. It's all too easy to get caught up in the hell I've been living in, and forget that the people around me are suffering too.

"I love you, Mom," I finally say.

"Love you too, sweetie." The call ends, and I stand there for a moment, breathing in slowly.

I hate to think about how much I've broken my parents with what I did and how I handled the situation.

I never meant to hurt them, but I did.

I really hoped seeing a therapist would help fix things.

Maybe soon, I'll be ready to go home and face all my fears —close the book on this chapter of my life and start anew.

twenty-two
• • •

"WHERE ARE YOU GOING?" Thea looks me up and down. "That doesn't look like something you wear for a night in with your roommate," she jokes, sitting on her bed cross-legged. She's already dressed in her pajamas. Her iPad is propped on the bed and I figure the second I'm gone she'll be on Netflix. Apparently, she's addicted to *Gossip Girl* and has a crush on someone named Chuck Bass. According to her, I am missing out on greatness.

"Your brother asked me to go to a party with him." I straighten the shirt I'm wearing.

"I wasn't invited? That isn't fair," she pouts.

I shrug. "Sorry."

"Whatever. Chuck is waiting, and he's so much more exciting than a party."

Somehow, I don't believe her, but in all honesty, I would rather stay in than go to this party. I am going to be surrounded by Huntley University's finest, people I don't know, and that gives me major anxiety since I am no social butterfly.

"Well, if there's another party, I'll make sure you can come," I add to appease her.

"Yeah, so I can feel like the third wheel," she grumbles, crossing her arms over her chest. "This past week has made me wonder why I wanted you guys to date. All the kissing is grossing me out."

I laugh, smoothing my hair back into a ponytail. "I'm sorry. I'll tell Cade to tone it down."

"Don't tell him anything," she warns. "It'll just make him kiss you more to gross me out. Brothers are assholes like that."

I finish my makeup and sit down beside her on her bed, since I still have some time before Cade was due to arrive.

"So, what's going on with you and Xander?" I'd asked her the same thing before, but I feel like we're better friends now and she might tell me more.

"Honestly, like I told you, nothing. I like him—" she shrugs "—and I think he likes me, but neither of us has made a move. Besides, I'm kind of over him. There's this one guy in my English class that I really like, and he seems interested."

I eye her. "Thea."

"What? Why are you saying my name like that? I feel like I'm in trouble."

"If you like Xander you should go for it."

She sighs. "We've been friends since we were kids, so that makes it weird, but he's also Cade's *best* friend which makes it complicated. I don't need that kind of drama in my life.

Besides, I don't want to end up on 48 Hours when Cade kills us for ... canoodling," she supplies, and we both dissolve into laughter.

I decide to let the topic of Xander drop. "Okay, so who's this new guy you like?"

Her cheeks flush, and I figure that was a good sign. "His name is Trevor, and he's really nice."

"Trevor and really nice? That's all you've got?" I laugh. "Come on, give me more than that." I gasp and grab her hand. "This isn't skinny jeans guy, is it?"

"What?" She laughs. "No! Besides, like I said, I'm pretty sure Cade scared him away from ever talking to me again. It's okay, though. He was kind of odd and those jeans were a turn off."

"So, are you going on a date with Trevor?"

I marvel at how easy our conversation is. It's so normal and easy. Two girls discussing guys and dates. I never thought this would be my life again.

"Tomorrow, actually," she admits.

"Tomorrow? And you didn't tell me? Thea!" I shriek, probably disturbing the girls in the room beside us.

"What? You didn't tell me about the party."

I frown. "That was an accident, truly. To be honest, I don't even want to go, so that's why I didn't say anything."

Her face softens. "You're forgiven."

A knock sounds at our door. Thea shakes her head. "That'll be my brother. No doubt he's sweet-talked yet another girl into letting him into the dorm. I swear, all he has to do his bat his eyes and they turn to goo. It's annoying."

Reaching her arms out to hug me, just as there is another knock, she adds, "Have fun, and call me if you're not coming back to the dorm. I don't want to worry."

"I will," I assure her, hugging her back.

A third knock sounds, and I holler, "I'm coming." To Thea, I roll my eyes and mutter, "He's so impatient."

I open the door and find the reason for his incessant knocking. A girl that lives on our floor, I think her name is Jessica, is hanging onto his arm and talking his ear off.

"Sorry," I apologize, slipping out the door.

"Thank God," he mutters under his breath, taking my hand.

"Bye, Cade!" the girl calls.

"Bye, Jessa," he groans.

I poke his side. "I'm pretty sure it's Jessica."

"Jessica! I meant Jessica!" he yells back as we start down the stairs. I can't help laughing. "She wouldn't shut up," he hisses to me, "and honestly, the talking was tolerable compared to how she kept feeling up my muscles. I was getting afraid that she might get adventurous and grab my junk."

"Oh, that would've been interesting." I laugh, picturing Cade getting mauled by the girls on my floor.

"Seriously—" he flails dramatically "—the girl's hands were relentless and it's not like I could forcibly remove her."

"Hey, you don't need to feel bad about it. I mean, I can't blame her." I wink. "Who wouldn't want to feel you up?" I ask playfully.

He laughs. "Apparently you."

I blush at that and duck my head. If only he knew how little experience I had in that department, he wouldn't make jokes so lightly.

Cade holds open the door for me and we stride out into the frigid night air. The sky is dark and cloudy, barely any stars shining.

"This way." He takes my hand, leading me to his Jeep. "I couldn't find a parking spot close."

"How long do we have to stay?" I ask, my nerves skyrocketing as I realize I am about to attend my first real college party. It's already nine, and I figured these things run late. I feel like such a grandma for not even wanting to go in the first place. I'd rather hang out with Cade in his dorm or with Thea.

Cade shrugs. "An hour or two. If you absolutely hate it, then say so and we'll leave sooner."

He can read me so well it's scary at times.

I climb into the Jeep, trying to think calming thoughts. My nerves are racing and my palms grow sweaty. These are Cade's teammates I'll be meeting and their opinion of me matters. I don't want them to think I am some weird freshman just trying to finagle my way into the "in" crowd.

"Your hands are shaking," he comments, turning up the radio.

I tuck them under my legs. "Sorry, I'm nervous."

"Don't be nervous." He rests one hand lazily on my knee, looking over his shoulder to back out of the parking space. "It's just a small party."

Small, I repeat to myself. I can handle small.

"Small? You call *this* small?" I shriek, sinking my hands into the fabric of the Jeep's seat. I stare at all the cars lining the street and the large amount of people hanging around outside despite the cold.

Cade shrugs sheepishly. "I may have underestimated the size."

I feel like I'm suffocating. Is this what a panic attack feels like? Oh, God.

I clutch at my chest, dragging air into my feeble lungs.

"Rae?" he questions. "Are you okay?"

"Give me a minute," I plead.

Even Rachael would've had trouble with a party this size, so Rae is in full-on freak out mode.

What the hell have I gotten myself into?

I want to climb in the back and hide beneath the seat.

"It won't be that bad," Cade says soothingly. "I'll be by your side the whole time. There's nothing to worry about. It'll be fine."

I chew worriedly on my fingernail.

"We won't stay long, I promise, but I have to show up or the guys will give me hell." He takes one of my hands in his, rubbing it soothingly. "Whatever you're imagining, I promise it's not like that."

He's making an awful lot of promises I am afraid he won't be able to keep.

I look at the house and back to him. "Okay."

If I don't get out of this car now, I never will, and I think

Cade senses that because at my word, he's out of the car and at my side in only a few seconds.

"Breathe," he tells me, pulling me against his side.

Breathe? What's breathing?

Oh, yeah. That thing where you force air in and out of your lungs.

Cade's hold on my hand is tight as we slither between cars and up to the front door. The people milling around outside don't seem to be paying us any attention. They are too busy smoking something that's definitely not a cigarette.

Cade doesn't bother to wait for anyone to come to the door. He just reaches out, takes the knob in his hand, and twists it.

I immediately want to slap my hands over my ears from the deafening sound of the music playing. The rumble of so many voices doesn't help my ears to feel any better. I realize as soon as the door closes behind us that there is no way Cade and I are going to hear a word the other said.

Cade pushes through the throng of people crowding the entryway, heading toward the back of the house. I can see the kitchen and figure that's his destination. I hold tightly to his hand, afraid if I let go that I will be sucked into a black hole and lost forever.

He looks back at me and seems to sense my fright, so he draws me closer to his body until I feel like I am glued to his side.

"Hey, Cade," someone I can't see calls.

Then a chorus of, "Hi, Cade," and "Hey, Cade," starts up.

He nods, not really acknowledging a specific individual.

We finally make it to the kitchen, and it's as packed as the living room and dining room we'd come from.

"Want anything to drink?" he asks me.

"Just water," I squeaks, lowering my eyes to the ground to avoid the stares of the people around us. And no, I'm not paranoid, because they are definitely staring.

"What? Hanging out with jailbait, Montgomery?" a male voice from the corner of the kitchen calls out. I look up, locating him immediately. He's a monster of a guy, taller and wider than Cade with black wavy hair falling messily into his eyes. He's smiling, but there's something off about it.

"Shut up, Eric," Cade growls.

The guy named Eric chuckles, draping his arm around the shoulder of a blonde that looks like her boobs were about to pop out and say hello to all of us. "Ooh, someone's testy."

"Ignore him," Cade mumbles under his breath to me. "That's what I try to do."

Try being the keyword there.

"Don't worry, beautiful—" Eric turns his gaze toward me "—I don't bite."

I step closer to Cade. I feel like at this point I am practically trying to climb him to get away from these people.

I suddenly wish I had my camera so I could hide behind its protective lens.

"Don't talk to her," Cade defends, moving his body in front of mine.

I might not have liked the guy, but I don't need Cade to get all Alpha male defensive on me.

I move so that I stand beside him once more. Eric glares at Cade, taking a few steps forward around the kitchen island that separates us. The blonde moves with him, his arm still draped over her shoulders, and every little bit he brushes his fingers over her breast. "What's your name, sweetheart?" he asks me, ignoring Cade's threatening glare. He smiles once more, and I still find it threatening.

I don't want to give him my name, but I know lying isn't an option. "Rae."

"Rae," he repeats my name slowly, like it was a flavor exploding on his taste buds. "Beautiful name for a beautiful woman."

Cade growls, his hold on me tightening.

"Don't get defensive, Montgomery. I'm just stating the obvious," Eric chortles. "Man, I've never seen you so worked up over a girl before. Haven't actually seen you with many girls. I was starting to think you were gay."

Cade jolts forward, his fist tightening.

I grab ahold of his arm, digging my fingernails into the skin. "Cade, stop," I warn. "He's just trying to get a rise out of you."

That makes him stop, but he still glares at Eric like he's ready to kill him.

"Come on," I coax, "let's grab a drink and go back to the living room." *Or leave*, which I don't say out loud.

He bristles, still glaring at Eric, but after a few more seconds, his body relaxes and he turns away from the other guy.

"He's just trying to piss you off," I hiss.

"I know," Cade mumbles, staring down at his shoes, "but it's working."

Cade grabs a bottle of water for me and a beer for himself. Taking my hand, he leads me from the kitchen. I feel Eric's eyes boring into my back. I don't tell Cade, but the guy gave me the creeps. There is definitely something off about him.

Cade finds an empty space of wall in one of the hallways and pulls me in front of him, my back to his chest. Almost every surface in the house is covered with bodies, and those that aren't look like they are covered in vomit and other mysterious stains.

I can feel a headache coming on from all the noise and reach up to rub my temples.

This is exactly what I'd pictured a college party to be like, and I don't want anything to do with it.

Even when I was still Rachael, I'd never been the girl screaming, taking her top off, and dancing on a table. And yes, that definitely just happened.

I'm not sure whether I should cover my eyes, Cade's, or both. Probably both—oh, God, she's going to knock someone out with one of those if she keeps swinging around like that.

I felt like maybe I should be the responsible person and step forward to try to stop her, but now a ring of people are forming around her, urging her on. Yeah, I'm not going to try and break through them.

Cade's hands grasp my hips, and I tilt my head back to look at him. "Is this what all your parties are like?"

He laughs. "This isn't my party, but yes, most of them are like this."

"Well, that's ... gross," I mumble, trying not to watch the show being put on.

Cade moves from behind me and drags me into the dining room where we can't see the girl anymore. I'm thankful for it.

The dining room isn't even decorated as a dining room. It's set up more like a den with a couch, chairs, and a TV with an expensive looking game box. The only thing that gives away the origin of the room is the chandelier in the center that must've come with the house, because there is no way college guys would've installed one.

I don't want to sit on the couch, because it is definitely stained with something funky, so Cade and I stand against the wall like we had in the hallway. The room had cleared out, thanks to the striptease going on—although, I'm not sure it could be considered *teasing* when you rip off your clothes.

I noticed Eric is still in the kitchen with the same girl. She is basically humping his leg and her mouth is glued to his neck, leaving a slobbery trail.

But Eric seems oblivious to the poor girl, who is clearly trying to get his attention. I know this because his eyes are on me. His eyes scan my body lazily, like he's memorizing every curve. Now I really do want to hide behind Cade.

"What are you looking at?" he asks, turning around to see for himself.

Eric has the good sense to look away in time, so Cade assumes I am just grossed out by the display.

Cade looks down at me, frowning. "Let's go."

We can't have been there more than thirty minutes, and I feel bad that he wants to leave because of me.

"No, I'm fine," I assure him. "These are your friends. Go mingle. I'll be fine here." I give his hand a reassuring squeeze.

He looks at me skeptically. "I think we should go."

"Cade," I say his name sternly, like I'm scolding a child. "I won't be the girlfriend that keeps you from doing things. I'm *fine*," I assure him. "Don't worry about me."

He sighs, swallowing thickly. "Give me fifteen minutes and then we'll go."

I nod as he lowers his head to press a soft kiss to the corner of my mouth.

As soon as he disappears from my sight, my anxiety skyrockets, but I know I made the right decision. I don't want to become a burden on him and keep him from his friends. I don't need Cade to become my shield from life. I have to learn to deal with uncomfortable situations on my own.

I fiddle with my fingers, feeling extremely awkward to be standing there by myself. It's clearly only upperclassmen at the party, which only serves to make me feel more out of place.

Maybe if I was still Rachael, I'd plaster a fake smile on my face and introduce myself to some people. But I feel frozen to the spot.

To have something to do, I fiddle with a loose thread on my shirt.

"Need some help there?"

I let out a startled squeak as I look up and see Eric. He stands there with his hands in the pockets of his jeans, angling his body toward me. He smiles in a way that I am sure was meant to comfort me, but only made me feel more unease.

"Uh ..." I let my hand fall away from the sleeve of my shirt. "No, I don't need any help." I take an unconscious step away from. If he notices, he doesn't act like it.

His smile widens. I'm sure that smile had lots of girls swooning into his arms, but not me.

"That's a shame." He chuckles, his eyes zeroed in on my breasts.

"Well, if you don't need anything, I'll be going." I move around him to leave, but he catches my arm, jerking me back in front of him.

"Ow," I groan, rubbing the tender area where my shoulder and arm connect. "Was that necessary?"

"Sorry," he apologizes, but there is nothing sincere in his voice. "I just didn't want you to leave."

I look over my shoulder where the blonde who'd been hanging onto him earlier glares at me. "I don't think you're lacking for company. I'm leaving.

This time when I move around him, he grabs both of my arms and shoves me against the wall so hard that it feels like my skull cracked against it. Tears sting my eyes and all the air leaves my lungs as he glares down at me.

"I wasn't done talking to you, bitch," he spits.

I flinch from his words, his hold, and the scary look in his eyes. It's like he's possessed. They are so empty and lifeless.

"Wh-what do you want to talk about?" I stutter, trying to appease him.

This is like the night at the club, but so much worse, because Eric is huge, and I knew there is no way I am getting out of this situation on my own. I have to hope Cade comes back soon or someone intervenes.

Eric is clearly drunk, but his hold on my arms is so tight that I swear my bones rubbed together. I am definitely going to have bruises in the morning.

"Why are you here with Montgomery?" he asks.

I hadn't expected that question. "Because he's my boyfriend," I whisper.

"Boyfriend?" He chuckles, the stench of alcohol on his breath making me feel dizzy. "That's funny."

"It's not a joke." I glare at him. "Now let me go," I say the words with as much strength as I can muster, but there is still a slight quiver to my voice.

He chuckles. "That's cute."

"What's cute?" My whole body starts to shake. This is so bad.

"That you think I'm going to let someone as pretty as you get away." He releases his hold on one of my arms, but before I can make a move to wiggle away, he presses his body firmly against mine. I feel like I am suffocating. "You're not going anywhere." When my body bucks against his, he slides his fingers down my cheek. "Shh, I won't hurt you."

I want to argue that he already had hurt me, but I know my words will only fall on deaf ears.

Glaring at him, I spit, "I never knew someone such as yourself had to force themselves on girls to get any action. That's called sexual assault."

His eyes burn, and I have no time to react before his hand slaps against my cheek.

I see stars and wiggle my arm, trying to get my hand to my cheek to soothe the burn, but I can't move.

I taste blood in my mouth from the impact, and while I might be scared, I'm also mad. I spit the blood out on his shirt, and he chuckles in response.

"You have sass, I like that."

"Get away from her," an icy voice says beyond the mountain that was Eric.

Eric doesn't step away from me; in fact, I'm pretty sure he draws even closer, tightening his hold to the point that I am sure my circulation is cut off.

Looking over his shoulder, he laughs menacingly. "Now why would I do that, Montgomery?"

With a roar, Cade charges forward, ripping Eric from my body. Eric stumbles back and Cade maneuvers his body in front of mine.

"Stay the fuck away from her."

Eric holds his arms out, laughing. He seems oblivious to the anger rolling off of Cade in waves.

"Do you really think I'm going to listen to you? I always get what I want, Montgomery, and I want her." He puckers his lips at me.

Cade loses it, and there is nothing I could do to stop him.

He charges forward like a bull, tackling Eric to the ground as if they are on the football field and not in the middle of a party.

There is a collective gasp and then sounds of, "Fight, fight, fight!" break out.

The guys roll around, fists flying.

I don't know what to do, but I think it's best if I stay out of the way. If I try to break up the fight I'll only end up getting hurt worse in the process and my head is already throbbing from the impact of Eric shoving me into the wall. I'm probably going to end up with a knot on the back of my skull the size of a baseball.

The crowd grows even more in size—apparently, fights are more interesting than boobs now, or else the girl has gotten dressed.

When I can't see the fighting men anymore, I eased out of the room heading for the front door.

I walk along the sidewalk and cross into the street when I spot Cade's Jeep.

He'll figure out where I went. Well, I hope ... and preferably soon. It's extremely dark, and none of the houses near his car have any outdoor lights.

I make sure to stay hidden before I land myself into any more trouble.

I want this night to be over. I hadn't expected much of tonight, but it had been even more of a disaster than I anticipated.

As I sit on the sidewalk by myself, tears spring to my eyes.

This night feels so much like the one at the club, but I was far more afraid of Eric than I had been of Icky Guy. I get the impression that Eric isn't used to girls denying him. And Eric has this mean glint in his eye that's worrisome.

I wipe tears from cheeks.

I didn't even realize I was crying.

I dry my face, but it's pointless. More tears replace those. I am a blubbering mess. I always try to be so put together, at least on the outside, but I am falling apart. Everything seems to be catching up with me.

I guess it's a good thing I told my mom I am ready to see a therapist again. My first appointment is tomorrow, and after this night, I am going to need it.

I'm shivering by the time I spot Cade walking to the car.

"Rae?" he calls into the night. "Rae? Where are you? Are you out here? Rae?"

"I'm here," I stand up, sniffling.

"Oh, thank God." He breathes a sigh of relief. He runs toward me and wraps his arms around me. "I was so worried. I tore that whole house apart looking for you."

"I had to get out of there," I blubber into his shirt. He's going to think I'm a crybaby if I keep crying all over him.

"I'm so sorry." He kisses the top of my head, smoothing his fingers through my hair. "I'm so sorry," he begins to chant over and over again. "I shouldn't have left you."

"I'm okay," I assure him.

"Are you sure?" He tilts my head back to look at me, and that's when I wince. "What the fuck did he do?" Cade growls, his face transforming to an angry grimace.

"M-my head hit the wall," I stutter.

He curses unintelligibly under his breath.

"We'll go to the hospital and get you checked out." He pushes past me and opens the passenger door.

"I really think I'm fine," I assure him.

"No." His jaw is set. "I'm not taking you back to the dorms until I know you're okay. We're going to the fucking hospital, even if I have to drag you kicking and screaming."

"Okay," I agree, figuring it's better to be safe than sorry.

"Thank you," he says softly before I get in the car.

I don't know why he's thanking me. I should be thanking him. He saved me tonight ... but really, he saved me before that.

"Everything is fine," the emergency room doctor assures Cade. To me, she adds, "There will be some soreness and a sizable bump, but you have no signs of a concussion."

"Thank you." Cade stands up and extends his hand for the doctor.

"Have a good evening," she says before exiting the room.

A nurse comes in a few minutes later with some papers for me to sign. Once that's done, we are free to go.

Cade keeps a hand on the small of my back as we head for his car. It's like he is still afraid I might fall over.

I climb into the big vehicle, and exhaustion floods my body. I want nothing more than to sleep for the next three days.

"Do you want to go back to your dorm or mine?" he asks, pulling out of the hospital parking lot. An ambulance zooms past us, illuminating the car with its flashing lights.

"Mine," I mumble, fighting the urge to close my eyes.

"Are you mad at me?" he asks softly.

"No," I gasp. "Why would you think that?"

"You said you didn't want to come back to my dorm—" he shrugs "—so I thought maybe you were mad at me."

I want to go to my dorm, because, frankly, I want my own bed right now, and I am seeing my new therapist early in the morning. I haven't told Cade about it yet. I'm not sure what he'll think, and I am a bit scared to say anything to him.

"Nope, I just want my own bed," I assure him. He looks at me doubtfully, so I add, "I swear, Cade. I'm not mad. Trust me, if I was mad, you'd know."

He chuckles. "Okay, I believe you."

"What's Eric's problem?" I ask suddenly. I've wanted to ask before, because there's obviously more there than I know, but there hasn't been a good opportunity.

Cade pinches the bridge of his nose, the red of the stoplight illuminating his face.

"Eric's just a fucking asshole," he spits. "He wanted to mess with you to piss me off. He's jealous because scouts are interested in me and not him, and, of course, the whole team knows I have no desire to join the NFL, so that only pisses him off even more." He sighs heavily. "I shouldn't have gone to the party. I only went because Adam and Brady were supposed to be there, and guess what?" He laughs humorlessly. "Neither of the fuckers showed up, so it was pointless for me to even go." He looks at me sadly. "I promise not all of the guys on my team are like that."

"I believe you." I force a smile because I'm too tired to offer a real one. "You're not like Eric, and neither is Xander."

He reaches for my hand, entwining our fingers together. "I really am sorry about tonight."

"Cade," I say his name warningly, "you don't have to keep apologizing to me."

"I know." He glances at me. "But I want you to know I mean it."

"I do," I promise. "Please, don't beat yourself up over this. Eric is just a shitty guy and that's not your fault."

"It's my fault for leaving you," he counters.

"And I told you to leave," I remind him. "It happened, and it's over with, okay?"

He sighs, tapping his fingers against the steering wheel to the beat of the song. "No promises."

I am too tired to argue anymore and drift to sleep. When I wake up the next morning, I'm in my bed, and Cade's scent lingers in the air.

twenty-three
...

I STAND OUTSIDE the therapist's door. It's my turn to go back, but I'm frozen. I am tempted to turn around and run out the door screaming, "I can't do this!"

But I never get that chance.

The door opens, and I stumble forward. A bright and cheery woman of no more than forty smiles at me. "You must be Miss Wilder."

"R-Rae," I mumbled, my heart racing with fear. With the way I'm sweating, you would've thought the woman was trying to kill me.

"Rae," she repeats, "it's nice to meet you. I'm Dr. Daniels, but you can call me Kathleen."

"Kathleen," I repeat, my pulse racing.

"Yes." She closes the door and sits down in a chair, not behind a desk like my old therapist had. "Sit, please." She motions to the other unoccupied chair.

I scurry over and sit down. I figure to her I must look like a frightened rabbit.

She grabs a notebook and pen off a table, depositing them in her lap. "How are you today?"

"Good, I guess," I mumble, staring out the window where morning sunlight streams in the window.

"You guess?" she repeats.

"I don't want to talk about it," I mumble. I don't know this woman, not yet, and no matter how kind she might look with her warm brown eyes and sweet smile, she's still a stranger.

"That's fine. Why don't we spend this session getting to know each other?" she suggests.

"Excuse me?" I reply, my brows rising. My last therapist had made it very obvious that he was the doctor and I was the patient. But this woman is different.

"I think we should get to know each other," she repeats. Sliding forward in her seat, she peers at me. "I'm here to help you, Rae, but that doesn't mean we can't be friends."

"Friends?" I snort.

She smiles. "Yes, friends. I'm not your enemy. I want you to get better as much as you want to get better."

"How do you know I want to get better?" I counters, looking around the room at the framed photos and memorabilia. It looks like she's married to a nice man with two children. She has a lot of books, and not all of them are medical books. Many are fiction. I even see a set of Harry Potter books, which makes me smile as I think of Cade.

"If you didn't want to get better, you wouldn't be here," she replies easily.

"What do you want to know about me?" I ask.

She smiles. "I think maybe you should ask me that first."

"Why?" My brows furrow together.

She smiles, crossing her legs. "Because, I want you to see that I'm not here to analyze you."

I want to snort at that, but I keep myself in check. "Okay then ... What are your kids' names?" I point at one of the framed photos.

"Tessa and Tyler," she replies. "We adopted them."

"You couldn't have kids?" I asks, and then promptly feel bad for asking. It isn't proper of me to pry, and I'm not sure quite how far I can take this question thing.

"Sadly, I couldn't." She frowns, her eyes growing distant. "But I love those two as much as if they were my own flesh and blood. They're my miracles." I can see the love she's talking about as she speaks. "You're in college, correct?" she asks. At my nod, she continues, "What are you studying?"

"Photography," I answer, my thundering heart slowing to a dull roar.

"Photography?" she repeats. "Wow. I'd love to see some of your photos sometime."

"I could bring some next time," I mumble.

"That would be great." She claps her hands together. "I always did have such an appreciation for the arts. I played the violin as a child."

The rest of the session goes much the same way. She wants me to come back on Monday after classes, and something tells me that she'll be ready to get down to the gritty stuff. I hope I'm ready.

"Rae, wait up!"

I stop at the sound of my name being called. Snow flurries flutter around me, sticking to my lashes. I'm glad I wore a beanie and scarf, even though the weather didn't call for more snow.

Cade jogs up to me, his breath fogging the air with each exhale. "I've been looking all over for you. You didn't answer your phone, and Thea said you left early this morning and didn't say where you were going. I was worried your head was bothering you and you'd gone back to the hospital."

"My head's fine," I assure him.

"I'm glad to hear that." He blows into the palms of his hands to warm them. "Where'd you go?"

I look away, toeing the ground. I expected him to ask, but I'm not sure I want to tell him. I can't lie, though. Lying will only make my problems worse.

"I went to see a therapist." I look into his eyes, waiting to see if he reacted in any way.

He smiles. "That's great, Rae. I think that will be good for you."

That definitely isn't the reaction I expected. Most people, when you tell them you're seeing a therapist, reply with, "A therapist? Like a shrink? Are you crazy or something?"

I should've known Cade wouldn't react that way. He

never did what I expected him to. He's constantly surprising me and in the best ways possible.

"Thanks, I hope so." I reach up, grabbing a strand of hair that sticks to the gloss coating my lips.

Dropping the subject from my therapy session, he asks, "Are you hungry? I thought we could go out for lunch." He rubs his hand around his stomach absentmindedly.

Now that he mentions it, I'm starving. In my haste to get to the therapist's office, I'd forgone breakfast.

"Lunch would be great."

"I know it might be too soon—" he rocks back on his heels "—but do you think you'd be up to meeting some of the guys on the team afterwards? I'm supposed to meet them at the gym at one. Eric won't be there," he hastens to add.

"Uh ..." I pause, thinking. "That would be fine."

He grins, and the dimples in his cheeks pop out. "They're going to love you, Rae."

I hope so. The last thing I want is to be known as the weird girl by the football team. But knowing me, I'll do something stupid to make them hate me. Or Eric has gotten to them and told them some disastrous lie about me.

"What's with that face?" He chuckles, reaching out to guide my chin up so that I am eyelevel with him.

"What if they hate me?" I frown.

He grins crookedly and lowers his head so he can whisper in my ear. "I'm going to let you in on a secret, Rae. You're impossible not to like."

I snort at that. I disagree completely with that statement. All I do is push people away.

But then why do you have friends now? a little voice in my head pipes up.

"What? You think I'm lying?" He pushes strands of his hair from his eyes.

I shrug. "I'm not the nicest person." Rachael had been nice. She loved everybody. Rae ... not so much.

Cade reaches out, tucking a strand of hair behind my ear. His fingers linger longer than necessary against the skin of my cheek. "You're nicer than you think you are. You're way too hard on yourself."

Sadly, I feel like most times I'm not hard enough.

"They're going to love you," he repeats. "Trust me."

Trust him? Doesn't he know I already do? I would never have told him about the accident if I didn't. I trust Cade in ways I've never trusted another human being before.

I reach out, grasp his jacket, and step closer. I tilt my head back and peer up at him.

His lips twist into a smile. "What are you doing?"

"Getting closer to you."

"Why?" He draws out the word.

"So I can tell you that I trust you. You should know that, Cade."

His smile widens until it's almost blinding. His smile makes my stomach flip. It's such an easy *happy* smile, despite the shitty things he's been through. I want to smile like that again.

He doesn't say anything in response. Instead, he kisses me, and it's exactly what I need.

His lips are slow and gentle against mine. Even though it

isn't a passion-filled kiss where we're clawing at each other, I still feel it through my whole body. Slow could be good. Slow is sweet. Slow is perfect.

When Cade pulls away, he places a gentle kiss on my nose, the snow swirling around us.

It's a scene straight out of a fairytale, but I am no princess, and his kiss can't save me.

Only time can do that and my own desire to shed the pain that clings to me.

Step One of healing had been telling Cade.

Step Two, I know without even discussing it with my therapist. I need to accept the events of that day, and understand no matter what I believe, I can't change it.

Step Three ... Well, that will be the hardest. I have to say goodbye to the people I lost. And goodbyes? Well, those are never easy.

Cupping my cheek and stirring me from my thoughts, Cade asks, "Are you ready to get lunch or do you need to go to your dorm first?"

"I can go now."

"Good, because I'm starving."

"This better not be the same restaurant you took me to for burgers before," I warn, trying to hide my smile. "If I end up with food poisoning again then I might have to reconsider your status as my boyfriend."

He throws his back and laughs, causing quite a few people to turn and look at us. "You're funny."

"No, Cade," I try to sound angry. "I'm dead serious."

"Don't worry, Sunshine." His hand finds the small of my back. "We're not going there."

"Thank God." I'm actually relieved. If he'd taken me to the same place, I would've run away screaming. Food poisoning is no joke, even if you do have a hot football player to take care of you.

He chuckles. "Did you really think I'd take you back there?"

"Well, you seemed to like their burgers." I shrug.

"I still feel bad about that," he admits with his lips twisting. "But I don't regret getting to spend the next day with you. I don't regret anything with you."

"Not even knocking me down?" I laugh, my hair blowing all around my face from the wind.

He stops walking and takes my face in his large hands. "Definitely not that, because without that moment, I might not have ever met you, and that would've been a real tragedy."

His words get me to thinking about how certain events in our lives lead to another and another. Take one of those events away and a whole new scenario would play out.

If I hadn't met Cade, I might never have been able to accept that I had to get better.

That's pretty crazy to think about.

We come to the Jeep, and I clamber inside, curious as to where we're headed.

Twenty minutes later, and I still have no idea.

He pull in front of a Subway, and I give him an odd look. "Subway?"

He chuckles, lowering his head. "Are you disappointed, Sunshine?"

"Well, it's better than that burger place," I tell him, ready to hop out of the massive Jeep.

"Don't worry, we're not eating here … Well, we're getting our food here, and then we're leaving."

"Leaving?" I question, raising a brow. "And going where?"

"It's a surprise."

Of course it is.

With a sigh, I head for the sub place.

It takes us no time to get our food and drinks. Another five-minute drive, and Cade exclaims, "Here!"

I don't know where *here* is. I look around, and all I see is an empty field of grass.

"What are we doing here? Isn't it kind of cold to be outside?" I ask, afraid to leave the warmth the Jeep provided.

"We won't stay long," he promises, reaching into the back for a blanket. "You can wait here until I get everything set up." He surprises me by leaning over and kissing my cheek, well, more like the corner of my mouth. Cade has no problem expressing his affection while I am a little more reserved.

He gets out of the car, and I watch him wade through the tall grasses and spread out the blanket and lay the food on top. He comes back to the car for the drinks and grabs yet another blanket. I look behind me wondering what else he has stored back there and see a duffel bag and football.

"You coming?"

I jump, realizing he's still standing there waiting for me to get out.

"Yeah," I mumble, my cheeks heating at getting caught being nosy.

It's cold—after all, it's practically December—but luckily, it isn't windy.

Cade leads me to the blanket spread out over the dried brown grass. He sets the drinks down and shakes out the other blanket he had tucked under his arm. He wraps it around both of us, which means that when we sit down we are impossibly close. My heart speeds up, and my breath stutters. Cade affects me like no guy had before. From the first moment I met him, deep down I knew he was different.

Cade hands me my food, his eyes lingering on the side of my face. "So, you think it went well with the therapist?"

I should've known he'd bring it up again. I shrug, staring out at the grass and trees beyond. It's easier to look at it than him when I say, "I do. She was nice and wanted to get to know me instead of trying to diagnose me or pry information out of me. I didn't expect that."

"I'm glad to hear that." The way he says the words, I know he means that genuinely. "I just want to see you happy."

Cade Montgomery is infinitely too sweet for me, but I am too selfish to let him go now.

"I am happy," I replies. "Right now, with you, I'm happy. I'm not happy every second of every day, but who is?" I take a breath, gathering my thoughts. "I'm trying to learn to appreciate the little things, those brief moments where …"

"Where what?" he prompts.

I turn my head toward him, my hair blowing around me. "Where I feel peace."

His lips quirk into a smile, and he reaches forward to grasp my chin between his thumb and index finger. "Do I also bring you peace?"

"You do," I admit. "When I'm with you, everything feels right." I hope I haven't given away too much of my feelings with my words, but with the way he smiles, it had been the perfect thing to say. I hate to ruin the moment, but I have something I need to ask him. "Have you ever considered seeing a therapist? You know, to talk about your brother and what your dad does to you?"

Cade looks away, his jaw clenching, and I worry that I made him madder than I predicted. After a few moments of breathing deeply, he looks back at me. "I probably should, but I don't know if I can. That's why I commend you for having the guts to go. I just ... I don't know if I can admit to a stranger that my dad hits me. It makes me feel so pathetic."

I lean my head on his shoulder. "You're not pathetic, Cade. Far from it. You're strong, loving, a protector, and so many other things. Pathetic is definitely not one of them. What your dad does, that's a reflection on him, not you. I ... I want you to know—" I reach for his hand, playing with his fingers "—that you can trust me. I'm here anytime you need to talk about things."

"Back at ya, Sunshine." He cups the back of my head and draws me closer so he can kiss my forehead. I close my eyes, soaking in the feel of him against me.

I worry about Cade. I know what keeping pain bottled up inside had done to me, and I don't want the same to happen to him. After all, if I hadn't seen his dad hit him, he would've never told me. But Cade is a different person from me, with a different personality, so maybe he can cope with things better than I can.

"Don't worry about me," he whispers, like he knows what I've been thinking about.

"I can't help it. I don't want you to hate yourself for things that aren't your fault. That's what I've done, and I know how miserable it can be." I look up at him and find him staring beyond at the trees.

"I'm okay, Sunshine. Really." He lowers his head to look at me. "Sometimes I want to blame myself and think that it must be my fault that my dad hits me, but then I stop and think, and I know that I'm wrong. I don't ask for it. He's just angry. But he's still my dad, as stupid as that sounds. If he wants to use me as his punching bag, that's fine." Cade's face becomes fierce all of a sudden. "But if he ever lays a hand on my mom, then we'll have a problem."

Reaching up, I curl my fingers against his shirt. "Does she know?"

"No." Cade sighs. "I think she wonders, but she doesn't want to believe it's possible. So, I let her think nothing's wrong." He shrugs. "Sometimes we have to protect the ones we love, and for me, that means keeping my mouth shut."

I try a different approach, not wanting to let it go. "What if you saw a little boy on the street corner and his father hit him?"

He winces. "That's different."

"No, it's not, and you know it," I say fiercely, determined to get him to see my point. "You need to stick up for yourself. If you won't seek help, then I think you should at least confront your dad about it."

He sighs, scratching his stubbled jaw. After a moment, he turns and gives me a small smile. "When did you become the one giving me advice?"

"When I started thinking like a normal person."

He chuckles, resting his chin on top of my head. "You were always normal, Rae, just a little sad."

He tilts my head back and covers my lips with his. The kiss is slow and sweet, but still manages to leave my toes tingling.

He brushes his nose against mine when he pulls away. "We better eat before we freeze to death."

"It was your idea to eat out here." I laugh. "And you've yet to tell me where exactly here is." I look around the field. The grasses are dry and brittle looking, but I am sure in the spring and summer it's bright green and soft. Maybe flowers even bloom.

"I'm not sure exactly." He shrugs, taking a bite of his sandwich.

"You're not sure?" I laugh. "What if this is private property?"

"Well, in the four years I've been coming here, no one has chased me off so I'd say we're safe. Now eat." He points at my food.

"Okay, okay," I oblige.

"Sometimes I come here when I want to get away from school and think ..." He pauses. "And get away from the football field. Out here, there's no one to bother me. I can sit for hours and just be me."

"You spend a lot of time by yourself, don't you?" I question.

"I guess so. I learned that it was easier that way."

I lay my head on his shoulder and inhale his familiar scent. "But you brought me here."

"I know." He lays his food down and wraps his arms around me. "I've begun to realize that no place holds any meaning without you."

My breath falters.

"Where do you see this going?" he asks. "Us, I mean?"

"I-I don't know," I stutter. "I'm not like other people. I can't imagine myself five years down the road. All I can focus on is the here and now, and you're a part of that."

"I'll take it," he whispers.

Breaking the seriousness of the conversation, I say, "Shouldn't we be getting back to campus so you can go to the gym?"

Cade curses under his breath. "You're right. We'll finish eating and head back."

By the time we pack everything up and get in the car, my fingers and toes sre numb.

"I think you should come to the gym with me." Cade glances at me out of the corner of his eye.

"Uh ... isn't that what I'm doing?"

He chuckles. "Yeah, sorry. I should've worded that better.

What I meant is, I miss our runs. Why don't you change, meet the guys, and stay for a while?"

I don't know what to say. It makes me nervous, that's for sure. I don't know these guys, and what if I hate them? At least if I was only going to meet them I could escape when I felt like it. Staying to work out with Cade would leave me trapped there. "I don't know, Cade," I mumble.

"Hey, if you get there and decide you don't want to stay then you can leave."

When he puts it that way, I don't see how I can argue with him. "Okay," I relent. It's hard to tell Cade no, but I also know I need to put myself out there.

His smile is huge which instantly makes me feel better for agreeing.

We reach campus, and Cade waits in the Jeep while I rush inside my dorm to change. Thea's gone, and I am kind of glad for that, so I don't have to explain anything to her.

I hurry back outside to the Jeep and clamber inside.

"That was fast." Cade chuckles, driving over to the building the gym was housed in since it was too chilly to walk that far—and I still feel a bit frozen from eating our lunch outside.

"I thought you were running late; I didn't want to hold you up anymore."

The closer we get to the gym the more nervous I become. I wipe my damp palms on the black material of my pants.

I spent my last year of high school alienating myself from all human contact, and now I feel like I am constantly putting myself out there. College has changed me for the better, molding me into the person I need to be. I still have a long way to go, though, but I now believed I'll get there. I don't feel so hopeless anymore.

When Cade parks at the gym, I hop out of the car before he can try to give me a pep talk. I'm okay. Nervous? Yes. But I'm not freaking out.

Cade grabs his duffel bag from the back and takes my hand. I breathe out slowly, trying to calm myself. I hope Cade is right and Eric is nowhere to be seen. I might run out of the building if I spot him.

Cade leads me around the equipment and to a back part of the building where the football players train separately.

He opens the glass door, and I think the amount of testosterone swirling in the air might suffocate me. Hot, half-naked, sweaty guys everywhere. It's every girls dream, but I find myself clinging tighter to Cade as my eyes land on every face searching for Eric. Cade is right, though, and he isn't here. I breathe out a sigh of relief.

"Guys," Cade calls in a loud, authoritative voice. They all stop what they're doing and look at us. I keep my shoulders squared and my chin high, refusing to be intimidated by the large men. "This is my girlfriend, Rae. She's going to hang out with us today."

Someone whistles, and then I hear a slap. Apparently, someone wasn't happy with the whistler.

The guy nearest to us stands up from the bench press he was occupying. His shirt is drenched with sweat and his dark hair is damp too. "Nice to meet you." Dimples, deeper than Cade's, popped out in his cheeks. "I'm Brady."

Brady ... I remember Cade mentioning that name.

I smile at the big bear of a man. "That's Adam." He points to another guy, and this one had coppery-brown hair. "Dane. Jesse. Rob. And Tyler."

"Hi." I wave weakly.

"Go change." Brady claps a hand on Cade's shoulder. "I'll watch her."

I wrinkle my nose. Watch me? Like I need a babysitter? Great.

"I'll be right back." Cade kisses my cheek. "Five minutes tops."

He eases out the door, giving me a reassuring smile.

Brady throws an arm around my shoulder. "We don't bite. You have nothing to be afraid of. Contrary to popular belief, most of us are quite lovable. Like big, muscular teddy bears."

I laugh, and he smiles.

"See? Nothing to be afraid of." He drops his arm and stands in front of me. "I remember you," he states.

"Remember me?" I ask, laughing. "But we've never met."

"I distinctly remember lover boy tackling you on the sidewalk." He smirks. "Who would've thought that would've spawned a relationship. The guy hasn't dated anyone in all four years he's been here. We would've thought he'd taken a vow of chastity if it weren't for the ... well ..." He winces.

"It's okay." I laughed. "We've talked about it. I know he's had hook-ups."

"Well, then, that's good. Otherwise this conversation could've been very bad for Cadie boy."

I like this guy. The others look on curiously as Brady continues to talk. He is obviously the chattiest of the bunch.

I'm surprised when Adam speaks up, sweeping his hair from his eyes. "We heard about what happened with Eric. That wasn't cool."

I flinch. I didn't want to be reminded about Eric.

"Coach heard about it," Brady informs me, sitting on the bench again. "Eric won't be playing in our last game next week."

My eyes widen in surprise. I hadn't expected that.

Cade returns, changed into his workout gear. "You better not have scared her way," Cade warns good-naturedly.

I smile up at him. "Not at all. Your friends are great."

"So," Brady says with a laugh, "does this mean I can bring my girlfriend to workout?"

Cade snorts. "Yeah, if you can get her to stop talking about her nails for five minutes."

Brady shakes his head, smiling. "Yeah, she does talk about them a lot."

Cade chuckles, bumping his friend's shoulder with his fist as he passes. I follow him over to the row of treadmills.

"It's not as good as running outside, but it will do."

I stand on one of the treadmills, and he climbs on the other.

Once we start running, there's no room for conversation, but that's okay. With Cade, I don't need to fill every moment with chatter; being with him was enough.

twenty-four

• • •

"I WANT TO KISS YOU." *Brett's voice skated over my skin. My heart fluttered like a little bird trapped beneath my ribs. My first kiss. It was finally going to happen. I'd always known it would be Brett. Even as a little girl, I'd known the boy next door was the man I was going to marry. He was my best friend, my everything. We shared everything together, so it seemed natural that we'd share the rest of our lives too.*

I stepped closer to him and draped my arms around his shoulders. Other couples swayed around us at the school dance, but I was oblivious to them.

Brett lowered his head, and his lips glided lightly against mine. It wasn't even a kiss, just a simple brush of his lips, but I already felt my knees weakening.

His hand at my waist tightened, and he deepened the kiss, slow at first, and then with more urgency.

He pulled away and murmured into my hair, "I love you, Rae."

Rae?

I looked up and saw Cade smiling down at me. The dance was gone and we stood on the football field. A sparkle caught my eye and I gasped at the ring on my finger.

"Thank you for giving me forever..."

"And then I woke up," I tell Kathleen. "What do you think it means?"

"It doesn't matter what I think," she sits back, crossing her legs. "All that matters is what it means to you."

I bite my lip.

"You can tell me," she continues. "This is a no judgment zone—" she waves her hands around, encompassing her office. I've been coming to see Kathleen several times a week for three weeks now, so I know she isn't kidding.

"I think it means I love him, that Cade's the one ... Maybe Brett and I were never meant to be." I fiddle with my fingers to have something to do. "I had my whole life planned out and then the accident happened and nothing made any sense."

"Could you tell me more about the accident?" she pushes.

I sigh. There's no point in beating around the bush. Besides, I've been whining to her about my woes for nearly a month now—might as well get to the point of all my problems.

"I was driving, got a text message, looked at my phone, crashed the car, and essentially murdered my boyfriend and best friends." I try to say the words casually, like it has no effect on me, but, of course, Kathleen knows better.

She taps her fingers against the arm of the chair she occupies. "And that makes you feel guilty?"

"Of course it makes me feel guilty!" I explode, the anger I feel rearing its ugly head. "I didn't have to look at my phone! But then I go and have dreams like that and I hear my mom's voice in my head telling me everything happens for a reason. So, then I wonder if I couldn't have prevented what happened. But then I think that's crazy, of course you could've prevented it by not looking at your fucking phone!" I gasp for air and sit back.

Kathleen watches me, not saying a word. "Texting and driving is a horrible thing, but it happened, Rachael. It happened, you've dealt with the consequences, and it's time to move on. Hanging on to the past is pointless. It's the past for a reason. It's gone. Done. Over." It's like she's trying to drill the words into my head.

"Sometimes I feel like they should've put me in jail."

"Do you really think that would've solved your problems?" she counters with a raised brow.

"No," I mumble.

"It's good that you feel remorseful for the accident, Rae. You're not a killer."

I close my eyes. That's exactly what I thought of myself for far too long.

"You were a girl who made a mistake. A mistake you've learned from."

My lower lip begins to tremble as sobs rack my body. "Sometimes I can still hear them screaming. I just want it to stop." I wipe at my tears.

Kathleen reaches out and clasps my hand. "You know how you make it stop?"

"How?" I ask, my voice shaking.

"You lay them to rest," she says simply.

"Huh?"

"You have to accept that they're gone," she clarifies. "Go to where they're buried, say what you need to say, and be done with it."

"I don't know if I can do that." I stare at a water stain on the ceiling. Lowering my gaze, I mumble, "What would I even say?"

"I can't tell you that." She shakes her head, tapping her pen against her lips. "That's something you have to figure out on your own."

Thea buzzes around our dorm room with excitement. Nova sits on my bed watching her with an amused expression on her face. Even though we've recently finished our project, we still hang out anytime we could.

"Is she always like this?" Nova asks me, brushing her long purple hair over one shoulder.

"Pretty much," I reply as I finish lacing my Converse.

"It's the last game of the season and Cade's last game *ever!*" Thea exclaims. "How can I not be excited? This is going to be epic!"

I look at Nova and shrug.

"It's football," Nova states in a deadpan voice.

"And it's amazing," Thea counters.

"At least I can take pictures." Nova holds her camera close.

"Pictures? There's no time for pictures!" Thea grabs a Huntley University sweatshirt and shrugs into it. "You have to watch the game!" She grabs a beanie and puts it on as well.

"Yeah, Nova, you have to watch the game." I laugh.

"Is Jace going to be there?" she asks, brightening.

"No." Thea grabs her shoes from the closet. "He never goes to the games."

"Well, I didn't either until today," Nova counters. "How did I get suckered into this again?"

"Well, Thea bribed you with coffee and suckered you into it," I reply, pulling my hair into a ponytail. It's windy, and the last thing I want was my hair whipping my face through the whole game.

"Dammit, coffee is my weakness."

"I'm ready," Thea finally declares.

The three of us head over to the stadium, and while I attended most of the games, I'd never seen one as crowded as this.

"Are there going to be enough seats for all of these people?" I ask Thea under my breath.

She laughs. "Of course, silly."

I'm still doubtful despite her positivity.

We take our seats, and my body gets that familiar hum of excitement.

"Hey, look." Thea points. "It's my dad!"

I lean forward, craning my neck to see the man she

pointed toward. Yeah, that's definitely their dad. I hope he didn't do or say anything to Cade. Cade is such a positive and happy person; he doesn't need his father trying to cut him down.

Nova lifts her camera, taking pictures of the crowd, the field, everything, really.

"I'm so excited." Thea rubs her hands together.

"I can tell," I mumble under my breath. Thea is always super hyper at football games, sometimes annoyingly so.

"I'm going to go talk to my dad, and I'll be back." Before I can reply, she slips out of her seat and down the steps.

"Is she going to be like that for the whole game?" Nova asks, lowering her camera to her lap.

"No."

She breathes a sigh of relief. "Thank God."

"She gets worse." I laugh.

"Fuck," Nova groans.

My thoughts exactly.

When halftime comes and the players leave the field, I can't help watching Cade's dad leave his seat, and I wonder if he is going in search of his son.

Despite the thrill of the game and the packed bodies, I am still freezing in the December air. Even though I wore gloves, my fingers are frozen. I try to wiggle them but they won't move. I wish I had a hot cup of coffee to hold. Yeah, coffee would be fantastic right about now. Or a small fire.

"I'll be right back," Thea tells us, standing and going to talk to some girls she knows.

Blowing warm air into her hands, Nova looks at me. "I think I picked the wrong game to come to. I'm so cold."

"We should've brought blankets," I agree, and we huddled closer together like penguins.

Halftime passes quickly, and Thea joins us once more.

The score is so close that I feared we might actually lose this game.

"You see that guy there by my dad?" Thea taps my shoulder and points.

"Yeah." I nod, squinting my eyes so I can see the man more clearly.

"He's a scout." She claps giddily, her cheeks flushing.

"Like for the NFL?" I clarify. I am clueless when it comes to this kind of stuff.

"Yes," she cheers. "Isn't it exciting? Cade could be on a professional team next year!"

I frown and don't comment. I know that is the last thing Cade wants, but Thea clearly doesn't know that. It makes me worried that Cade might pursue that path just to please his family. It isn't something we've discussed in-depth. I know he doesn't want to be a part of the NFL, but he never told me if he knew for sure he wasn't pursuing it.

Thea seems to sense my change in mood and leaves me alone—although, she still cheers obnoxiously loud. The girl puts the cheer team to shame.

"Are you okay?" Nova asks.

I open my mouth to answer her but gasp instead.

Cade goes down, his knee slamming into the ground. He rolls over clutching his leg.

"Oh, my God!" I gasp, my hand flying to my mouth. "Cade!" I cry, trying to push by Thea to reach him—like as if they'd actually let me onto the field. "Cade! I have to get to Cade!" I plead with Thea when she grasps my shoulders.

Panic swarms through my body at seeing him lying on the field. I want to get down there and do something. I need to help him—even if it's just to hold his hand.

"Rae, he's okay, see?" She points to the field where a teammate is pulling him up. He's walking with a limp but appears to be shaking off the injury.

"Oh, thank God," I breathe, hugging her.

My moment of panic begins to fade. I clearly overreacted, but the thought of Cade being seriously hurt had been crushing, and it was within that moment that I finally grasped the depths of my feelings for Cade and the truth my dream had been trying to reveal to me.

I am in love with Cade Montgomery

Not the kind of puppy love of someone infatuated.

This is true, deep, irrevocable love.

I know it's probably too soon to feel that way, but these things can't really be controlled. When something is meant to be, it's unstoppable.

"You can check on him after the game, but I promise he's okay," she assures, urging me to sit down.

I watch his teammates guide him to the bench, and I wish desperately that I could be there for him the way he's always there for me.

But I have to wait, and that really fucking sucks.

My eyes flicker for the rest of the game from Cade on the bench to his father in the stands. Even from this distance, I can see the hard set of the man's shoulders. He's pissed. I'm terrified that the man is going to inflict even more damage to Cade, both physically and mentally.

When the game ends, I have no idea who won, but from the cheers on our side, I assume it's us. I push Thea out of my way so I can get to the aisle. I don't care if I offend her with my gesture or not. I have to get to Cade. Now.

I glance behind me and see his dad racing for the exit as well.

I know I need to beat him.

I'm able to cut him off and run for the locker rooms.

I reach the locker room door, ready to burst inside. I slam my shoulder against it and flinch when it doesn't budge. Fucking locked.

Tears prick my eyes, and I whimper in desperation.

I look behind me and see his dad approaching.

Double fuck.

I stand against the opposite wall of the locker room door and slide down until my butt touches the floor.

His dad stops, looking from me to the door. He gives no indication of recognizing me. Just looking at him is getting my blood boiling.

"You're an asshole, you know that, right?" The words bubble out of my mouth before I can stop them.

"Excuse me?" He stops pacing and stands in front of me. His hands are shoved into his pockets.

"You heard me," I sneer. "I know what you do to him."

"Do to who, sweetheart?" He chuckles, completely unaffected.

"To your son, Cade. Remember him? The son you like to hit? I saw you," I seethe, standing up once more. With my height, I'm eye level with him, and I refuse to cower from his domineering presence. "I saw you hit him, so don't even deny it," I spit. "He's a good guy, which is more than I can say for you." I look him up and down. "You're scum and like to take your anger out on your son. Who does that?"

"You have no idea what you're talking about." His face grows red and a squiggly vein on his forehead threatens to burst.

I glared at him. "I'm not stupid, so don't treat me like I am."

Anger radiates off of both of us as we stand staring, neither of us willing to back down.

His fists clench at his sides, and I briefly wonder if he might hit me.

We startle apart when the locker room door opens.

"Rae?" Brady asks, taking in the scene in front of him. "Is everything okay?"

"I don't know," I answer honestly.

Brady hesitates. "You want to come see him?"

I nod, brushing past Cade's dad. Before the door to the locker room closes behind me, I catch it with my hand. I turn back around and speak calmly but with authority. "Watch what you say to him, I mean it. I won't watch you tear him apart." He doesn't say a word, just stands there. I push the door open wider. "Are you coming?"

He finally cracks a smile ... a small one, and not very nice, but a smile nonetheless. "Am I allowed or will you yell at me for that too?"

I roll my eyes. God, this man is a piece of work.

I turn around and let the door swing closed. It locks behind me, barring Cade's dad from entering the locker room.

Brady stops me, his eyes wide. "What the hell was that about? Did you get into it with Malcolm?"

"We were having a discussion." I straighten my clothes. Brady looks at me like he doesn't believe me. "Honestly," I add.

"Mhm," he hums, not believing me at all. "He's this way." He turns down a different hall and points to a room. "You can go on in."

I push the door open and find Cade sitting on a padded bench like you'd find in a doctor's office. He's already changed into sweatpants and a sweatshirt. His pants are rolled up exposing his right knee. A doctor gently probes the area, and Cade doesn't flinch, so I hope that's a good sign.

"Hey," I whisper, and he looks up at me.

He smiles beautifully, like I light up his whole world. He reaches his hand out for me, and I step closer.

"How bad is it?" I ask, and I'm not sure if I'm addressing him or the doctor.

"Not too bad," the doctor answers. "There's some swelling and it will bruise, but I don't think anything was torn. It's going to require rest and elevation to help with the swelling. Don't overdo it, I mean it," he warns Cade. He turns to the freezer in the small room and grabs an icepack. "Sit tight for a little bit," he directs. "I'll be back in a few minutes."

Cade sighs and rests his head against the wall, the icepack on his knee.

"Come here." He pats the empty space beside him.

I hop up, afraid to get too close in case I cause him more harm.

"Closer," he growls, wrapping his arm around my waist and drawing me fully against him. "I'm not going to break if you breathe on me."

I laugh, leaning my head on his shoulder. "You scared me."

"I did?" He seems surprised.

"Yeah," I whisper, and tears start to fall.

Seeing Cade injured on the field had reminded me of the helplessness I'd felt seeing my friends dead in the car. When you love someone, and I knew I loved Cade, it was terrifying to see them hurt. You want nothing more than to take their pain away.

"Don't cry, Sunshine." He reaches over and swipes my tears away.

"I can't help it."

He presses his lips against my forehead, and my eyes close. "I'm okay."

"But it could've been worse." My voice shakes with emotion.

"But it wasn't," he counters, rubbing his hand up and down my arm.

I look up at him, staring into his kind blue eyes. In five months, this man has become my friend, my boyfriend, and so much more. He saved me.

"I love you."

His eyes widen, and his mouth parts, like he doesn't quite believe I said it.

I'm not ashamed for having admitted my feelings. Instead, I feel stronger. Love doesn't make you weak, it gives you strength and a purpose, so when you find it, it's only proper that you shout it from the rooftops.

"Love is a very powerful word," he whispers, cupping my cheek. He brushes his nose against mine. His hair tickles my forehead and his lips are dangerously close. If I was a braver person, I would grab his face and kiss him until we begged for oxygen. Instead, I am still slightly terrified of his rejection.

"I know, that's why I used it, because what I feel for you is a very powerful thing." My hands begin to shake, and I'm tempted to run away. But I hold my breath and stay, waiting to hear his reply.

He grins, pressing his forehead against mine. "I love you too, Sunshine."

I gasp, but he silences the noise with his lips. He tilts my head back, his tongue finding mine.

My hands wind around his neck, and I squeak when he grasps my thigh and pulls me onto his lap.

We move against each other, and I can feel him pressed against me, his desire evident, which only increases mine.

He moans into my mouth, gasping my name.

"I love you," I murmur again and again. Now that I've said it, I never want to stop. I want him to know that I mean it and I'm not going to retract my words.

He bites my bottom lip lightly, his hand cupping the back of my neck. He pulls away, and our gasps for breath become the only sounds in the quiet room.

"What did I do to deserve you?"

I reach up, brushing my fingers over his slightly stubbled cheek. "I'm the one that should be asking that question," I murmur.

"You underestimate yourself, Sunshine." He runs his thumb over my bottom lip. "You can't see what I see, and that's a damn shame."

The clearing of a throat has us breaking apart.

The doctor tries to hide his smile behind his hand. "That doesn't look like resting to me."

My cheeks flame with color, but Cade is unaffected.

"My lips may have been moving, but my knee was stable, Doc. Don't worry."

The doctor shakes his head, muffling a laugh. "Get out of here."

Cade tosses the icepack at the doctor and takes my hand.

After grabbing his duffel bag, we head for the exit. I can't stop myself from looking for his father.

"What?" he asks, noticing that I'm distracted. "Are you looking for someone?"

"No," I whisper.

I'm silently thankful that his dad left. It means I spared Cade from being hurt by cruel words and maybe even a fist to the face. A small part of me hoped that maybe my words had affected the man somehow and he could find it in his heart to seek Cade's forgiveness.

Forgiveness could heal immeasurable pain, and it's time that I forgave myself.

twenty-five

· · ·

"ARE you going home for the holidays?" Kathleen asks before I can even sit down in the chair. "I'm sure your family would love to see you."

Her words scream ambush, but I keep myself calm. After all, I have no proof that she talked to my mom, but with a question like that, it sure sounds like it.

"I haven't decided yet." I shrug, picking a piece of lint off my black jeans. "Maybe."

And that's the truth. My mom had started calling me every day, and it is becoming harder and harder to say no to her. My parents have been nothing but supportive since the accident, so I have no real reason to stay away except for my own insecurities.

"Have you thought about visiting your friends?" she questions, chewing on the cap of her pen.

I know what she's asking. Did I decide to visit the cemetery where they were buried?

"I haven't made up my mind." I sigh. "I didn't even go to their funerals. I was still in the hospital and afterwards it just ... It felt wrong," I mumble, closing my eyes at the onslaught of memories. Oh, God, the hate I received had been crippling. My friend's parents needed someone to blame, and I was the only person they could fault, and rightfully so. But I was only human. I had feelings. I bled. I cried. I hurt. But they didn't think about what I was going through, only themselves. Going back to school had been just as bad. People looked at me differently, whispering under their breath as I passed. It had been horrifying, and I was completely alone. But I always felt so selfish anytime my thoughts strayed down that path. I was *alive,* and I should be thankful for that, any rude comments thrown my way shouldn't even matter, but they did.

Kathleen stares at me, twisting her lips as if she thought deeply about her next words. I hold my breath, waiting for what she might say.

"You act as if because you were responsible for the accident that you don't have a right to grieve their deaths."

I flinch, turning away.

She continues, "You're allowed to mourn them, Rae. You lost them too."

My hands begin to shake, and I feel the telltale burning in my eyes that indicates the threat of tears, and lots of them. Kathleen is exactly right.

"You have to let yourself mourn them." She reaches out, gently placing only the tips of her fingers against my knee. "Say goodbye to them and put this all to rest. I'm not saying you need to forget them, or that this will magically heal you, but it is a huge step. This will always be a part of you, Rachael, but it doesn't have to define you."

She sits back and grabs a tissue. She holds it out to me and I accept it, dabbing at my now damp face.

Right after the accident, I cried all the time, especially when I woke up in the mornings and realized it wasn't a nightmare. My tears had dried up about six months after the accident, but coming to college seemed to have stirred them up again.

"It's okay. Let it out."

And I do.

A year and half's worth of tears burst forth, and nothing else had ever been so cleansing.

"I can't believe Cade isn't coming home for Christmas," Thea whines, neatly folding her clothes and packing them in a suitcase. "It's winter break! Who wouldn't want to go home? Well ... except for you two, apparently." Her mouth falls open with a sudden gasp. "Oh, my God, are you two planning like a romantic getaway or something?"

I snort. "Absolutely not. I don't have a romantic bone in my body."

"But my brother does." She eyes me with a hand on her hip.

I raise my hands in surrender. "Honestly, we have no plans. I just don't feel like going home and he doesn't either."

"Whatever," she huffs, zipping her suitcase. "You're both so boring." Her phone beeps with a text message and she reads the screen. "That's my mom. She's picking me up since Cade obviously won't be taking me home. I need to get my own car," she rambles. "Anyway—" she walks over to me and holds her arms out —"I'm going to miss you, and I'll see you when break is over."

I hug her back. "I'll miss you too," I say and mean it. I've become so used to seeing Thea every day, and listening to her prattle on about random nonsense, that it will be weird to be without her for two whole weeks. Maybe while she's gone I can have a ceremonial burning of all the pink shit on her side of the room. With the way she's dressed—leather jacket, torn jeans, and boots—I doubt she'd mind seeing the stuff gone.

"Text me!" she calls over her shoulder as she leaves the room.

I'm not prepared for the amount of loneliness I feel the moment Thea is gone. She's always so fun and energetic, and while at times it's annoying, I have grown comfortable with her exuberance.

I spend a few hours editing photos, talking to Nova on the phone—she flew home to California—and watching Netflix.

College life. What can I say?

I'm not surprised when there is a knock on my dorm room door around dinnertime.

I open the door to find Cade holding an armful of food and other bags.

"Moving in?" I joke.

He laughs. "If you let me."

I close the door behind him, and he sets the bags on Thea's bed. He begins unpacking them, and I see that he brought Chinese and ... "Candles?" I question. "Why did you bring candles?"

He turns to me and smiles, that same smile that always makes my knees quake. "I may be a guy, but I thought girls liked candles."

"Candles are fine, I just wondered why you brought them." I shrug, my stomach rumbling as I inhaled the scent of the food. "Besides, I think it's against school rules to light candles in the dorms.

"Rules were made for breaking," he counters.

He grabs the fluffy blanket I keep on my bed and spreads it on the floor along with several pillows. He then sets the food on the blanket and scatters the candles around. He pulls a lighter out of his pocket and lights all the candles before dimming the lights in the room.

He surveys the room with his hands on his hips. "What do you think?"

Cracking a smile, I say, "I think we're going to burn down the building with all these candles."

"I guess we just can't roll around." He winks, causing my insides to squirm. The last week, ever since I told him I loved him, things have changed between us yet again. The intensity between us has become electrified like we're combustible.

He steps forward, closing the distance between us, and ghosts his fingers along my cheek. I'm sure he can feel the heat there from my blush.

"Don't get shy on me," he whispers, brushing his lips softly against mine.

A small moan escapes me, and I grasp his shirt in my hands, pressing up on my toes so I can kiss him fully.

I've always tried to keep things from getting too out of hand between us, but it is growing increasingly difficult to do that. I want Cade in every possible way, and I'm not sure how much longer I can wait. But I know Cade, and he won't be the one to initiate things in that direction. He thinks of me as a skittish cat that might run if he makes one wrong move. If things are going to go farther than kissing, I will have to be the one that presses for more, and that scares me. I've always been more comfortable letting someone else take the lead.

His hand that rests at my waist skates beneath my shirt, and I shiver at the feel of his hand against my bare back.

He backs up, and my legs hit my bed. I sink down, and he followed. The bed is far too small for the two of us, but I don't mind.

He's careful to hold his weight above me. Always so gentle with me. Sometimes I miss the Cade that he was when we first met, the one that wasn't afraid to joke with me. I'm not as breakable as I used to be. I am growing stronger every day, and I wouldn't be able to say that without having him in my life. I wish he could see that.

"I love you," he growls, his fingers tangling in my hair.

I don't respond; my lips are otherwise occupied.

My body grows warm with the heat we're generating, and I pull my shirt off. He hums in approval, peppering small kisses over my breasts.

I close my eyes, soaking in the moment.

The room could burn down around us, and I would never even know.

I curl my body around Cade's and lay my head on his chest. His warmth winds around me.

Our make-out session ended long ago. We've eaten and cleaned up, and now we're ready to go to sleep.

There's no discussion about whether or not Cade will stay the night, we both just knew it would happen.

I've changed into my pajamas and Cade had stripped down to his jeans—like I'd pitch a fit if he wore his boxers.

He rubs his fingers lazily against my arm, humming under his breath.

He clears his throat suddenly, and I lift my head to look at him. My hair brushes against his bare chest, and he shivers.

"I was thinking that maybe we should go somewhere tomorrow." His voice is soft and hesitant.

"Sure," I agree readily. "Where do you want to go?" Getting away for a little while sounds like a good idea—even if it's only a day trip. A change of scenery would be nice.

"Xander's dad has a cabin close to here. I was thinking maybe we could stay there for a few days," he suggests, tangling his fingers in my hair.

"A cabin? Is there plumbing?" I wrinkle my nose, envisioning some shack in the woods.

Cade starts laughing and then can't seem to stop. Tears

stream down his cheeks. He wipes them away. "Of course it has plumbing, silly girl."

"Hey, it was a fair question," I defend, giggling.

Lying there wrapped in his arms, laughing about plumbing, I feel like Rachael again.

Cade gave me myself back, and I will never be able to repay him for that. I only hope that my love is enough.

twenty-six
. . .

I STARE at the outside of the cabin, wondering if it is really as nice as Cade claims it is. It seems so tiny—and I am now questioning whether or not he lied about the whole plumbing thing.

Cade looks at me over his shoulder with a small smile as he slides the key into the lock. As the door swings open, he uses his large body to block what lies beyond from my view.

Finally, he takes a step to the side to let me pass.

I step into the cabin and my jaw drops. "Cade! This is amazing!" I gasp in awe. I hadn't expected this, not at all.

While small, it's stunning.

A fire already roars in the stone fireplace where two leather chairs were angled to face it.

The bed is in the corner and covered in fluffy white bedding.

There is a closed-off area that I assume is the bathroom and there's even a small kitchenette area.

"You like it?" he asks, setting our bags down.

"I love it." I spin around, taking in the wood clad walls and rustic chandelier. "I can't believe you thought to bring me here."

He shrugs. "I knew it was close and I felt like we both needed to get away. Breathe fresh air, that kind of thing." There is a sadness to his voice that has me worried.

"Cade?" I probe. "What's going on? Is something wrong?" I ask worriedly. I love this man, and I don't like seeing him so heartbroken. I wrap my arms around his neck, forcing him to look at me. "Talk to me."

"I feel bad ..."

"For what?" No way am I letting him off that easy.

"For not going home, for not going pro and disappointing my dad, for lots of things. But despite that—" a slow smile curves his lips as his hands wind around my waist "—I don't regret being here with you right now."

I close my eyes, leaning my head against his chest where his heart beats. "You don't?"

"No." He kissed the top of my head. "This where I belong, but that doesn't stop me from feeling guilty."

I look up at him, staring into his eyes. "Don't ever feel bad for making the choices that are best for you. When you start living your life for someone else, it's not your life at all."

"You're right," he agrees with a sigh.

"You're a good man, Cade." I move my hand to cup his stubbled cheek. "Too good, sometimes."

He chuckles. "You flatter me."

"No." I shake my head. "I'm honest."

He grins, giving me a quick kiss on my lips. "You know, a few months ago, I never thought we'd be standing where we are."

"Really?" I laugh, lightly poking his ribs in jest. "You sure were relentless in your pursuit to make me like you."

He throws his head back and laughs. "Yeah, I guess I was," he agrees. Lowering his voice and running his fingers lightly over my cheek, he says, "But that's only because I knew there was something between us—something that was once in a lifetime. I wasn't going to let you get away so easily."

Before I can respond, he crashes his lips to mine.

There's nothing sweet about this kiss. This is pure passion, and I love it. I want more, so much more, with him.

"Cade, please," I beg, hoping he knows what I want and need. I am too scared to come right out and say it.

He tilts my head back, his tongue flicking against mine. "Tell me what you want, Rae." He nips at my bottom lip. "Whatever you want I'll give it to you."

"You," I breathe, slowly blinking my eyes open. "I want you, Cade."

"You have me," he murmurs, taking my lips once more.

I push lightly at his shoulders, and he pulls away enough to look at me.

"You know what I meant." My breath comes out in soft pants. In this moment, I feel so young and inexperienced, like a blushing twelve-year-old girl.

He brushes his thumb over my bottom lip, his blue eyes darkening. "Are you sure?"

"Yes," I gasp, hating that there is an almost begging quality to my voice.

Cade stares at me, and it's like he's giving me a chance to change my mind. When he sees that I'm certain, he picks me up, and my legs wind around his waist. Our lips meld together. I smooth my fingers through his hair as he carries me to the bed.

I know he didn't bring me here with this intent, but this place is perfect. I want to give him this final piece of my heart and not in some dorm room. This ... this is *right*. This is the moment I didn't know I'd been waiting for.

He lays me down carefully on the bed's surface. His movements are tender, like he's afraid I might crack or break.

He kisses me slowly and sweetly, but I can feel the desire building.

My hands find their way under his sweater and he tugs it off, throwing it somewhere behind him.

He spends minutes just kissing me, and I wonder if he's trying to torture me on purpose.

I remove my shirt, and when his hands move to the button on my jeans, my hips buck.

"Cade," I moan his name, whimpering. My body is a bundle of nerves, and his touch sets me on fire. I never experienced anything like this in my life. This is one moment where no memories from my past will linger, because there's nothing to compare it to. This moment is ours.

His eyes flick up to meet mine and his gaze is so intense that goosebumps break out across my skin.

He moves up my body, sprinkling small kisses along the way.

His lips join mine in a sensual dance, and my hips lift to meet his. Sweat dampens my skin as I wrap my arms around his neck.

When he pulls away for a breath, a confession tears from my lips. "I'm a virgin," I pant.

His whole body stills, and he moved his head to look at me. His breath tickled my face as he weighs his words carefully. "Are you serious?"

I want to laugh at his silly question. "Why would I joke about that?"

He stares down at me with a mixture of awe and confusion. "H-how? You had a boyfriend."

Running my hands up his solid chest, I confess, "I was never ready, but I am now." I lean up just a little bit and whisper in his ear, "It was always supposed to be you. I see that now."

"Fuck," he groans, his fingers grasping the fabric of the bed covers beside my head. "Are you sure about this? I can wait, Rae. I swear to God, if you tell me to stop I will."

"I'm ready," I speak with certainty.

He removes the rest of my clothes slowly, covering every inch of my body with kisses.

His touch is infinitely gentle.

When we come together, there is a little pain at first, but Cade is patient with me, letting me get used to it.

Once the hurt disappears, I knew there has never been

anything more magical in the world than sharing this moment with him.

I rock my hips against his and cling to his damp shoulders.

Tears prick my eyes—not because I'm sad, but because I'm so *happy*.

Later, when I lie wrapped around his body, I don't feel like Rae or even Rachael. I feel like me, and that's pretty great.

"This is nice," I murmur, leaning my back against Cade's solid chest. The heat from the flames in the fireplace warms my outstretched hands. I feel content; there is no part of my mind lingering on the past. Right now, I am living in the here and now. I haven't been able to do that in a long time. Cade gave me my life back.

"You think so?" He nuzzles my neck, making me laugh when his scruff tickles my skin.

Sitting here with him, I feel so free. Like I could do and be anything—like I have a future that is no longer defined by an accident.

"This is perfect. *You're* perfect. How'd I get so lucky?" I lean my head against his shoulder and look at him.

His eyes grow serious. "Most people would argue that we've both been very unlucky in life, but I often find myself asking the same thing, and it's all because of you. You're my

Rae of Sunshine, and I mean that. Before you, I was a ghost in my own life. You woke something up in me."

I feel like I've done nothing for him, but seeing the sincerity written all over his face keeps me from rebuking him.

We've both been through a lot in our lives, and our time together has changed us for the better. It wasn't by sheer dumb luck that I met Cade. It was fate, pure and simple. I owe a lot to that fumbled football and the man that crashed into me. He said I woke something up in him, but he'd done the same for me. My life changed the moment Cade stepped into it. I'm not that girl hiding away from prying eyes anymore. He makes me want to *live*, because I got this second chance at life. My mom had been right a long time ago when she told me just because my friends were dead it didn't mean I was. I couldn't see it then. I'd been too sullen and depressed. But now everything makes sense.

"What are you thinking about?" Cade asks, brushing his fingers through my hair. It feels good, and I lean into his touch.

"My mom," I reply, closing my eyes, "about how she was right about so many things and I didn't want to see it at the time."

"We rarely want to listen to our parents, but the truth is, they usually know what they're talking about." His lips brush against my ear with his words.

"I want to go home," I confess, scooting away from him. It's something I'd been considering since my last appointment with Kathleen. "I want to see my parents and spend

Christmas with them." He saddens at my words, and I hasten to add, "I want you to come with me. They'd love to meet you." Actually, my parents know nothing about Cade, but that needs to change. I have to stop trying to block them out of my life. We'd been close before the accident, but I pushed them away.

"Really?" Cade brightens.

"Yeah," I nod, smiling. I am growing more excited by the second as I think about getting to see them again. "They'll love you." While they might not know about Cade right now, I know I'm not lying. They'll both be thrilled that I moved on and Cade is such a good guy.

He rubs his hands together. "I'm thinking I should wear my sweater vest to meet them."

I pause, holding in laughter, unsure if I heard him right. "Sweater vest?"

He frowns. "Don't parents like a guy in a sweater vest? It means he has his priorities in order."

I have no idea what to say to that. Finally, I respond with, "Why do you even own a sweater vest?"

"Halloween party a few years ago; I went as a nerd."

I snort. "Of course you did." Patting his shoulder like I would a child, I say, "I think you should leave the sweater vest here."

He chuckles. "Fine, no sweater vest. Bummer." He stands up, reaching his hand down for mine. "I think it's time we ate some dinner." Lowering his voice and grazing his lips against my ear, he adds, "You know, restore our energy."

My cheeks color as my mind is flooded with images of

Cade above me and the feel of his body moving against mine. Despite the pain, it had been better than I imagined.

He takes my hand and leads me to the kitchen. The refrigerator is fully stocked, and he places the items he wanted on the counter. He directs me to chop the vegetables while he makes his "secret sauce" and slathers two chicken breasts with it.

It's all so normal. It makes me imagine more moments like this with him, maybe one day at our own place, and even further in the future with cute blue-eyed children running around.

I can't help smiling at the thought, and then tears prick my eyes.

From the moment of the accident, I stopped thinking about a future for myself. I thought there was no life left for me, but I was so wrong.

I could have it all.

And just like everyone was always trying to tell me, moving on didn't mean forgetting my friends, or Brett, or even my actions, it meant *acceptance*.

"Hey," Cade murmurs, noting the single tear coursing down my eye. "What's wrong, Sunshine?"

I know I could lie and tell him it's the onion making the tears, but I don't want to. I always want to be honest with Cade.

"They're happy tears, Cade," I tell him, leaning up to kiss his cheek right where his dimple is when he smiles wide. "I know now that I'm going to be okay, and it feels so good to be free of it. I chained myself to that broken car, and for a long time, I thought my life couldn't move past that, but it can. I know now that I'm going to be all right," I rambles. "I don't feel like I'm a horrible person anymore."

He wipes the tear away and tilts my head back to place a small kiss on my lips.

"You're a remarkable person, you know that?" He leans his forehead against mine. "I'm so glad you can finally see what I've seen from the beginning. You deserve to see your true beauty, because it shines through in everything you do, Rachael."

Beauty.

Happiness.

Sunshine.

It's all sort of the same thing, isn't it?

They've been masked by a dark cloud for me for a long time now, but the storm has passed, and now this Rae of Sunshine can truly *shine*.

twenty-seven
...

WAKING up next to Cade is something I can get used to, especially when he makes me feel so good. My body feels languid and relaxed. I'm so comfortable, in fact, that I completely forgot about our plan to visit my parents until he mentions getting ready.

It's so nice in the cozy cabin that a small part of me is sad to leave. I hope we can come back one day.

We clean up and head back to campus. If we're going to be gone at least a week, we need to pack more than we brought to the cabin. Cade drops me off at my dorm before heading to his and tells me he'll be back to pick me up in twenty minutes.

I hurry around my dorm room, packing everything I think I might need. Really, I am just busying myself so I don't worry about going back home and what I know it means.

I have to visit the graves.

Kathleen was right, saying goodbye and acknowledging that they were gone is what I need to gain true closure. I still feel terrified, even though I know in my heart that this is the right thing to do.

I don't bother to call my mom and tell her we're coming. I just can't seem to bring myself to do it, even though I know she will be thrilled. A part of me is still scared that I'll get there, panic, and demand that Cade turn the car around and take me back to campus.

I sit on my bed, taking deep breaths.

You can do this, Rae. There is nothing to be afraid of.

My little speech seems to help, and I finished packing. I sling my duffel bag over one shoulder and my camera bag over the other.

Cade is already waiting in the parking lot and he jumps out of the Jeep to help me with my bags.

"What the fuck are you wearing?" I stop dead in my tracks.

He look down at the blue shirt and sweater he's wearing. "What's wrong with this? I didn't think it was appropriate to meet your parents in my jersey. I was trying to dress up."

I can tell I've offended him so I immediately feel bad. "It's just ... I've never seen you dressed like that before. I like it." In fact, the dorky sweater is actually growing on me. There's something about it that is very much Cade in a weird way.

He puts my bags in the back and I climb in the car. Bags of Cheetos, Trail-Mix, and Doritos cover the middle console.

"Where did you get all this?" I ask.

"My room." He shrugs, messing with the radio station. "Sometimes I get hungry and I like to have options."

"I can tell." I laugh, eyeing all the bags.

"I brought drinks too." He points to the cup holder.

"You've thought of everything."

He grins, his dimples showing. "Of course. What road trip would be complete without snacks and hydration?"

"It's only a three-hour drive, that's hardly a road trip."

He raises his brows at me before flicking his gaze back to the road.

"It is when you're a guy and you're hungry all the time. Now, hand me the Cheetos."

I hand him the bag, and he starts munching.

Between bites, he says, "And since this is a mini road trip, I think we should sing at the top of our lungs to every song on the radio."

"I can't sing," I warn him.

"Neither can I." He flashes me a smile, orange flecks of Cheetos clinging adorably to his lips. "So it will be perfect. One of us won't outshine the other."

"All right, fine," I agree, not wanting to dampen the happiness between us.

He turns the radio up, and we start singing.

I had to admit that it is pretty fun, even if we are both horrible.

Life should be filled with more of those simple moments, where for a few minutes everything is perfect.

Cade parks his Jeep in the driveway of the two-story brick home. It looks exactly as when I left, just a little more festive. My dad hung the multi-colored lights and wreaths dot every window.

My hands shake with nerves, but I don't feel like running away, which is good. This is my home, and I've been wrong to think it was anything but.

Cade glances at me but doesn't say a word.

He's waiting for me to make the first move.

I can't help glance to the right, where beyond the stretch of field lies Brett's house. We used to run through the fields as children, laughing, scraping our knees, and enjoying life.

I place my hand against the window and close my eyes. If I think hard enough I can hear his laugh as we fell and rolled around in the tall grass.

I startle when I feel the slight pressure of Cade's hand on my knee.

I look back at the house, and without saying a word, slip from the car.

Cade follows me as I trek up to the front door, his hand hovering comfortably at my waist. I could've gone in through the garage, or used my key at the front door, but it didn't feel right. They don't even know I'm coming.

I feel horrible for not coming home for Thanksgiving, and not calling enough.

I've been a lousy person, and I have a lot of making up to do.

I raise my arm and press my finger to the doorbell. Even from the outside, I can hear the loud ringing.

I hold my breath as I wait.

I hear footsteps approach the door, and I reach for Cade's hand. He gives mine a reassuring squeeze and I know everything would be okay.

The door opens, and I look straight at my mom. She gasps, "Rachael! Is that really you?"

Before I can reply, she jumps at me, throwing her thin arms around me. I close my eyes, inhaling her familiar scent of sugar cookies—of *home*. I start to cry, my tears soaking into her shirt. It has only been four months since I left home, but it really feels like so much longer than that.

She finally pulls away and grasps my face between her hands, just looking me over. "You look beautiful, sweetie."

I know what she is really saying; I look like myself.

"And who is this?" Her smile is wide as she reaches up to hug Cade.

He seems surprised by the gesture but is quick to return it.

"This is Cade my ... boyfriend." It still feels weird to say that. Maybe it always will, because Cade is so much more than that to me. He's my savior.

My mom's eyes widen in surprise and she claps her hands together. "That's wonderful! Come on in." She waves Cade inside and then grasps my arm. It's almost like she's afraid if she lets me go for too long I'll disappear.

We head to the back of the house where the kitchen is.

Baking ingredients clutter every surface, with cupcakes, pies, and cookies, all in various stages of completion. I didn't noticed before, but she even has some flour in her hair and on her cheek.

"I like to bake," she says, when Cade keeps staring at the mess.

"She makes the best cookies," I boast, "have one." I point to a plate on the table. "You'll never want another cookie ever again."

Cade chuckles and moves over to the table.

I look at my mom, who keeps glancing between Cade and me with a look of awe. "Where's dad?" I ask, half-expecting him to pop out from behind me.

"He ran to the store to get more flour. I dropped a bag."

Well, that explains why she has flour on her.

"These are delicious!" Cade exclaims, reaching for another cookie.

"Told ya." I move away from my mom to wrap my arms around him. He grins at the gesture.

My mom watches on happily with a smile on her face.

She sits down at the table and gestures for us to sit down as well. She launches into a million and one questions like the typical mom, about school, friends, and particularly how Cade and I met. She finds that part quite funny.

The door leading into the house from the garage opens, and I jump up with excitement.

When my dad turn into the kitchen, I practically knock the poor man down.

"Rachael?" He peers down at me, in shock that I am actually here. "I didn't think you were coming home for Christmas."

"Change of plans." I grin.

He hugs me again. "I'm so glad you're home."

"Me too," I agree, squeezing him tighter.

After he gives my mom the flour, it's time to introduce Cade.

Even though I know my dad will approve of Cade, it's still nerve wracking. I've only ever brought one guy home.

"Nice to meet you." My dad extends his hand to Cade.

"Nice to meet you too, sir." Cade clears his throat, shuffling his feet nervously. It's cute to see Cade so uncertain when he's normally so confident.

"Cade plays football," I blurt, knowing my dad will be thrilled with that information.

"Really?" His eyes widen.

"Yes, sir," Cade responds.

"Let's go talk in the family room." My dad claps Cade on the shoulder, leading him out of the room. Cade looks over his shoulder, pleading with me to save him. I laugh, shaking my head. My dad is harmless.

"Can I help?" I ask, stepping up to stand beside my mom.

"You can frost those cupcakes for me." She points to a plate of cooled chocolate cupcakes. "Frosting is over there." She points again.

I takes off my jacket, tie an apron around my waist, and go to work.

We're both quiet, focused on the task at hand.

Eventually, she asks, "So ... Cade?"

"What about him?" I ask.

"How do you feel about him?" she asks, crossing her arms over her chest.

"Honestly?" I smile, tucking hair behind my ear. "I love him."

She doesn't say anything for a moment, just stared at me, as if weighing her next words carefully. "I saw it, but I wondered if you were aware of how you felt about him."

"Very aware." I duck my head, feeling a bit embarrassed. "I never thought I'd love anyone else after Brett, but then I met Cade and everything changed. He scared me but exhilarated me all at the same time. I told him the truth and ..." I search for the right words. "It didn't matter to him. He still saw me as ... well, *me*."

"I like him. I can see that he's good for you, and that makes me happier than you'll ever know. I love you, Rachael, and I've only ever wanted the best for you. I worried after the accident that we'd lost you." She reaches out, touching my cheek in a gesture that makes me feel like a little girl again. "In a way, we had, but seeing you today ... laughing, smiling, looking at him with so much love ... it's wonderful. I'm glad you've been able to move on."

I reach out and hug her, probably getting frosting on her shirt, but she doesn't seem to care.

"Cade has helped me so much, just by being him. Kathleen, my therapist, has helped too. She's the real reason I was able to come home, and because of her, I'm going to say goodbye." I don't need to elaborate further. My mom knows exactly what I mean when I say I need to say goodbye.

She takes a steady breath, and her eyes filled with tears.

"You're a strong girl, much stronger than you believe." She reaches up and taps her forehead. "Mental strength is harder to come by than physical. You have it, and don't ever forget it." Touching her fingers to her heart, she adds, "You feel deeply and care immensely, that makes you a beautiful person inside and out. I would've been more worried about you after the accident if you acted like you didn't care. Sometimes we all have to suffer through terrible things to find the light in the dark."

I can't help looking over my shoulder, almost as if I feel him, and find Cade standing in the doorway.

Staring at him, I whisper, "I finally found my light."

I'm not surprised when my mom puts us in separate rooms that night. I am even less surprised when Cade sneaks into my room a little after midnight.

"My dad might like you, but I'm pretty sure he'd still kill you if he found you in my room," I warn Cade as he slips into bed beside me. The bed is a queen size, but even then it feels too small for Cade's large body.

Wrapping his arms around me, he pulls me onto his chest. He runs his fingers through my still damp and tangled hair from my shower earlier. "We'll just have to make sure he doesn't find out." He chuckles, cupping the nape of my neck and leaning up to kiss me. "Thank you," he whispers against my lips.

I blink my eyes open and give him a quizzical look. "For what?"

"For trusting me, for loving me, for giving me you." He rolls us over again so he is now above me. "I never knew what I was missing until you," he murmurs, nuzzling my neck. "You make me see the world in a whole different way."

Warmth soars through my body. It feels good to hear him say that. I never wanted to be a weight tied around his ankles. I wanted to lift him up the way he did me.

He runs his thumb over my bottom lip, his eyes darkening with lust. "Thank you for showing me that my demons don't define me."

"Cade—" I reach up, putting my hand on his arm "—I didn't show you anything."

He shakes his head. "You did. Before you, my life was so dull. I played the part but I didn't *live* it. Now, I do. Everyone else saw what they wanted to see when they looked at me, but you? *You* always saw *me*."

With only a few words, he stole my breath. I will never understand how I got so lucky to have this man come into my life, and I hate how badly I treated him at times. I vow in that moment to spend the rest of my life—or as much of it as he'll take—making it up to him.

"I love you," I whisper.

"Not as much as I love you, Sunshine."

"Does your mom ever stop baking?" Cade whispers in my ear as we sit at the kitchen table watching her whip up more treats.

"Nope." I laugh. "I'm pretty sure she even bakes in her sleep. Our house is always overflowing with sweets."

"If we don't leave soon I'm going to gain fifty pounds," Cade warns, reaching for another cookie.

I lightly slap his hand. "Lay off on the cookies. It's not even noon."

He grins. "It's not like they have alcohol."

"True," I agree, "but I've also lost count of how many you've eaten."

He frowns, lowering his head like a little boy in trouble. "Okay, no more cookies ... until after dinner."

I giggle, shaking my head at him. "I think I'm going to have to hide them."

"No!" he cries.

My mom peered around her mountain of baking supplies and says, "Why don't you two find something to do? Bundle up and go outside for a bit."

I looked over at Cade and crack a smile. "That's code for she wants us out of her way and we're getting on her nerves."

"It is not!" she protested.

"It is," I whisper. "Don't worry, Mom, we'll get out of here." I start thinking about what my mom suggested, and say to Cade, "I'm going to grab my camera, I'll be right back and then we'll go outside."

"Sure, I'll be here." He points to the table, eyeing the cookies.

"Don't even think about it," I warn, before running out of the room and up the stairs.

I grab my camera bag and shrug into a jacket then bound back down the steps. I'm surprised to find him standing at the bottom of the stairs tossing a football in the air. Noticing my look, he explains, "Your dad found it."

"Don't expect me to play football," I warn, grabbing a blanket from off the back of the couch. "You know I can't catch."

"I said I'd teach you." He winks.

I know that Cade's form of "teaching" would involve lots of hands-on activity. Not that I would mind.

"Besides," he adds, following me to the back door, "you're probably better than you think you are."

"Well, I guess you'll have to actually teach me this time instead of rolling around in the grass," I joke.

He grins wickedly and winks. "Ah, but rolling around in the grass with you is so much fun."

I laugh, shaking my head as a light wind stirs my hair around my shoulders.

For the time of the year, it isn't that cold, and luckily, there's no snow, so we won't freeze to death.

Cade follows me down the deck steps and into the yard.

"I like it out here," he says, staring beyond the yard to the field of tall grass.

"I think you hate being cooped up inside," I joke, watching where I step so I don't trip.

"That would be an accurate statement." He looks over his shoulder at me, grinning. "I blame it on the fact that my dad kept me outside playing football all the time and ..." He pauses, his face twisting with pain. He takes a deep breath, as if bracing himself. "Before Gabe died we were an active family. You know, skiing, snowboarding, swimming, always outside and on the go."

I keep quiet, not sure what to say. Cade doesn't talk about his brother a lot, and I know it's a testy subject, so the last thing I want to do is say something to upset him. I hate seeing him hurt, though, and I wonder if he often feels the same way when he looks at me.

I spread the blanket down on the ground, set my bag beside it, and lie down staring up at the sky.

Cade joins me, lacing our hands together.

He turns his head toward me, and I look over at him. "When I think about Gabe, and the years after that, and all the shit I went through, it makes me so grateful to have found peace—to be able to enjoy this moment, right here, with you." Bringing my hand up to his chest, he continues, "I no longer feel scared to defy my dad. I know I'm ready to do my own thing, be my own person, consequences be damned."

"What are you saying?" I whisper.

"I'm saying that when I graduate I'm going into architecture. I won't pursue football. I want it to remain a hobby that I love, but not something I'm forced to do." He reaches out, grabbing a piece of hair that had blown across my face, and tucks it behind my ear.

"It makes me happy that you're doing what you want," I admit. True, it's scary that Cade is graduating in the spring and I don't know where things would go, but life doesn't come with a map for a reason. You aren't meant to know where your future will go, but you are supposed to enjoy the journey—even when you have to climb mountains.

"It does?" he questions, seeming almost unsure.

I nod. "I will always want you to do what makes you happy, Cade. I'll support any decision you make because I love you, and when you love someone you don't hold them back from their dreams, whatever they might be."

Before I can take a second to breathe, he crashes his lips to mine.

His kiss is consuming, his touch electrifying.

Despite the chilly air, I feel warm all over as my body floods with heat.

Cade pulls away, his breath fanning across my cheek. His stare is intense, and I find myself drowning in his blue eyes.

Cracking a smile, he says, "Let's go exploring."

I can't dim my smile. "Sounds good."

I hop up, but Cade is a little slower. His knee is still healing, and a part of me worries that he might always have problems from the injury. But Cade is confident that it only needs more time.

I leave the blanket where it is but grab my camera bag. I pull my camera out, following Cade into the brush. He's ahead of me, with the football clasped in his hand. I can't help taking a picture of him.

He looks over his shoulder and smiles, so I take another.

"You're lucky I'm not shy," he warns with a laugh, "because you're kind of intimidating with that thing."

I lower the camera, sticking my tongue out at him.

"I'm serious." He chuckles, reaching out to shove some of the tall dead grass out of his way. "You're kind of a bad ass." He stops and turns around, waving his hand at me.

I roll my eyes. "I'm definitely not a bad ass."

He grins crookedly and steps forward, cupping my cheek. "You are ... and you're also my Rae of Sunshine."

"I thought you forgot that shitty nickname."

"Never," he gasps, faking offense. "It's an awesome nickname, and I will use it as often as I can for the rest of your life, so get used to it."

"Oh, really? For the rest of my life?"

"Yeah." He smiles, leaning his forehead against mine. "Did you think you were going to get rid of me or something? I want you, always, Rae. I mean that."

I close my eyes and lay my head on his chest. I can hear the steady beating of his heart, and I know he means what he said. Sometimes it's still hard for me to believe that he loves me and sees a future for us. I want those things too, but sometimes it's all too easy to doubt that he wants them too. It feels good to hear him say it.

I step back and smile up at him. "Come on." I start forward and he follows.

He nods his head toward the house beside ours. "Is that where ...?" he trails off.

I nod. "Yeah." Steeling myself, I add, "We used to run through these fields playing as children." I force the words past my lips. I don't want to be afraid to talk about Brett, Hannah, or Sarah. I want to remember them and be okay with it all. Pointing to the swing set that sits broken in our yard—and honestly, I don't know why my parents haven't gotten rid of dingy thing yet—I say, "Sarah and Hannah used to come over when we were little and we'd play out here for hours and run over to Brett's house to make trouble."

Cade gasps. "Rachael! Were you chasing after a boy?" he jokes.

I laugh. "Hey, it was only one boy." I bump his shoulder. "I wasn't one of those girls that had a new crush every week. It's only ever been ... well, you and Brett."

"And selfishly," he lowers his voice, "that makes me very happy." His lips graze my chin, and I shiver from the feel of his stubble rubbing against my skin. "Enough serious talk." He grins, backing away from me. "Let's play some catch."

"Cade," I groan.

"Come on," he coaxes, "it'll be fun."

I set my camera down where it isn't in danger of being stepped on and pray to whatever God is listening that I won't get hit in the face with the ball.

"Ready?" Cade asks, lifting the ball.

"I think so ..." I scream when he throws it before I finish speaking. I jump up, catching it, and then turn to run when he starts chasing me.

He catches me around the waist and spins me around, before we promptly fall to the ground, and roll until he hovers above me.

"I win." He kisses my nose.

"You didn't even give me a chance." I frown.

"My bad." He grins crookedly. He stands up slowly and

offers me his hand. "This time you can throw first." He lowers and picks up the football, handing it to me.

He jogs away, and I toss it to him. He has to run forward to catch it since I didn't throw it far enough. He turns away from me and runs.

I jog after him, and when I get close enough, I jump onto his back.

He starts laughing, reaching back to grab my legs.

"I got you," I chime, pressing a kiss to his neck.

"You got me a long time ago, Sunshine."

I smile widely at his words as he heads back to where we left the blanket. He drops the football on the ground, and I hop off his back. I jog back to where I left my camera, and as I approach, I call, "Smile!"

He grins and my stomach flutter. Cade's smile does crazy things to me.

After snapping a few more photos, he takes the camera from me. "My turn."

I blush, lowering my head, suddenly shy at having the tables turned.

"Don't hide from me," he warns, his voice husky.

I look up slowly and find that he's lowered the camera.

"You have nothing to be afraid of, Rae."

"I know." I stand up straight, squaring my shoulders, and level him with a smile.

He grins. "Now that's more like it."

I take the camera from him then and sit down on the blanket, going through photos. Cade leans over my shoulder looking as well.

He points to one. "Hey, you made me look good there."

I laugh, leaning against his chest. "That's because you look good no matter what and you know it."

He chuckles, lying on his back. "That's true."

I set the camera aside and curl my body around his.

We grows quiet, and Cade strokes my hair.

"Are you ready?" he asks softly.

I stop breathing, and my heart skips a beat.

It's time. I know it. He knows it.

I have to take care of what I came here to do.

"Yes."

Cade holds my hand as we walk through the cemetery. My mom told me where they were buried, so I don't have to search the headstones.

The closer we get, the faster my heart races.

I know this is it.

The beginning of something new for me—a life without fear.

"I want to go alone," I tell Cade.

He nods and releases my hand. "I thought you would. I'll be over here." He points few feet away. I know what he's saying—if I need him, he'll be close.

"Thank you." I lean up and kiss his cheek.

I give him a reassuring smile as I head to Brett's grave. Hannah and Sarah were just as important as Brett, but he's the one I need to speak to and say goodbye.

Kathleen and Cade might've given me that final push to gather the strength to come here, but I'd known all along that this was what I had to do. I'd fought the inevitable for far too long.

As I stride through the graveyard, I take several deep breaths to calm myself. I can do this. I'm strong, and I won't break—not anymore.

I stop in front of the grave, a choking panic overcoming me.

Brett, the boy I'd grown up and loved once upon a time, is gone and what is left lies here beneath my feet.

I suddenly feel bad for not bringing flowers or *something* to leave for him.

I sink to my knees, tears coursing down my cheeks as I reach out to touch the cold stone surface of the headstone.

"Hi, Brett," I choke. "I'm so sorry it took me so long to visit. I'm sorry about a lot of things, actually." I laugh humorlessly. "I'm sorry I stole your sweatshirt when we were ten and lied about it ... I really wanted it." I laughed, and this time it doesn't sound forced. I reach up and dry my face with the sleeve of my shirt. "I'm sorry for eating all of your cotton candy when we went to the carnival. I'm sorry for ruining your art project in eight grade when I tripped and fell on it. I'm sorry for making you pose for hours while I took your picture. On second thought, I'm definitely not sorry for that. You know what, forget it, I'm not sorry for any of it. I'm not sorry for being your friend or for loving you. I *am* sorry that because of me you're not here right now," I sob, "but I wouldn't take back any of the memories I have of you for anything. I'm thankful I got to have you in my life for as long as I did. I will always regret what I did, but I won't let it rule my life anymore. I wish things were different, but wishing gets you nowhere. I know one day I'll see you again, so even though I came here to say goodbye, I was wrong. This isn't goodbye, Brett. This is me telling you I'll see you later." I take a deep breath and stroke my fingers over his name. "I have to live my life, and I know you'd want that for me."

I sit there crying. There is so much more that I want to say, but I can't find the words. I know in my heart they are unnecessary.

I press my lips to my fingers and place them against the headstone.

I stand up and dust the grass off my jeans before I walk forward and am met by my present, my future, my forever.

epilogue
...

SIX MONTHS LATER...

"That's the last one." Cade grins, setting the cardboard box on the floor. He comes around the kitchen island and wraps his arms around my waist from behind. I lean my back against him, smiling. "Now we have our own place."

"*Almost* our own place," I remind him.

After graduation, Cade and I decided to move in together, but since Cade wanted a house, not an apartment, and we couldn't afford a house on our own, we're going to have roommates.

But not just any roommates.

He groans, "Way to burst my bubble, Sunshine."

About that time, Xander and Thea stroll in. Each of them is renting a room from us so they can live off campus.

Thea still insists that nothing is going on between them. I guess only time will tell where those two end up.

Thea wrinkles her nose at us. "Am I going to have to watch you grope my best friend all the time?"

Cade chuckles. "Probably." He nuzzles my neck, and I giggle.

"Bleh," Thea gags. "I think I liked her better when she was mopey and didn't talk to anyone, because this—" she points at us "—is getting majorly gross real fast."

Xander starts to laugh and chimes in with, "Well, what do you think is going to happen when they start having loud, obnoxious, bang the walls down sex?"

"Oh, my God!" She slaps her hands over ears. "I didn't even think of that!" She runs from the room and up the steps. "Moving in here was a *bad* idea!"

The three of us laugh at her over-dramatic antics.

"I'll finish unpacking the stuff in the family room." Xander tosses his thumb over his shoulder and backs out of the room, leaving us alone.

"Are you happy, Sunshine?" Cade asks me, cupping my cheeks in his large hands. His eyes are serious, almost worried, like he thinks I might say no.

As cliché as it sounds, he makes me happy when my skies are gray. With Cade by my side, even the bad days don't seem so bad anymore.

I place one of my hands over his. "I couldn't be happier," I promise. "I'm ready for whatever the future holds for us."

"Like babies?"

I start laughing. "How about you let me graduate college first and *then* we'll talk marriage and babies?"

"Deal." He grins.

And we seal it with a kiss.

www.ingramcontent.com/pod-product-compliance
Lightning Source LLC
LaVergne TN
LVHW031608060526
838201LV00065B/4776